CRUSH ON A DRAGON

Vivienne Savage

Crush on a Dragon is a work of fiction.
Names, characters, places, and incidents are the product of the
authors' imaginations or are used in a fictitious manner. Any
resemblance to real persons, events, and locations are coincidental or
used in a form of parody.

Table of Contents

Chapter 1

According to the journalist on Astrid's television, human-on-metahuman violence spiked over the summer months. Veiled insinuations from the polished, pretty and blonde morning news anchor claimed paranormal creatures had it coming for openly displaying their talents by poolsides and in their yards where neighbors were able to see their unnatural shapes. How could America, or even the rest of the world, adjust to the changes overnight?

Astrid knew better. She blamed it on intolerance. In the six years since the emergence of magical beings, tension had only grown. She'd expected humans to live in harmony with their quirky neighbors, not haze them and drive them from peaceful communities.

Some werebeasts chose to reside in shifter-only villages constructed by wealthier members of their community, while others, like Astrid, flew under the radar by changing their name and identity and bribing the press. Anytime in public, Astrid fervently hoped no one recognized her from the happy-go-lucky little girl who once visited the president and first lady at the White House.

It worked as suspected. At times, she'd receive skeptical eyebrow raises, but when asked her name, she had a list of aliases at her disposal. She'd been anyone from Ingrid Hofferson to Astrid Ellis, sometimes carrying a phony ID card to match.

Within a few moments of turning on the television, she wanted to turn it off again. "Neighbors remember the victim as a friendly man who mowed lawns for the elderly members of the community. Police have confirmed it as a hate crime and have no leads at this time."

She frowned. Such a needless loss, all because the man was a witch.

"Well, that's enough of that, don't you agree, Cleopatra?" she asked the kitten prowling by her television. After turning off the news station, she gave herself a final look in the mirror, fluffed her curls, and grabbed her purse. "Play nice with the others."

If Astrid didn't own her business, she'd be officially running late. By the door, she stepped into a pair of strappy, gold-toned sandals, and then surveyed all she commanded inside her apartment. Her father may have helped her realize her dream, but it was hers, and a profound sense of pride resurfaced.

Her recent residential acquisition claimed the building's corner lot, a studio apartment with ample space for two workstations—one for jewel crafting, another for sketches and art. She had no carpeting, only polished floors in a warm, chestnut brown wood and silk rugs gifted by her Aunt Mahasti. The expansive windows, flanked by gauzy blue curtains, revealed a clear summer day in San Diego.

"Keep everyone in line, Isis. Love you," she called over to the Bengal sprawled out over the back of the couch. The older cat was the only one she owned. The three fluffy kittens bouncing around her home came from the shelter where she volunteered as a foster mom.

While it was difficult to relinquish her foster babies, she knew they'd be happy, well-adjusted kittens going to good homes.

An elevator took her from the top level apartment to the ground floor where she crossed paths with one of the building's security guards. Other residents claimed he never smiled, but he often did for Astrid. The big bear, a grizzly she assumed, rarely allowed anyone to see beyond his gruff exterior.

"Morning, young lady. Late start for you today."

"Morning, Charlie. I overslept," she admitted. "How are the grandbabies?"

"They're great. Beth finally got around to sending pictures to my phone."

His bear shifter daughter had married a human, and recently she'd given birth to twin boys. Astrid leaned close while he dragged a large, scarred finger over his cell phone screen to reveal two plump, rosy-cheeked infants. She fell in love with their chubby faces.

"They're adorable!"

"They are," he said proudly.

Before leaving, she promised to finish his commission within the week. She'd finally dreamed up the perfect gift: a gold bracelet for Beth with a pair of bear cubs made from yellow topaz chips.

Warm sunshine and a cool breeze kissed her cheeks as she stepped outside. She headed down the already busy sidewalk at a leisurely pace, soaking in the laid-back atmosphere. She preferred San Diego's easy pace over Los Angeles's hustle and bustle.

Like clockwork, Astrid arrived at her preferred coffee bar after the morning rush. Thirty minutes ago, men and women in smart business suits packed the cafe from the counter to the door. Now there were only a couple, a few fellow artists she recognized, and one very fine-looking sailor in his dress whites. He stood in front of her in line—a tall, broad-shouldered figure clad entirely in white, from his pristine shirt to his shoes. He'd tucked the cap beneath his left arm, the bill facing her. For a moment, she enjoyed the view, until her phone beeped and drew her attention to an incoming text.

Mom: Hi, Astrid! How's work? Are you okay?

Her mother must have seen the news report. That was the only reason Astrid could surmise for the early morning inquiry to her welfare. She rolled her eyes and chuckled, swiping her finger across to reply.

Astrid: Doing good. Getting my caffeine fix.

Mom: Call when you get the chance. I have something to give you.

Astrid: Yeah? What's that?

Mom: You'll have to come home to find out. Friday maybe?

The customer ahead of her completed his order and maneuvered around her with a courteous smile, white teeth against warm-toned skin of an indiscernible ethnic heritage, and bright green eyes. They were the greenest eyes she'd seen since her friend Javier Arcillanegro. Like her, he'd been born half dragon, half human, and their parents had hoped fervently for a match between them.

Instead, he'd been like a brother to her or even a close cousin—an annoying one who hadn't yet left his teens. Javier was still a child by dragon standards, nearly a decade her junior.

Astrid: I'll call when I'm at work and by my calendar. Love you.

"Morning, Astrid. The usual?"

She tucked her phone away and gave the barista a sunny smile. "Let's be adventurous and try something new today. Large s'more frozen latte with a double shot of espresso and coconut milk, hold the whip, please. Oh, and a trio of those mini raspberry white-chocolate scones too, thanks."

"No charge," Wendy told her from behind the counter before she could insert her card into the machine. "The sailor in front of you must have been feeling generous. He paid ahead with a twenty for the next couple people."

Astrid blinked and swiveled her head to search the man out. He stood at the far end of the counter, waiting for his order. An impressive assortment of colorful ribbons in neat rows stood out against his pristine uniform, and his various pins gleamed.

"Did he really?" she asked.

"Uh-huh." Wendy giggled and lowered her voice. "His name is Nate. He comes in here sometimes from the base. I think he's a lieutenant or something."

"Thanks." Astrid edged down the counter to wait for her drink and food, giving the officer another once-over from the corner of her eye. He didn't seem to pay her much mind beyond offering a polite smile.

"Thank you for the whole pay-it-forward thing," she said to break the ice. "You didn't have to do that."

"It's no trouble, ma'am," he replied easily, his voice deeper than implied by his deceptively youthful features. He couldn't be a day over thirty. "You looked a little distracted, so I thought I'd save you the hassle."

"Astrid," she offered. "I'd say ma'am was my mother, but she'd probably make a face and tell you she's way too young to be a ma'am."

"Pleasure's all mine, Astrid. I'm Nathaniel, or Nate for short if you like."

Their orders arrived back to back, their names scrawled across the white cups. "Scone? It's the least I can do since you bought them. Though…" She eyed his uniform. "You might be pushing your luck on the whole bravery thing, getting coffee and icing on yourself."

When she tipped the brown paper bag toward him in offering, Nate graciously accepted one of the sweet delights. Her skin tingled when his green eyes roved from her golden sandals to the pale blue, off-the-shoulder dress. His observant gaze made her pulse race.

"I like to live dangerously," he quipped before raising his steaming cup. "I guess it comes hand-in-hand with working in security on the base."

Under normal circumstances, Astrid would have thanked him again for his generosity and left, but his kind green eyes held her attention. Like a bird with a shiny new toy, she lingered for conversation, all the while observing the sailor for subtle signs of him being a man on the run.

"So I guess the base doesn't have good coffee?" she asked.

"It's not bad, depending who starts the pot up, but then I wouldn't have an excuse to enjoy this fine day," after a pause, he added, "or your chipper company for that matter. Though I could say the same thing for you. Coffee overpriced at the university?"

"Ha. I haven't been to the university in over a year, but you'd be right about their prices."

Nate glanced at the door when a group of noisy teens entered. They eyeballed Astrid in passing, focusing on the hem of her bohemian chic dress.

"Wanna get out of here? I'll walk you back to car," he offered with a nod to the door.

"Um, actually I walked but my job isn't far."

"After you."

Nate held the door like a true gentleman. As she brushed by, an electric buzz zipped up her spine. The sensation startled her, making her grateful for her frozen drink. Otherwise, she'd have coffee splashed over her hand. Her skin felt flushed and warm. Her dress, while short and breezy, suddenly had too much fabric to bear.

What the hell was that about? Am I sick?

"Which way?" he asked.

"Oh, um, I work over this way." Still fumbling over the unexpected spark, she gestured down the street and found herself staring again as Nate put his cap on. In the sunlight, his eyes stood out against his light brown skin even more, and she spotted freckles scattered across the bridge of his nose and upper cheeks. They didn't detract from his handsome looks, neither did the slight bend to his nose and thin scar at the corner of his mouth. They made him interesting. She wanted to take his slim face between her hands and cover it with kisses.

"Let me guess… Bookstore?"

She laughed. "Books? What makes you jump to that conclusion?" Did she look like a book junkie? A librarian? Around them, the Gaslamp Quarter operated under the lull of the quieter morning hours. Most people worked, although a few tourists wandered the sidewalks.

"I don't know," he admitted with a quiet, good-natured laugh at his expense. "Clothes?" Nate studied her again, and when he appraised her, it set off a series of flutters in her tummy, unlike the disinteresting college boys in the cafe.

"Wrong again." She laughed and came to a halt outside a shop nestled between a clothing boutique and a wine bar. Gold letters painted across the window declared the shop to be The Dragon's Hoard. The O in Hoard resembled a gold coin in metallic paint.

With her keys in hand, she let them in and disabled the security system. Automatic lights activated, casting a subtle glow over carpeted floors and spotless, glass displays.

Nate whistled. "Wow, talk about sparklers."

Glossy cabinets with black velvet-lined shelves displayed handcrafted jewelry and delicate crystal figurines. Oil canvases depicting dreamy landscapes hung on the walls. The spacious building provided the freedom to create art in the back while maintaining an eye on the storefront.

"Only you? No other employees?"

With eyes gleaming in genuine interest, Nate drifted to a shelf decorated with tiny, jade figurines. She'd learned the art of gem sculpture from her grandfather Maximilian, and made him proud when she excelled at his preferred craft.

Gems were her calling, the natural gift she'd honed over the years of seclusion at Drakenstone Manor. With only Javier's infrequent visits, a friendship with Svetlana, and a bond she'd developed with a witch in Texas, most of her childhood passed in isolation.

"Just me," she confirmed. "One of my girlfriends will stop in sometimes, and I trust her with the register when I'm in a creative zone, but yeah, just me. It only ever gets busy if there's an event downtown or something. Even then, I'm never packed. People wander in, look, then wander out again. Some buy, some only look." She shrugged and tossed her purse behind the front counter.

He whistled. Items on the open shelves bore tags with digits in the hundreds. The ones behind glass sat beside small folded cards directing the buyer to speak with the attendant, their worth too valuable for the average shopper.

"Next, you'll be wanting to tell me you're also the artist responsible for filling this place with jewelry."

Astrid cocked her head. "How'd you know there's only one artist?"

"It's all in the same style. I'm right, aren't I?"

"Yeah, I am," she said in a daze. She set her coffee down and turned on the stereo to her preferred station before preparing the register.

"That's some talent. So, if it's not too personal, when you aren't making art, what do you do for fun? Or are you completely addicted to your work?" He cracked a wide grin.

And then Astrid's entire world changed; the floor dropped out from beneath her. Sweat moistened her palms, prompting her to wipe both hands against her dress.

Handsome, check. Good job, check. Knows his art, check. The best smile she'd ever seen on any man, check.

The expression on his face stood apart from his casual smiles, stealing her breath away. For her, it was the emergence of the sun from behind the clouds after a week of stormy skies.

"Astrid?"

She snapped out of it, and heat surged to her face. "Sorry," she muttered. "Obviously, I'm not caffeinated enough. Uh, anyway, I was going to say that art *is* fun. What about you? Something tells me you aren't one of those party hard sort of sailors." She squinted and sized him up again. His complexion had a healthy, bronzed glow. "Surfing," she guessed. "Or, wait, no… volleyball. Beach volleyball, *Top Gun* style."

Bad idea. Thinking of the iconic beach volleyball scene in one of her mother's favorite movies made her imagination skyrocket to fanatical levels of visualizing Nate shirtless and gleaming under a sunny, California sky. She shook it off and tried to focus.

"Nah. I like to—" He cut himself off and seemed to reconsider his answer. "I guess you could say my family is into the fish and wild game thing. Not for trophies. When I was a kid, Dad would take me camping, and we'd fish the entire weekend and survive on what we could catch. And maybe I am known for waterskiing on occasion. The rest of my time is divided between chillin' out and taking my girl Echo to the dog park for a game of fetch, you know?"

"Huh. Waterskiing." Not a guess that had crossed her mind at all. While he loitered, she moved to a worktable and pulled out her sketchbook, then returned to the front counter and took a seat on the stool. With her pad propped up on her lap, she started to sketch out a necklace idea featuring some green and blue gemstones she'd been holding on to for ages. Nate had inspired ideas.

"So did you all survive off fish only or did you get rabbits and stuff to go with them? My dad takes me hunting almost every summer." Her lips quirked up at the corners. "We fish, too."

"Nobody can field dress a rabbit quicker than me." He shifted his weight and leaned forward to snoop. His cologne, mixed with his natural musk, wafted around her and threatened to tear her attention away from her drawing. Damn her shifter sense of smell. "Your dad sounds cool. Some guys aren't into doing that with their daughters."

"Both my parents are outdoorsy." Not a lie at all, either. "So lots of our vacations revolve around stuff like that. Camping," *in the middle of the furthest, wildest reaches*, "rock climbing," *on mountain ranges most humans couldn't hope to scale*, "or just relaxing on the beach and snorkeling," *at my uncle Teo's exclusive island resort. With hippocampi*. She smiled and angled her sketchbook away.

"Only child, eh? Me too." He put his back to the counter and gazed out the storefront window. "So how into the beach are you?"

"No, I have a younger brother," she corrected, "and I'm quite fond of the beach. California born and raised. You?" Little by little, she tried to learn more, without coming across as an overeager girl.

"I'd have to be comfortable around water to enlist in the Navy."

"You'd think so, but a friend of mine dated an engineer from the base and he hated the water." *Not this guy, though if he enjoys waterskiing.*

She found Nate mysterious, the way he only gave teasing glimpses of himself. He didn't brag and boast, a trait she found admirable.

"Engineers don't count. They're all strange hermits," he replied, never losing his smile. "You should come with me down to the shore sometime. For a day."

Impulse drove her to counter his vague offer with a better invitation. "How about a morning at the beach followed by an evening at the county fair?"

"Sounds good."

Yes!

"As luck would have it, I managed to get some time off this weekend to unwind and decompress. We can meet up, or I can swing by and get you if you want."

She eyed him again, trying to get a read on the man. What harm was there in letting him pick her up? She could always get a cab home if the need arose. Or make her own way if things went south.

"Sure," she agreed. "Will Sunday work? I have a couple of buyers coming in on Saturday, so I'll be here. You could pick me up at the coffee shop. I'll bring the caffeine."

"Only if you'll catch a movie with me after your business is done with your buyers."

Her brows rose. Nate had plenty of confidence, a refreshing change from other men she'd dated in the past. But why? Did he have an ego to put her Uncle Teo to shame? Was he used to women saying yes? Or was he experiencing the same undeniable pull of attraction?

"I feel I have to warn you then. I toss sour gummy candies into my popcorn."

Surprise flickered across his features, its source undeterminable. It could be anything from her acceptance of the date to what Ēostre called a "strange, abhorrent snacking habit."

"While gross, that won't be the worst movie theater food choice I'll have witnessed. My mom likes to sneak Taco Bell inside her purse," he confided, dropping his voice to a whisper as if there were others nearby to overhear their confidential chat.

"Yeah, okay, she wins." Her nose wrinkled, and she turned her attention back to her sketch. Something reminiscent of waves, she thought. A flowing design in silver with touches of gold framing the stones.

"So... no boyfriend?"

"I'd hardly be agreeing to a movie date if there were." Though some of her friends were known to date around. A few seconds of consideration brought clarity to his question. After a headshake, she smiled and added, "No. No boyfriend. You?"

"Haven't had the time in a while, but I do now." The reassuring smile surfaced again.

"Well then, looks like we're both single, so a weekend spending time together doesn't seem like a terrible idea. Swing by here Saturday afternoon when you're free, and we can figure out what to go see."

"Sounds good." He bent into an exaggerated bow, hat held in one hand. "Then I bid you adieu, fair lady, till we meet again," he said on his way to the door.

Astrid giggled. His dramatic exit had already burrowed a little notch into her heart. "Hey, Nate?" He paused with a hand on the knob. "Thanks again for getting my coffee today. I'm glad we ran into each other."

Fate had funny ways of bringing people into a person's life, and everything in her body buzzed and hummed, urging her to stop him from leaving. It was a strange, alien sensation, and she was human enough to resist the wild call to leap over her counter and grab him. So she remained where she was, and swallowed back a thick lump in her throat.

"Me too. Take it easy, Astrid." He shut the door behind him and pulled his hat over his head before disappearing past her windows.

The weekend couldn't come fast enough.

***

Nate's father, a huge bear of a man, greeted him at the door to their meeting house. At six foot five, Daniel Kirkpatrick stood two inches taller than his son and broader in the shoulder from a lifetime of heavyweight lifting while in the Marines. They had few other similarities beyond the color of their green eyes and their freckles, which were more prominent in the younger Kirkpatrick than his biological father.

Before Nate's eyes could adjust to the dimmed lighting, Daniel shooed him toward the open central meeting chamber. "Come in. It's about time you arrived. We've all been waiting for you." The man glanced over his son's attire. "You look nice in your dress whites."

"Sorry. Traffic was hell." The rare compliment from the old man unnerved him, but he flashed an uncertain smile and allowed his father to herd him into the open space where their monthly meetings took place.

An enormous table dominated the center of the lodge's primary room, large enough to sit twenty-five men in a circle. Every man in the order had an assigned seat, his name engraved in the stone. Nate strode past five empty seats to the right of his father before finding the place of Sir Galahad.

For Nate, it was only a name attached to a life he could no longer recall. Sometimes, he had vague recollections of sitting beside King Arthur, but the fragments of fading memory dissipated like smoke.

If Arthur currently inhabited a body, he'd occupy the chair to Nate's right—if their king wasn't missing. According to the knights with all of their memories, Merlin's Cycle had excluded him from reincarnation for over a century. No one knew why.

"Welcome back, brother." The man across the table flashed a polite, brittle smile. In this life, Sir Bedivere used the name of David Mitchell. He was swarthy-skinned and dark-haired with intense blue eyes.

"Thanks."

The chorus of polite and friendly greetings continued among the small gathering of knights, their ages ranging from a youthful seventeen to a distinguished seventy-two. Of the twenty-five, nineteen lived a current life. Seven were present in person, three were children too young to participate, and the rest joined via video conference.

According to his father, there hadn't been so many of them among the living at one time in centuries. Nineteen different men had been born in different parts of the world and drawn together again through the magnetic, magical force binding them. Their ethnicities ran the gamut of fair to deep espresso. They didn't have the luxury of choosing their bodies.

Daniel, who sat behind a nameplate inscribed "Sir Kay," tapped a button on the laptop in front of him. The curved, plasma television dominating one of the walls powered on. "Let's begin the meeting then, shall we?"

Astrid's picture appeared on the screen. Nate had taken the photo himself a week ago, capturing the young woman outside her shop on a breezy afternoon. Her golden hair blew back in the wind, and her dress billowed around her legs. She'd looked beautiful.

The intruding thought made him squirm in his seat, but no one seemed to notice anything amiss.

"Did you make contact?" Bedivere asked.

"I did. I walked the target to her job and convinced her to spend time with me over the weekend."

A few heads nodded in acknowledgment.

"What you're doing is a brave thing, son. I'm proud of you for enduring this," Kay said.

Nate's brows raised. "That's funny because I don't remember anyone giving me an option."

His father's smile faded. "We discussed this and our reasons for selecting you, Nathaniel." Expressions of approval and pride became solemn and taciturn, neutral during the conflict between father and son. It was a common occurrence between the old and the young, the knights of Nate's generation too fresh to recall their many past lives and lacking the wisdom of the years.

"Right. She's into green eyes and uniforms." According to their files, her last relationships had been with a firefighter, a police officer, and a Marine. "Why not Lancelot?"

The knight to his left jerked upright in his seat. "I'm married, bro. You don't want to know the shitshow we'd all have to put up with if I took this mission. I learned my lesson about adultery centuries ago."

"You're lucky Arthur's forgiven you," Nate muttered. Or rather, he had before his disappearance over a century ago.

The knight formerly known as Lancelot grinned back at him and winked. "Hey, she's dead and gone. We're still here with a job to do."

Kay nodded in agreement and then leaned forward, spreading his hands in a gesture of defeat. "You two are the only knights of appropriate age and appearance guaranteed to attract the creature. I'm a little too old to be playing the part of the handsome bachelor, or I'd do it myself."

"We don't even know if she's one of them yet. For all we know, she's some poor human child adopted into a crap situation," Nate said. "They're not like other shapeshifters. We have no proof dragons and humans can interbreed with our kind."

Bedivere crossed his arm over his chest. "Do your job and we will."

Their desire to know Astrid's human status would change the way the Knights of Merlin operated forever. Not only would they have to deal with dragons, but also their half-human progeny, who by all appearances seemed normal. How many women could a single male dragon impregnate? How could they identify and eliminate them as well?

Ever since she'd dropped out of the spotlight six years ago to attend an ivy league, private college, Astrid Drakenstone—now Astrid Ellis—had gone to exquisite lengths to guard her new identity, down to dyeing her hair a dull shade of dishwater blonde while in at the university.

No respectable journalist had any interest in uncovering hidden supernatural creatures. Unearthing secret identities often met with deadly consequences, as well as jail and immense fines for the snitch.

Five years ago, President Maximilian Emberthorn had signed into law the Paranormal Beings Right to Privacy Act, guarding all of his hidden friends from unwanted exposure. All attempts to overturn it had failed.

Their statuses as magical beings were as confidential as their medical data.

"Look, I'll do it, but I'm telling you, she's normal. Another 'all-American girl next door' type." *With a glowing personality.*

While Astrid was beautiful, she wasn't unnaturally flawless. Her eyes were blue, not some terrifying, smoldering shade of green, gold, or liquid silver. Their president's amber eyes practically gleamed red in the right lighting. But Astrid resembled her human mother. Her human mother who either paid frequent visits to her plastic surgeon or brewed her coffee with water from the fountain of youth.

"I don't care what you have to do or how far you have to go. Find out with 100 percent accuracy whether or not she was born from a dragon's seed," Kay said.

"And if she is a dragon's child? What then?" Nate asked, chilled. Goose bumps raised over the backs of his arms. He had yet to engage a dragon in battle in his new life. Until hanging Astrid in her shop, he'd never been alone with one either.

"We do what we do best. Slay her and any others sired by the wyrms."

Chapter 2

Days later, when Friday arrived, Astrid was humming with excitement for her date. It wasn't until she checked her messages that she was reminded of her mother's cryptic text in the coffee shop.

Saving herself the long drive west of Los Angeles, she called Aunt Mahasti instead and was swept away on streams of magic into an instantaneous teleportation to the estate.

A fog scented with jasmine and heady, Middle Eastern oils reinvigorated her senses. They were the same fragrances Mahasti preferred to wear on her skin. Astrid breathed it in and sighed.

Home sweet home. No matter how much she loved her apartment in San Diego, returning to the manor always renewed old memories of growing up in their eclectic household.

"Oh, it took you long enough to come visit!" cried a cheerful voice to her rear.

Astrid spun to see her mother approaching from the direction of the stairs. "Mom, what's the big deal about this surprise? Didn't you guys already give me a birthday party?"

Chloe hugged her. "I know we already gave you a party, but there's something we forgot to do."

Her dad cleared his throat as he emerged from the den.

"Something I neglected to do," her mother admitted.

Although Chloe was in her fifties, she remained forever frozen at the age of Astrid's birth. Dragon's blood had proven to be the catalyst to unlocking supernatural potential in her, and carrying Astrid had imbued her with long life. Possibly immortal life.

"Where's Brandt?" she asked, looking around for her brother. He almost always greeted her first.

Saul, her father, hugged her with one arm and chuckled. "He's with Max. They'll be over for dinner. But there's another special guest here to see you."

Astrid perked up. "Who?"

The voice of her beloved uncle reached her seconds later. "Has living in the city dulled your nose, little one?" The door to her father's den framed the flawless water dragon.

"Uncle Watatsumi!" With unconcealed delight, she darted across the room and gave the Asian dragon a hug, wrinkling his ornate kimono in the process. He chuckled and enfolded her in his arms, used to her exuberant greetings. "It's so good to see you again!"

"You saw me only weeks ago, child."

"Several weeks too many," she pointed out.

She never tired of visiting him across the ocean.

"Okay, what's this all about? You all look so serious."

"I have something that belongs to you, Astrid," her mother began. She pulled a familiar, rectangular case from beneath the couch then opened it to reveal the beautiful weapon within. Nestled against a bed of red velvet laid the most dangerous sword to dragonkind next to Excalibur.

Ascalon.

"Mom's sword?"

"No, sweetie. Your sword. I've been holding it all of this time for *you*. It was never meant to be mine."

All of her life, she'd been given explicit instructions to steer clear of her mother's sword, and never touch it. She knew the story behind the blade, that it was once used to battle a female dragon named Brigid, but nothing else. The fabled dragonslaying weapon hearkened back to the ancient days when dragons razed the countryside and devoured defenseless villagers.

"I don't understand."

"It is a sword meant for a half-dragon, Astrid," Watatsumi said. "In the old legends, Saint George slew many dangerous wyrms with this blade, dragons who would have done him and others great harm."

"I don't want a dragon-killing sword," Astrid said, petrified of it. "Why would you give it to me?" She'd never killed any creature she didn't intend to eat, and she couldn't imagine taking the life of one of their kind. She considered herself a dragon and a human. She'd been raised to live in both worlds and couldn't choose.

"And I hope you never have to use it, baby, but the truth of the matter is, it belongs to you." Chloe gave her a reassuring smile.

Her uncle stepped forward and took the weapon from Chloe. Its ornate sheath was beautiful. In fact, she'd drawn the weapon before in her personal artwork, but still, she had never touched it, never ran her finger over its polished blade or felt the cool metal under her skin. Something about her mother and father's earnest plea to never touch it had carried with Astrid through her entire life.

Her hands raised for it, almost of their will despite her trepidation. Her heart hammered, pulse too rapid to count the individual beats.

"I dreamed of this day many years ago before you were born, Astrid," Watatsumi said. As he removed the blade from the scabbard and laid it over her spread palms, power radiated through the steel and rushed across her fingers. The metal gleamed, and an otherworldly glow encompassed its length.

Chloe gasped. "It's never done that."

"Then it's true," Saul said. "It was meant for Astrid."

She curled her hand around the hilt, the grip so comfortable and natural it was as if it had been made for her.

"There's one more thing I must tell you," Watatsumi said.

"What?"

"There is a great change on the horizon for all of dragonkind. Our futures hang in the balance of uncertainty, and I see two paths before you."

"I don't understand," she said, cradling the blade on one palm. The power surged again, warm and alive. It comforted her.

"Many of our kind were adamantly against you gaining possession of this weapon. They fear it spells doom for all dragons. That you will bring destruction upon us, and… it could very well come to pass."

"What? No! I would never—"

"However, down your other path lies our salvation."

She tried to swallow back the thick lump in her throat, but her mouth was bone dry. "Tell me how to pick the right path."

Saul reached over and gave her cold hand a squeeze. "That isn't how it works, sweetheart."

Watatsumi nodded. "I can speak nothing more on the matter, for fear it will change what is destined. Some things *must* happen, Astrid, or there can be no change for good or for ill. Remember my words when the time comes."

Chloe ducked away and returned with another package. She unwrapped it to reveal a dark leather sword belt printed with the silhouette of horses and kittens. "Here. This is for you," she said.

"Mom, I can't exactly wear a sword around."

"Nonsense," Saul said before his mate could respond. "People wear guns to Walmart now."

Both Astrid and her mother shot Saul a look; then Chloe continued with what she had planned to say. "I know, but in case you ever need to, you'll have it."

Astrid stared at it. Her parents were insane. "It's really pretty. Colorful." All it needed were some bedazzled tiaras, and it would be fit for every girl's princess costume collection.

"I thought the kittens were a nice touch," Watatsumi said.

Saul beamed with pride. "I thought so as well."

Allowing her no chance to protest, Chloe girded their gift around Astrid's hips. The sword hung from her right side, an ominous weight and reminder of the terrifying destiny awaiting her. They'd always implied something great lay ahead of her in the future.

"Max and Ēostre should be here soon. When you told me you were coming, we called everyone to join us for dinner."

"You didn't have to do that, Mom."

"I wanted to. You're so busy with your new life in San Diego that we never see you anymore."

"I'm sorry," Astrid said, chastened.

"That wasn't a complaint," Chloe said. She smiled warmly. "I'm glad you've been happy there. Come on. Help me out in the kitchen and tell me about what you've been up to."

A conversational hour passed while they prepared dinner together, during which Astrid considered the encounter with Nate. She didn't feel ready to share that bomb with her parents, not when she still wasn't certain about it herself. So she focused on other things, telling her mom about her recent sales in the shop and her latest girls' night out with her former college roommate.

"No boys?" her mother asked. While she lacked magical powers, she'd always been intuitive to her child's needs.

"Nothing serious, no."

"Nothing serious means there's something," Chloe pointed out.

She rolled her eyes. "I have a movie date with a guy I ran into at the coffee shop. That's it."

"Is he cute? What's his name?" Her mother shifted away to wipe the counters, cleaning their mess.

"Seriously, Mom, if you start with an inquisition in here, I'm gonna have Mahasti poof me home."

"What? Can't I be curious? You haven't dated anyone since that Jasper fellow."

"Jason, Mom, not Jasper. That's what Dad kept calling him."

Chloe giggled into one hand. "I know. Your father only did that because the boy was such an asshole, you know."

"He was," Astrid agreed sadly. "I don't think he cared about me aside from wanting to have a tour around Drakenstone Studios."

Her mother paused. "Does this one know who you are, or are you using my name?" Her lips pursed before she asked, "What does he do for a living?"

Despite her intentions to keep both parents in the dark, she found herself growing eager to discuss him. Warmth blossomed in her chest as the memory of his smile flit through her mind. "I'm using your name for now. He's in the Navy. An officer. He did one of those pay-it-forward things at the cafe, and so we ended up talking while waiting for our drinks."

"Better than how you met Jasper."

"Mom."

Chloe grinned impishly. "I promise I won't tell your father a thing. Keep me updated."

"No promises. I'm not in any rush." It was a lie, and it wasn't. Until her startling encounter with Nate, she hadn't been in a rush. Now she had no idea what to think.

"He is cute, though," she admitted. "No, not cute. Handsome and—"

A tremble seemed to reverberate through the house, a palpable sense of magic adding a charge to the air.

"And what, sweetie?"

"Grandma is here!"

Astrid abandoned the kale and spinach salad she was tossing and hurried toward the large family room. A shimmering portal hung in the middle of the door between the living room and the hallway. Astrid looked through it into the family wing of the White House.

A tall, rangy man with black hair stepped through first then reached through and signaled for the others to follow. Andrew Connelly had been one of Max's bodyguards since he ran for the presidency. The werewolf was practically family by this point.

"Astrid!"

Her little brother barreled through the portal after Andrew, nearly knocking him aside in his haste to reach Astrid. He collided into her, hugging her legs. "You came home!"

"Sure did, kiddo."

"I missed you," he gushed. "I built my Legos and put a T-rex in the Nether."

"That sounds awesome. You can show me after dinner, okay?"

"Okay!"

Her grandfather stepped through the portal next. Max was a handsome man, and as a human, he appeared to be in his forties. In his arms, a red-haired toddler wriggled for freedom. "Branwen, please. A moment, little one."

"Down! Papa, Papa, want down!"

"In a moment," he told her again.

Ēostre entered last with a boy clinging to her. He resembled his mother, with curls of pale blond atop his head and expressive, liquid silver eyes.

"Astrid, you look lovely." Ēostre waited patiently to receive her embrace, Max beside her after Chloe relieved him of his daughter. The portal behind them closed.

"Thanks, Grandma."

Over dinner, Max regaled them with his plans for retirement from the White House and they all took turns asking Astrid about each facet of her life in the city, from her new shop to her plans for the weekend. Chloe chuckled when she replied with a vague comment about possibly seeing a new movie with a friend.

"Oh! Grandpa Max, can I still have those green opals you offered last time we visited your hoard?"

"Of course," he replied charitably. "I set them aside for you." His brows raised. "I couldn't convince you to take them last time."

Astrid cleared her throat and had a sip of wine. "Thank you. Um, I finally have an idea for a piece that they'd be perfect for. That's all."

After more family bonding, she returned to her apartment with enough leftover spiced lamb to carry her through the weekend. Once she'd stowed her food in the fridge, she settled at her computer desk.

Isis curled around her ankle then a kitten bounded over to plop beside them and reveal her belly. Of the three she'd chosen to foster, Cleopatra struck her as the one with the most personality. She'd been tempted to apply to keep her.

Maybe. She had enough love for two cats and one man, didn't she? A smile curved her lips as she logged onto Facebook and found a new message on her shop's page.

Nathaniel Kirkpatrick. The profile photo featured a stern-faced Nate in his uniform.

"We forgot to exchange numbers at your store, so I found you here to confirm our night out. I hope this isn't too presumptuous of me and that I haven't offended. Feel free to ignore this and assume I'm a weirdo if I have," she read aloud.

Offended? She clicked his name, went to his profile, and sent a friend request. As soon as the page registered with his acceptance, she tapped out her number to his personal message box and hit send. Seconds later, she received a beep on her phone with an unrecognizable number. The body of the message simply asked, "Astrid?"

Astrid: Yup, it's me. Your FB pic is super serious. Doesn't the Navy believe in smiles?

Nate: LOL Smiles? What are those?

Astrid: You know what those are. You gave me a stunner in the shop.

Nate: You gave me a reason to smile.

Her cheeks warmed. For a moment, she stared down at the phone, trying to think up a witty response.

Astrid: Hopefully I'll manage it a second time.

Nate: I'm looking forward to it. See you tomorrow around six?

A nervous tremble made it difficult to tap out an answer. Yes, she replied, only to rethink her answer and tell him to pick her up at five instead.

They ended their text exchange after parting wellwishes for a good sleep, and then Astrid rose from her computer. The sword scabbard tapped her thigh. Somehow, she'd forgotten it was there, and wearing it felt more natural than she wanted to admit.

"Well, you certainly aren't going along with me on my date. I don't care what Mom says."

She unfastened it and set it on the dresser.

Chapter 3

"C'mon, Astrid, hang out with us tonight. The others are at the bar up the street, and Phil's band is playing."

On any other day, her best friend, Toni, would have made a compelling argument to drag her away from her shop for an evening of fun with their mutual circle of friends, but Astrid had plans of attending a movie with a hot sailor from the nearby base.

"I can't. I already made plans."

"What plans?" Toni blew her purple-streaked bangs out of her face. "Staying here all night painting? You can do that anytime."

"No, I'm meeting up with someone to go to a movie."

"Bullshit." Her friend crossed her arms and stared her down. Her lips pursed. "When I asked about it last week, you said there wasn't anything you wanted to see. And if you had a date, I'd know about it because you would have *called* me."

A brief flicker of guilt brought heat to her neck and cheeks. She and Toni shared everything, especially when it came to guys. They'd been roommates in college and were as close as sisters.

"I'm telling you about it now?" She said the words like a question, uncertainty wavering her voice.

"Astrid, honey, you don't have to make up a story if you don't wanna come out and drink—"

The bell over the door chimed. Both women swiveled toward the entrance, and while Toni gaped, Astrid smiled. All at once, that same rush of giddiness swept through her and chased the anxiety away.

"Nate, I almost didn't recognize you out of uniform."

"Heh. Despite what the guys on base would tell you, I have a life outside my uniform."

Her gaze crept up his jeans and untucked, buttoned shirt. The vertical, blue stripes intensified his green eyes, making the slow grin spreading over his face even more brilliant.

"Oh, hey, sorry. If you're not finished with your buyer, I can disappear for a few and come back."

Shaken from her stupor, Toni barked out a laugh and shook her head. "Are you kidding? I wait for birthday gifts if I want something from Astrid's hoard. And I was just leaving anyway, so you two kids have fun."

At the door, behind Nate's back, Toni mouthed the words "wow" and "call me," gave Astrid a thumb's up, and then took off.

"Let me lock up. Then we can head down to Horton Plaza. Did you find parking okay or did you take the trolley from the base?"

"Nah, I found a spot in the garage up the way. I don't live on base."

As they started down the street, Nate's hand engulfed hers, his warm skin calloused and firm. Reveling in the security of his grip, she beamed up at him then turned her eyes toward the crossing ahead of them.

"I'm glad we could do this today," she told him. "What should we see?"

"Let's pick when we get there."

They scanned the movie posters, and an amicable debate ended with a confident decision. Of the three movies they were willing to see, only one had a showing within the next twenty minutes. Astrid unfastened her purse and reached inside to approach the ticket window, but Nate touched her arm and shook his head. Between his fingers, he held two evening passes.

"They passed these out to some of us on base. It's on me tonight. Snacks are on me too," Nate decided. "I get a military discount."

Astrid laughed. "Fine. You get to feed my sweet craving."

Before Nate's invitation to the theater, she'd had no interest in any of the movies currently showing. She still lacked interest in the flick they'd chosen as a tentative compromise between romance and action, but once they settled in their seats with a bevy of showtime snacks, he made the movie interesting. She giggled at his occasional quips and swatted his shoulder. He even let her steal some of his nachos, and then they shared a pack of Red Vines.

About an hour into the movie, she lowered her cheek to his shoulder. She breathed in the scent of his skin and closed her eyes, relishing the moment when his arm surrounded her. He was solid muscle beneath her, built like a lean swimmer.

He smelled divine, his skin infused with the scent of sandalwood and bergamot. She could have breathed in his cologne all night along with the natural musk she associated with him.

"Not a bad movie. Ready to go?" The movie had ended, but he hadn't moved. She stirred at the sound of his voice but didn't lift her cheek from his shoulder.

"There's an end credits scene," she told him.

"You sure? Everyone's leaving."

Astrid chuckled. "Yeah, trust me."

True to her word, a brief clip came on at the end, a promising teaser for the next installment of the franchise. Only a few other couples had remained in the theater.

"The mall is closing up, but if you aren't in a rush to be rid of me, we could walk around a bit. Maybe grab a drink?" she suggested as they stepped out of the theater.

"Trust me, I'm not in a rush to get anywhere." He slanted another of his heart-melting grins down at her. "Come on. We can cut through down this way. A buddy told me about a place if you're game."

"Sure."

Shops in the open-air mall were closing their doors and flipping their signs for the night. Nate and Astrid cut through the center and meandered toward the parking garage exit. The stench of old, stale urine assaulted her nose as they took the stairwell down to the road level. She knew the area well and sometimes brought clean blankets for the homeless men who cycled in and out for shelter.

"Hand over your purse."

A man shambled out of the shadows beneath a broken streetlight and stepped into their path. Beside her, Nate tensed and drew her back. The stranger drew a gun from his pocket and aimed at Astrid.

"Look, we don't want any trouble." Nate angled his body in front of her.

"Shut the fuck up, man, and gimme your wallet. You, Blondie, the purse. Now."

Although the gun looked legitimate, the subtle traces of gunpowder were absent from the weapon. It smelled like cheap plastic. And juice. Like someone had spilled fruit punch on it and hastily wiped it clean.

A kid's toy, she wondered? Was anyone stupid enough to rob a couple using a replica?

"Look, you can give me the purse, or I can pump some holes in your boyfriend here. You make your mind up." He swept the gun from her toward Nate.

Astrid's eyes narrowed. A surge of rage tightened her fingers on the handle of her clutch, and she held it out in offering toward the robber. He'd threatened Nate. Not her. Four years of school and dealing with university boys had hardened her enough to weather threats from men with the appropriate recourse.

Leiv had always taught her to use the least amount of force necessary when facing a human opponent. Never kill when a wound would suffice.

With that in mind, Astrid, under the guise of passing over her purse, slammed the leather satchel against his wrist in a sharp, overhand blow. Before the gun clattered to the ground out of his grip, she stepped in and hooked both hands behind his neck and slammed his face toward her rising knee.

Growing up with a Russian uncle with a fondness for wrestling and a penchant for doing it in his bear form had given Astrid an advantage. She took their assailant down to the ground as Nate rushed for the handgun.

Astrid pressed the gunman's face into the cool, wet ground. A light, five-minute shower of rainfall during the movie had kissed the concrete with moisture.

Nate turned the gun over in his hands a few times. "This isn't even real. What the hell?"

"Look, I'm sorry!"

Her date dropped the imitation handgun on the ground and stood back with his arms crossed. He shook his head. "I'm calling the cops."

"Don't bother," Astrid said. She didn't weigh as much as the man trapped beneath her, but she had leverage and supernatural strength. She could always blame his helplessness on the former.

"What?"

"I don't want the police involved."

"Astrid, this asshole had a gun in your face. You're seriously going to let him go?" Nate demanded.

"It wasn't a real gun, so he didn't actually break a law."

"It's still attempted robbery." Nate glanced at the man on the ground. He scowled, while the would-be-thief gazed up at him with startled eyes. "We need to—"

The man on the ground had eased one hand beneath him and pushed up with surprising strength. He didn't smell like a shifter to Astrid, but raw power emanated from him, and it stunned her. A flash filled the space between them in ivory radiance. Dazzled, she stumbled off of him, only to become vaguely aware of Nate shielding her with his body.

"Nate? Nate!" she cried, feeling for him with both hands. "I can't see!"

"Neither can I," he called back.

Astrid felt blindly with her hands, and they found one another by voice. It was like a flashbang grenade without the auditory effect. Blinded, she clung to her date with both hands and waited for her vision to return, certain at first that it never would.

"I can't see!"

"Shh… Give it a moment, okay? Don't panic yet. I'm already getting my sight back."

Nate was right. Astrid blinked and spots formed in front of her eyes, but the vague, blurry shape of the street swam into her view.

"Can you see now?"

"Some," she replied shakily.

"He must have been some kind of witch or warlock. Whatever they call them," Nate concluded after a moment of stony silence passed between them.

"Maybe… but I know witches, and I've never seen one of them do anything like that," Astrid said. "Most of them don't want any trouble. If he were a sorcerer, why would he rob anyone?"

"Does it matter? Let's talk about that stunt you pulled. What the hell, Astrid? Attacking a man with a gun was a foolish thing to do."

An uncomfortable flush crept up her neck. "We're alive, and that's all that matters. I don't want to spend hours in a police station."

It pissed her off that he doubted her. The rational part of her forced her to acknowledge she'd kept her true identity secret from him. Would Nate have protected her like a damsel in distress if he knew she was a dragon?

"I'm walking you home in case that creep is still around," Nate muttered darkly.

"I'll be fine." The stubborn part of her wanted to call an end to their fiasco of a date, still raw about his chastisement even though she knew he was right. From his viewpoint, knowing nothing about her, she *had* been foolish. Her mother and grandmother, women who had battled angry dragons, would have agreed.

"Look, I'm sorry for snapping at you. Very sorry, Astrid."

"It's okay," Astrid replied in a gentle voice. She glanced toward the sidewalk, hoping to appear contrite.

Nate took her left hand without prompting and stroked the back of it. "Are you all right? I should have asked straight off, but I was so mad about what that asshole did."

"Yeah, a little shaken is all. We should go before someone comes to see what the light show was about."

"Good idea. You live around here, right?"

He hadn't released her hand, and she found his casual, soothing touch eased the tight feeling in her chest. "Take me to my shop instead. I'm not ready to go home for the night." And not ready to take him to her home either.

Their walk back was somber, without the lighthearted chatter they'd shared on the way to the movies. She led the way into the shop but didn't turn on the front lights. Instead, she locked the door behind them and led him to the back. She drew the curtains shut and flipped on the lights.

"Just grab a stool from the easel if you want. Is Coke okay? I think I still have some rum back here too unless Toni finished it off the last time we hung out."

"Whatever you have is fine."

She took a few minutes to make their drinks then carried them over.

"Are you sure you'll be okay? You want to call your mom or dad or someone to talk?"

Nate had begun to fret, and it was surprisingly cute. She raised her chin to look up at him and smiled.

"No. I'm good," she assured him with a hand on his shoulder. "Just needed a moment. I've never had anything like that happen to me before. I mean, my dad always warned me it could happen in the city, so did Mom. I'm just glad you were there with me. I think the blinding was scarier than the gun in my face."

"Brave girl," he murmured.

He hung around in the shop with her for a while longer, and she showed him some of her current projects, including the charm bracelet for Charlie and plans she'd sketched out for the clients who visited that day. They wanted a bridal tiara for their only daughter's upcoming wedding, and she'd begun designing the headdress while waiting for him to arrive for their date.

When midnight arrived, she had just coaxed him into sharing a few Navy stories. She'd never been on a ship out at sea, and his tales of sailing to Australia and Dubai excited her.

"I better save Dubai for next time," Nate remarked as he looked at his watch. "It's after midnight."

"And we have another date tomorrow," Astrid said. "We still have that date, right?"

"Hell yeah. As long as you aren't backing out on me."

After she collected their glasses and tossed them in the dishwasher, he walked her back to her building a few streets over.

They parted ways on the sidewalk outside, and as the elevator took her to the upper level, Astrid mourned that she didn't have the courage to bring him inside.

***

It didn't take Nate long to find him since the gunman looped around the block and circled back after Astrid was safely inside. They met on a quieter side street a few blocks over from her building.

Nate shoved Lancelot against the wall. "What the hell was that stunt tonight?"

"Kay told me to test the girl for magical power or strength, okay? I didn't expect her to have mad wrestling skills instead. She almost broke my nose."

Startled by the knight's admission, Nate released him and stepped back. "Kay sent you?"

Lancelot nodded and rubbed his shoulder. "Shit, it still hurts from when she wrenched it. Didn't feel like anything supernatural, though. I'd probably have lost the arm altogether or, at the very least, I'd be at the hospital if she were a dragon. She wouldn't need to power up and transform to do that."

"True. True."

"Since I'm still alive, I'm inclined to agree with you about her being a human trapped in a shitty situation. She's hot, though."

"You were really going to toss away your life to prove me wrong?"

Lancelot shrugged. "Not without a fight. I'm too attached to this life to let it go yet, and unlike you, I remember the ones I've already had. I *know* I have it good now. Figured if she did dragon out on me, you'd have my back and we'd take her down together."

Among the mortals, Lancelot was known by the name Jared Bennett. He was a personal fitness trainer to the stars and made thousands guiding aging actresses and flabby actors through intense workouts to fulfill the physical requirements of their action roles. He had a wife and two girls, neither of which had the soul of a knight. Their order had been all male since its inception, and that wouldn't change, much to their relief.

"Did you seriously expect her to go into dragon mode in the middle of downtown?"

"Anansi did."

"Anansi was an asshole," Nate muttered. "But that's a completely different situation. That was a small African village. This is San Diego. It would be all over the news in seconds."

"Right. Meaning the public would go into an uproar about getting rid of the dragons once and for all. Even the president couldn't smooth that fiasco over the way he did when old Fafnir resurfaced."

"You're an asshole, man. You know you caught me in that radiance spell, too."

Lancelot shrugged, but he had the good sense to appear chastened before muttering, "Sorry. You could have told her to let me go."

"How would that have looked after you just had a gun in her *face*?"

"Chill, man, it was Kylie's. I just sawed off the little tip and painted it black. The most it would have done was shoot bubbles in your girlfriend's face."

"She's not my girlfriend. She's a target."

"Yeah? What took so long for you to ditch her?" Lancelot tilted his head and eyed him with skepticism. His blond brows raised. "You get laid in there?"

"No! Christ, no. No," he repeated softer. "But I could hardly hope to secure more time with her if I ran off like a douche after she was mugged."

"True."

"Next time you two geniuses have a brilliant idea while I'm on a mission, you let me know first."

"Sure, whatever you want, man. I'm sorry about taking you by surprise."

Lancelot agreed easily with genuine remorse, but that came as no surprise to Nate. The guy was his original birth father, the man who conceived him centuries ago. Lying to him felt wrong.

"I wasn't entirely honest with you about why I'm upset," he confessed.

Lancelot raised a brow. "Tell me something I don't know. I was giving you the chance to decide you were ready to talk."

No surprise. No one knew Nate better. He sighed and leaned against the wall. "I don't feel like we're doing the right thing anymore."

"What do you suggest we should do? Stop hunting them altogether?"

"What harm are they causing?" Nate countered.

"There's that black dragon in Ghana with the harem of underage girls. I'd call that plenty of harm."

"I'm not saying we should ignore the ones like him. What I'm saying is that those dragons are the only ones deserving our attention."

"How can we determine who deserves it until we investigate, son?" The modern slang fell away and the old Lancelot emerged. He studied Nate with the caring eyes of a father. "I understand why you feel this way, because you aren't alone."

"I'm not?"

Lancelot shook his head. "When Kay created his harebrained scheme to assassinate Belenos of Gaul, Percivale and I disagreed fervently with him. Unfortunately, we were alone."

"I would have stood by you both."

"You were deployed at sea, Galahad. The three of us alone wouldn't have swayed his judgment."

Nate sighed and looked at the time. If he was going to meet with her and some of his Navy pals at the beach, he needed to get to bed. "Yeah. I know."

"What are your next plans with the girl?"

"Beach and the carnival tomorrow. I'll report in afterward, okay?"

"Come on, I'll give you a lift to your car. But a word of advice to you, if you're willing to take it."

Nate raised his brows. "What?"

"Speak to some of the other knights about your concerns, in private. I'd start with Degore, Bors, and Dagonet. Maybe even Gawain."

"Gawain is still a teen."

"It makes no difference. Chat with him before he's poisoned by Kay's influence and hatred."

A grin spread over Nate's face as he considered the possible repercussions of going behind Kay's back. Screw it. He wasn't known for his courage for nothing. "You know what. You're right."

"Of course I'm right." Lancelot threw an arm around Nate's shoulders and grinned back at him. "I'm always going to be the best father you've ever had."

Chapter 4

The reality of hanging out with a gang of Navy officers on the beach had been different than her expectations, but still fun despite the lack of volleyball. Instead, they'd enjoyed hilarious attempts at bodysurfing and an impromptu sandcastle competition.

One of the female sailors, a werewolf named Maria, flashed Astrid a knowing smile. Shifters often recognized each other, by scent if not by mannerisms alone. They kept one another's secret and chatted amicably about life in San Diego until one of the guys returned with a pair of rented jet skis.

Later, they abandoned the beach as a group and moved on to the county fair for an evening of greasy food and carnival rides. By midnight, the magical hour when she finally forced herself to part from his side, there was only enough vigor in her bones to stand drowsily beneath the shower and crawl into bed with damp hair.

Over the next few weeks, their thriving relationship progressed to visits over lunch at the cafe or her shop and evening picnics beneath the stars at Balboa Park. For a military man, he had a formidable grasp of romantic gestures, and before bed each night, they chatted over text messages or on Facebook.

He even charmed her friends.

Dating became a gratifying experience, but time with Nate mentally and physically exhausted her. After a night on the dance floor, she crawled into bed without washing off her makeup, afraid she'd pass out in the shower.

Two days later on a Monday morning, the alarm company monitoring her shop awakened Astrid from a dead sleep in the early, pre-dawn hours. She arrived to find a surprise awaiting her at The Dragon's Hoard. In bright red paint, someone had sprayed the letters DRAGON'S WHORE on the glass. The door, which had been a custom order featuring a stained glass window, had been reduced to a mass of splinters attached to broken hinges. Colorful glass shards covered the rug beneath her feet.

A police officer was already on scene, a sympathetic, middle-aged man who had a shifter daughter of his own. He patted her shoulder and concluded that the vandal must have been frightened by the noise wailing from the alarm.

He asked her about any possible enemies, relationships recently ended with bad blood, or angry customers unhappy with the results of her work. He took photographs for evidence, and once she'd called the insurance company and the home improvement store to order a temporary replacement door, Astrid retreated to the rear of her shop and sobbed.

Toni appeared by noon with frozen vanilla lattes. She worked at the same cafe where Astrid and Nate met. She'd begged off of her shift an hour ahead of schedule, citing a family emergency.

"Girl, I'm so sorry I couldn't get out of work earlier to come. Maybe we can get it off with a Mr. Clean Magic Eraser? I'll run down the road and buy some."

"I already called a cleaning service. I don't even want to look at it anymore."

Would her customers remain loyal if the truth emerged, or would her store become swamped with curious people hoping for a glimpse of the billionaire movie tycoon's dragon child? Ever since she'd changed her name and Max had enacted laws of privacy, she'd had a chance to enjoy her life without restrictions.

The press had called the law a dictatorial move, but everywhere across the United States, shifters had wept in relief and celebrated the opportunity to keep their lives secret. Normal. Human spouses and parents of shifter children rejoiced, free of the fear they'd receive a terrifying call in the night.

Despite all of her protection, someone had defiled the sanctity of her greatest possession, the only thing she truly owned of her hard work and love. She felt violated and no longer wanted to sit inside the shop.

"Did you call your parents yet? Let them know? If the press gets wind of this and the news runs with it, they'll find out soon."

"We bribe the press not to run any stories about us like this," she said numbly. "Keeps my identity safe now."

"Still, give them a call."

Toni hugged her and tossed away their empty cups before hefting the bag of trash to take out to the dumpster.

Heeding her friend's advice, Astrid called home. Chloe picked up on the second ring. "Hi, sweetie, what's wrong?"

"Everything."

She gave her mother an accounting of the events beginning with the first call from the security company to the police officer's comments. She'd spent hours counting inventory and noticed nothing missing.

"Oh no," Chloe breathed on the other end of the phone. "We're on our way. All of us. Sit tight and we'll—"

"Don't bother, Mom. There's no point in coming, and it will only draw more attention. Toni and I are about to go and get some lunch anyway." Though she had no appetite and would only pick at her meal. "Actually, can you ask Aunt Mahasti if she'll come weave some spells around the place?"

A heavy silence dominated the line.

"Mom?"

"Sweetheart, Mahasti *did* leave a ward around your store," Chloe said.

"What?"

"You know how your dad is, but he didn't want you to think he doubted your ability to protect yourself. It's—wait, hold on a moment. You think what?"

Astrid overheard Mahasti's voice in the background and strained to hear the genie speak.

"Are you sure?" Chloe said in a panicked voice.

"Mom, what? What is it?"

"Astrid, love, do the police have the person responsible for it? Were they at the scene of the crime when you arrived?"

"No, Mom. If they had him, I would have told you right off. There's no sign of the vandal and only a blurry image on the security cameras."

"They left without any sign of injury?"

"Yeah, the police couldn't find any physical evidence here or anything."

"Mahasti believes there's magic involved. The moment someone broke through the integrity of your door, the wards should have immobilized them until long after the cops arrived."

***

If Nate wanted to be successful, he had to rally the knights behind him before Kay became aware of his plans.

He drove early into town for the meeting before any of the knights appeared at their lodge. In his Jeep, he listened to music and watched the parking lot until Gawain, the only underage knight among them who attended meetings, arrived in the company of Sir Bors. Like Kay and Nate, the two were father and son in their present lifetime.

After killing the engine to the Jeep, he stepped outside onto the pavement and called out, "Hey guys! What's happening?"

"Oh hey, dude!" Gawain called back.

"How's it going?" Bors asked him pleasantly.

"Well enough. Hey. You have time for a quick chat?" Nate asked.

"Of course. I've always got time for you, Nate," Bors replied with a jovial smile. "What can we do for you?"

"I want to know what you think about Kay's recent outbursts and my current mission. What you really think, not what you'd say at the round table to avoid division among us."

Bors opened his mouth to speak but the teenage knight beat him to the punch. "I think it's lame," Gawain said. "It's not cool to lie to a woman like that, man, and I felt bad for you when Kay gave you the job."

Nate nodded. "Agreed. And you, Bors?"

The middle-aged knight sighed. "Agreed, but what can we do when Arthur left Kay, Gareth, and Pelleus in charge during his absence from the world?"

"Do any of us know for a fact that Arthur gave him the leadership?" Nate asked.

"Hell no," Gawain said. "I don't have my memory back yet either, but we'd all know if Arthur wanted someone to lead. Everything I've ever read about Arthur suggests that he keeps detailed notes. He'd have left something behind for us."

Bors pursed his lips, and a thoughtful look came to his brown eyes. "You're quite right, Gawain. But of course, Kay only has Gareth and Pelleus to corroborate his claims."

"Who both have something to gain from him leading the knighthood in Arthur's absence. Don't you find this a little suspicious? Arthur never agreed with hunting peaceful dragons."

"No, he did not," Bors agreed. "And he would take special offense to the stalking of Astrid Drakenstone. It surprised me when you accepted the job."

"I didn't want Pelleus to do it," Nate admitted. "I'm going to be honest with you both. Whether or not she's a dragon doesn't matter now. I think we can have peace between us all. A genuine lasting peace now that they have a dragon in the White House with something to lose if their kind go on the rampage."

"Then if I may be so bold, Nate, what do you need from us?" Bors asked pleasantly.

"Your support when the time comes. I don't know yet what I'm going to do, but I have a feeling that change is coming."

"Sure thing, man," Gawain said. "Hey, there's Sir Tristram. I bet he'd want in on this."

He did.

As a group, the four knights chatted to the side of the building as more members of the knighthood arrived for the gathering. Most of them waved in passing and continued inside, but Sir Percivale paused to study Nate's congregation.

"I don't know if I'm willing to defy Kay," Tristram said with reluctance. "While I know in my heart what you speak is right, I don't want to see our knighthood divided."

Fear of division seemed to be the concern each of them had. A knighthood without unity would collapse on itself. "Then take some time to think about it," Nate pleaded.

"I will."

Kay's SUV came into view, cruising down the road toward them. Their group broke apart and they moved inside.

One by one, the slayers took their seats at the round table. Beginning with the oldest knight to the youngest, they recounted their actions of the month in the debriefing. Nate was among the last to report.

Kay's baleful glower seared into his son. "It's been nearly a month, Galahad. Three weeks and what do you have? Nothing."

As uncomfortable as the name made him, Nate refused to squirm in his seat. Echo set her head in his lap, and he rubbed her ears beneath the table. *Good girl*. "She hasn't said anything to implicate her status, Echo hasn't reacted violently to her scent, and I'm not in a position to outright ask and receive an honest answer."

"I have to say, I'm with him on this one," Lancelot added his support. "She didn't show anything supernatural during my attack, only a good handle on skills any woman can learn in a proper self-defense class." He frowned. "Really good. Props to whoever taught her."

His father drummed his fingers on the table. "What about her family? We've been trying to get a bead on Saul Drakenstone for years, but he always manages to slip away."

"She doesn't speak about her father or mother unless it's a vague reference to family affairs. She doesn't use names." Nate shrugged and spread his hands in defeat. "What do you want me to do? I can't even tell you what the inside of her apartment looks like."

For good reason. A week ago, she'd tiptoed around the subject of him coming up for coffee after they'd gone for a casual night socializing with her friends. He'd feigned ignorance and mumbled an excuse about needing to visit the base.

"Then ramp up your charm, or we'll get someone who can. Pelleus from Italy has been put on standby now that he's finished with that blue in Greece. His third kill in this incarnation."

Pelleus from Italy was a womanizing douche who would have peeled Astrid's panties off of her on the first date and had no qualms about putting his sword through her chest afterward. Nate straightened and pushed his shoulders back. No woman deserved that. Dragon or not.

His father knew how to egg him on.

"Three kills, and you've yet to get one. When will you contribute to our cause, Galahad?" Bedivere asked.

"He isn't Galahad anymore," Kay said. "Not yet anyway. Not until his memories are back. And that starts when he's finished this mission and spilled some dragon blood."

"Then stop getting in my way," Nate shot back. "You want me to get the info you need, then don't go behind my back and send Lancelot to scare her or Gareth to vandalize her shop."

His father glowered at him.

There was a small part of him that had hoped Astrid would call, that she'd need him after finding her shop entrance in tatters. Worse, he'd wanted to comfort her.

In the past, Nate would have remained a passive but obedient spectator, but something about Kay's words stirred a fire in him. He straightened and stared directly at Kay, meeting his eye. "To be honest with you. I think this entire thing stinks. Why are we hunting this family? When was the last time Saul Drakenstone has razed a village? Has he *ever* attacked a human? Nothing about this fits our usual modus operandi. We've been reduced to street thugs mobbing girls in alleys and stalking harmless supernaturals. I thought we were supposed to go after threats?"

"We can't determine whether or not they're a threat until you proceed with your duty," Kay snarled back.

"What duty? The one you're constantly calling into question and interrupting?"

"Man's got a point," Percivale said. "How is he supposed to work while she's terrorized by your antics? We're professionals. Let's act like it."

Nate sighed in relief. It was good to have someone on his side. The other knight smiled warmly at him from across the table.

"Fine." His father leaned back in his seat. "You have until our next meeting to produce worthwhile intel or we go to Plan B. This meeting is adjourned."

Nate and Echo caught up to Percivale outside as the knight was en route to his vehicle. He was an older fellow, a decade Nate's senior, but younger than their current leaders. Killing the fire wyrm, Anansi, in Ghana had earned him the respect to move up in their ranks.

"Thanks for having my back in there," he said.

"No problem. I know where they're coming from, but sometimes I think Kay forgets we're here to slay dragons. And only slay dragons. Stalking little girls and harassing them like this? It bothers me, Nate. There are better ways to flush them into the open. This is childish."

"It is. And there are more dangerous dragons to hunt. Everyone agrees Anansi needed to go down." The dragon had been demanding tributes in first-born daughters from the villages and collected quite the harem of abused young women. He'd tricked parents by promising riches, wealth, and good luck to those who obeyed his commands. Death came to anyone else.

Finally, Percivale pinned him down and ended his long reign of terror in Africa. Even his own kind wouldn't miss him.

"What's Saul Drakenstone done to be loathed like this? He abuses no women. He harms no one. Hell, he makes good movies," the knight muttered, rubbing his bearded chin. Gray peppered his black hair, and his skin was weathered, dark brown from a lifetime of work outdoors.

"You've watched his movies?"

"Who hasn't watched his movies, Nate?"

Percivale was among the small handful who used Nate's current name as an act of kindness, not as a taunt.

Maybe the name Galahad would feel right after he'd recovered his memories. Maybe it never would. How could he possibly know until he'd murdered a dragon?

Until he'd killed one of Astrid's possible relatives or friends.

"My father."

"Kay is stuck in the past. Times are changing for the dragons, and if we want to survive without losing our sanity over the next thousand years, we have to adapt." He shook his head. "What shall we do once the last dragon is dead? Will we turn to shifters? Ah, we've wasted enough time. I need to get on the road, kid."

Nate grimaced. "Where are you going in a hurry?"

"San Francisco. Kay's ordered the usual routine surveillance on Loki Agnarhorn."

"I'll come with you if you don't mind. I need to clear my mind."

"You sure? I won't be coming back for a few days."

Nate shook his head. As for work, mortal members of their brotherhood worked everywhere, and a single phone call would account for his absence at the base.

After grabbing his gear from the tool chest in the back of his Jeep, Nate joined the other dragonslayer, and they headed to the airport.

***

Gathered around an open pizza box, Astrid sprawled on the floor with three of her closest friends. Toni was the only human among them. The twins, Heather and Melanie, were coyote shifters. After her harrowing day, a night with her pals was a must.

They all adored Nate. One evening out with them and their current boyfriends had cemented a bond between the sailor and all of her pals. Eventually, she'd be introducing him to her family.

Astrid imagined Saul staring down his nose at her boyfriend before the interrogation began. Within seconds, she'd killed her buzz with anxiety.

With a mischievous look on her face, Toni leaned forward and murmured, "So. You and Nate. Spill the beans."

"Toni," Astrid groaned. "What more do you want me to say?"

"Have you two kissed yet?" Heather asked.

Melanie refilled their wine glasses. "When's he taking you out again?"

"No, and I don't know. We haven't had the chance to talk in a couple days."

"Why not?" Toni demanded. "Doesn't he know your shop was vandalized? He didn't show up?"

"No, and I didn't want him to since I haven't told him my real name."

"What the hell? Woman, you have to tell him. Eventually, he's going to find out about your—" Toni mimed flapping wings.

"Not necessarily," she hedged. "Most people assume Mom had me thanks to artificial insemination."

"Still, if you two are gonna get serious, he has the right to know."

Astrid took another sip of wine and reached for more pizza. "I know. I guess I'm just trying to stretch it out, you know? Before the inevitable change happens where he either runs away or starts seeing my monetary value."

"We don't care about your monetary value," Melanie reminded her. "Or do you think that about us now, too?"

Astrid tossed a bunched up napkin at the coyote across the coffee table. "Of course not. I'm just thinking about my track record with men. You all liked Scott, too."

"Yeah, that fireman was hot." Heather fanned herself.

"But not too brave, freaking out about you being a dragon. You'd think a dude who battles wild brush fires wouldn't almost piss his pants over you being able to breathe it." Melanie winked at Astrid.

Heather frowned. "Anyway, how are you holding up after the break-in? Did they get anything?"

Astrid shook her head. "Doesn't seem like it. I did a full inventory afterward. I don't think it was a theft. It was..." Someone sending her a message. Chilled, she shivered and raised her wine for another sip. She felt safe in her shop and had even slept there before when the work flowed easily, keeping her up until late into the night. She wouldn't allow someone to take that from her.

"They spray painted the windows, but whoever it was, the cameras didn't pick up their face."

"They didn't try to get inside?"

"That's when the alarm went off, most likely scaring them away. Grandpa Max insisted on that alarm system. He said it's so loud Daddy would be able to hear it at the studios in L.A., and I agree. Now that the professional window cleaner finished his work and I had a new door installed, everything has gone back normal again."

Toni leaned over for the television remote. Her discreet tap of the channel button came too late to hide a newscast of the recent events in Greece. Someone had murdered another dragon shifter in cold blood.

"It's okay. I know about it already," Astrid assured her. Though it was no less disturbing to know it was open season on shifters and that dragons were no longer unstoppable behemoths.

"Did you know him?" Toni asked.

"No, but my dad did. He's upset about it. Mom says today is the first day he's come up from his hoard since they found out. He goes there to sulk usually over not getting his way with Mom, but now it's like his mourning shrine every time we lose a family friend."

"Ugh. I'm sorry you guys even have to go through this stuff. Slayers seem to leave the rest of us shifters alone mostly," Melanie said. "It's bad enough some asshole tried to mug you and Nate, now you have problems with bigots, too."

Astrid hesitated before speaking. Giving voice to her concerns made them real, gave them power, but clinging internally to her terror had twisted her stomach into knots. "I think it was a slayer who tried to mug Nate and me during that first date. I keep going back over it in my head and there's just no way a sorcerer would attack someone with a gun."

The twins stared at her until Toni spoke up with a gentle reminder. "But you said it was a toy."

"I know. It was weird, but nothing else makes much sense."

"So why didn't he spear you and call it a day?" Toni asked.

"Who knows. Maybe he didn't want to hurt Nate, too, since Nate is a human. Maybe they were testing me. Maybe it's the same guy who came up and kicked in my door. I guess my parents had my aunt put charms on the place when I first opened up, but this guy bypassed all of it. We have a family friend who's a witch, and she came out here to check into it for us, right?"

"Right?" Heather said, waving her hand for Astrid to continue.

"All gone. It was like this guy cut through my aunt's spells. And she's a genie, so that should have been impossible unless..."

"Unless it was a slayer," Toni said in a strained voice.

"Astrid, that's terrifying. If this is a slayer, what's going to stop him from coming back?" Melanie asked.

"She left a few hidden traps around my shop that she says should even give a dragonslayer a kick in the ass."

Chapter 5

Nate collapsed into a desk chair inside of the slayer safe house and brought the computer out of sleep mode. Within seconds, he'd brought up the dossier on Loki Agnarhorn, a digital file consisting of scanned pages written centuries ago and recent data acquired during the age of technology. The handwriting and style varied over the years as different slayers took over the task as their keepers of history.

"Half of the older stuff is in Old Norse," he muttered. "Hell if I know what this means."

"How's your Middle English?" Percivale asked.

Nate gestured with a hand and shrugged. "Decent."

The older knight passed him a manila folder. "Here. These didn't get scanned into the database yet, but I have copies. Most of it's repetitive, the same information repeated from age to age. Loki the Trickster, God of Mischief, the selfish one, the annihilator. Bringer of Ruin."

"Impressive list of titles for a man who makes shitty cellphones now."

"And therein lies the trick." Percivale grimaced. "I bought one of his phones about sixteen years ago before the knighthood found me and I discovered all of this. The title fits. And his phones are still trash."

"Apple products, man, it's the only way to go."

Nate read over the old accountings. Like Fafnir and many of the other dragon elders from the past, Loki had raided villages, demanded tributes, and became notorious for his mischief ruining lives across Europe.

In the past two or three decades, however, he had been relatively quiet. He made no schemes, and while his name popped up from time to time in the technology sector, the world had no idea he was a dragon.

"It says here he was among the dragons who voted to remain in secrecy. How the hell did we get ahold of this intel anyway?"

Percivale shrugged. "Ask Kay. He won't reveal his sources, but you'd think he had a front row seat to their supernatural shindig."

"Be straight with me, Perce. Are they planning to slay the trickster along with the other malevolent wyrms now?" Nate asked.

"Seems like it. Anansi was only the start, but to be honest, we could have taken Loki out by now if Kay wasn't obsessed with the Drakenstones. I went and did that on my own time because it was the right thing to do and our honorary leader is out of his damned mind."

Nate shrugged. Percivale hadn't told him anything groundbreaking. "He's offended one of them managed to become president. He'll never let it go until Emberthorn is dead."

"We need Arthur to reincarnate. It's been over a century since anyone's seen him, but if he were here, he'd put an end to this madness. What I wouldn't give to see us return to the good days of glory and righteousness. Guns and rifles. Explosives in dumpsters." He snorted, disgusted. "It's no way to battle a creature armed with only his or her claws when we have magic of our own."

Nate glanced to his left and raised a skeptical brow. "In a minute you'll be telling me about how it was back in your day when we had to walk five miles in the snow to slay dragons."

"Twenty miles. And hell, it was *your* day, too, Nate. You just don't remember it yet."

After a good laugh, they concocted a plan for monitoring the wyrm's activities. Loki followed a transparent schedule known to the closest members of his household staff and his corporate associates. A typical nine to five Monday through Saturday followed by quiet evenings in a sprawling fifty-acre compound.

"Christ, he even works during the weekend."

"He's a dragon. Their concept of time is different," Percivale said.

Loki maintained a small staff of loyal shifters on his property, but he had no friends, a loner who attended events with no woman on his arm.

"My informants tell me he's going to be at some craft beer tasting down at Fisherman's Wharf this evening."

"Least it's not wine," Nate muttered.

"You haven't had wine until you've enjoyed a good rosé on a fine summer afternoon, Nate. Expand your horizons."

"Tastes like pink swamp water."

"All right, all right, smart ass. Before we go, let's see you summon that sword."

Nate sighed. "I told you, I can do it now."

"I want to see it with my own eyes."

Percivale stared him down until he relented. With a groan, Nate muttered the oath under his breath, "When called upon, I draw thee to defend the rights of the weak with all of my strength."

In a radiant flood of light, the sword emerged from nothingness and appeared in his hands. Light shone from the crystalline, white metal.

"Not bad. You're still reciting the oath to do it, but that's better than nothing. Think you can take out a dragon if he loses his shit?"

"I can do it." Nate made a sheathing gesture with the sword and it vanished again. It was part of his spirit and bound to him throughout all of his many lives.

"C'mon then. Load up your gear and let's get moving."

Nate fastened Echo's service dog vest into place and collected their supplies. When it came to reconnaissance missions, slayers didn't leave their base of operations without the tools necessary to take down a dragon.

Beer wasn't so bad, but Percivale wasn't open to acquiring tickets to the event, so instead, the men and Echo sat on the wharf with binoculars under the guise of birdwatching. It fit. A little. With their magnificent feathered wings, dragons resembled a splice of bird and reptile. Their durable skin ran a wide gamut of colors from pearlescent silver to black opal and mimicked the texture of alligators when they reached maturity.

Younger cubs and new adults sported softer hides, and those were the easiest to pierce with mortal weapons.

One of the restaurants on Fisherman's Wharf hosted the tasting in their outdoor patio area. People mingled and took seats at round tables while waiters came around with their first pours. A few guests stood at the railing and pointed at the sea lions basking in the early evening sunshine.

"Our target's at the back in the black and green polo."

"That's Loki?"

Nate's brows skewed as he peered over at the lone man sitting at a rear table, beer glass in one hand, pretzel in the other. In his khaki slacks and company polo, he blended with any other San Franciscan at the wharf for a pleasant summer evening.

"Sure is."

"He looks so…" Nate tried to find an appropriate word but came up blank. "Did Kay really send you up here to watch the man piss away his day with a couple of beers? This doesn't tell us anything. He's not even talking to anyone. No mischief. No spells. Nada."

"What did you expect? For him to bewitch the server for a free glass? We've only been here for five minutes."

"All I'm saying is, this is crap. Except for the rare few like Anansi, these guys haven't done anything to merit a quick death in the last fifty years. Loki's especially behaved according to the files. Apparently, I watched him in my last life, with nothing to report except the start of his new business venture."

He still found it disconcerting to see his signature on old reports. His handwriting hadn't changed, the loops and lines of each word identical despite the name changing.

A broad grin spread across Percivale's face. "And that hasn't changed. Kay sent me here to verify that's the case, but as you can see, he's a rehabilitated dragonman. Glad I'm not the only one who sees it, because he's a tough one. The dragon sorcerers are like cockroaches. They never go down unless there's a half dozen of us to stomp them."

"Yeah, well, with age comes power. If all mages were immortal the way Merlin is, I imagine we'd be living in a completely different world. Lucky for us, they reincarnate the same way we do."

"True enough. The smart ones, though, they do the same as us and store things away for their next life."

As the night passed with no examples of strange behavior, Nate grew disinterested in the job. His phone buzzed, alerting him to incoming texts in addition to the ones he blew off to avoid Astrid dragging him into deep conversation in his comrade's company.

His phone burned a hole in his pocket. Damn, he wanted to talk to her.

"I think we can both agree this dragon isn't a danger to anyone," Percivale said. He lowered his binoculars and glanced to his right at Nate. "Aren't you going to answer those?"

Nate cleared his throat. "What if it's only a show?"

"A show for who, kid? He doesn't know we're here, and if he did, I don't think he'd care."

"We can't report that to Kay. He'd never accept it."

The older knight chuckled and rose from his seat. "Coming from me, he won't have a choice. There are better dragons to fry, and we're wasting our time."

They grabbed fresh coffee from a cafe on their way back to the car. Percivale started the engine, but he didn't take the vehicle out of park.

"What's really on your mind, Nate? You were itching to get away, but you've been distracted and edgy since we arrived to monitor him."

Nate hesitated.

"You can tell me. I'm not Kay. Hell, maybe I should have raised you this time around."

"You're barely older than me," Nate pointed out.

"Old enough I could have done a better job. So what's on your mind?"

"The girl."

"You two getting close?" Percivale asked.

"Yeah. I guess we are. Closer than I intended at first. It doesn't feel right to keep her in the dark about it, but I can't exactly open up and tell her I'm one of the guys responsible for her race dying out."

"You've never slain anyone who didn't deserve it."

"So you tell me."

"Read your own notes, kid."

"I have. I do all the time, but it's still unfamiliar, like a damned dream or something. Hanging out with Astrid, it's fun. Easy. I don't want to give that up."

"No one is saying—"

"You heard Kay. He was quite clear on the matter."

Percivale went quiet, lips pressed into a thin line. Nate recognized the look and let him think in silence.

"Kay's been a different man for a couple cycles now, a hothead when it comes to the Drakenstones, but he does raise a legitimate concern. If they're replenishing their numbers by mating with humans, we need to know. I'm not saying the girl is a danger, but she could be something new. Unknown. We need to know what we're dealing with."

"I don't want to hurt her."

"Then don't."

"Easy for you to say. You're not the one lying to her."

The older slayer set his coffee aside in the drink holder and gave him a look. "So this is what your change of heart is about. Living in harmony with dragons. Letting the rest of them slide and letting bygones be bygones. I heard you've been chatting up a couple of the younger guys. Gawain seems to think that we can be friends with the dragons."

A surge of pride swelled in Nate's chest. He grinned. "Maybe. Nothing says we can't all form some kind of understanding. Settle a truce and agree to let the bitterness remain in the past where it belongs. It'll lead to a happier future for everyone, you know?"

"So you thought you'd try to campaign for peace, eh? Christ. You've got a crush on a dragon, and that's why you're all tore up over this. Look, Nate, I don't know what kind of game you're trying to pull, but Kay is going to figure out sooner or later that you're not being completely honest with him."

"Don't tell him."

Percivale shook his head. "Nah, I wouldn't do that to you. I care about you too much for that, but I know what's going to happen when he figures out you're holding back intel."

"I'm not. All I have are hunches, but no proof. She hasn't said or shown anything about herself that points to being magical at all."

"Give it time. What will you do if it turns out she's some creature born from one of them and a human?" The older slayer raised his brows.

"I don't know." Nate sighed and leaned back in his seat. Fretting, he closed his eyes and pinched the bridge of his nose. "I honest to God don't know."

***

Nate didn't call her that week and paid no visits to the shop. She'd hoped to find him on Facebook, but his profile was strangely absent of any posts, not that he spent much time on social media to begin with.

He didn't share memes often, and the few posts he made usually related to mentoring at the Boys & Girls Club in L.A. where he visited his mom at her job.

Still, he was quiet. Growing concerned, she sent a text message and received a clipped response hours later.

"Maybe he's busy on base?" Toni suggested. "I mean, are they even allowed to take cell phones on those ships?"

"I dunno. He isn't on a ship and doesn't often speak about his work."

"Well, cell phones aren't secure, girl. The man has to be busy. Text him again tonight and ask if he's okay."

A few hours later, she did as Toni bid her and received a terse affirmative before Nate mirrored the question back to her.

Nate: How are you doing?

Astrid: I'm good now.

Nate: I'm glad. Miss talking to you.

She sagged in relief, before giving in to her curiosity and asking what he was doing.

Nate: Secret stuff. Should be home soon.

No matter how long she waited for the magic to fade, it never did. There was something indescribable about her attraction to Nate, and it became more concrete with each meeting.

She looked forward to his goofy smiles, his humor, and the way he leaned against her store counter in his uniform. She hadn't seen his dress whites again, but fondness branded the image into her memory. She couldn't forget it.

When she called her grandmother the next morning to see if she could use their beach house for a day, Ēostre offered it for the entire weekend instead, asking if she wanted company.

"Um… not this time. I'm bringing a friend."

"Oh. A nice girls' evening out? How fun. Well, there's wine in the cabinet, so enjoy."

"A guy friend."

Ēostre said nothing at first. During the silence, Astrid's heart pounded in an erratic jackhammer and the sound of it drowned out everything else. Sharing news about Nate made her nervous, like a wish she couldn't voice if she wanted it to come true. The more people who knew about him, the more it would hurt when their relationship inevitably collapsed.

"That is *marvelous* news, sweetheart. Is he a nice boy? In that case, I'll be sure to tell your father and grandfather you're having a nice evening in with the girls in front of the home entertainment system. It'll keep them from playing the busybody and checking into your affairs."

Astrid exhaled in relief. "Thank you."

"Now tell me about him. What's he like? Is he hot?"

"Grandma!"

"It's a legitimate question."

It was, so after she'd confirmed Nate's attractive qualities, they chatted for another hour before she hung up and phoned the man to make her offer.

While twisting a blonde curl around her finger, she waited for him to answer. The moment the call connected, she blurted, "So I was headed up to Carlsbad this weekend and wondered if you want to come with me."

"Huh?" came the tired voice on the other end in a drowsy slur. "This weekend? Sounds great."

"*Really?* I mean, great. My grandparents keep a beach house up there, and I usually keep an eye on it for them. Pop in sometimes. There's a grill, too. We could bring steaks and stuff. Have a relaxing day watching the water from the deck."

"Sure. I'll look forward to it. Supposed to be clear, too."

Her keen hearing picked up the sound of mattress springs creaking beneath the weight of a moving body. Suddenly, the lethargic voice made sense. She glanced at her stylish, ornate grandfather clock, an antique from her grandmother's hoard. It read eleven twenty. "Did I wake you? I'm sorry. You were probably on duty last night or something."

"No, no, it's fine. I kinda overslept." After a pause, he added, "I can't think of anything better to wake up to than the sound of your voice anyway."

"Flattery will get you everywhere." Chuckling, she relaxed on the stool. "Right. So I'll do some shopping, and if there's anything specific you want, feel free to bring it or send me a text."

"Sure thing, baby girl. Talk later?"

"Yeah. Get some more rest."

The rest of the week flew by on gilded wings. Before she knew it, Saturday had arrived, and they were en route to her grandparents' beach house in his Jeep. Nate claimed he couldn't fold himself into her tiny hybrid car.

"It's that one," Astrid said.

Her family had built great memories in the beach house her grandmother had purchased a few years ago. Now she and Max vacationed in it occasionally, but they'd given her keys and all of the security codes. After instructing Nate to park in the vacant garage, she leaped out and deactivated the home security alarm. The light changed from red to green, and the gentle, prolonged beep ended.

"Grandparents into surfing?" He gestured to the four boards hung over a shelf loaded with beach toys.

"You'd be surprised. Plus, they let the whole family use the place. So, um, make yourself at home."

Nate approached with a duffel bag over his shoulder. He'd brought steaks and board shorts for the beach. "Big family?"

"Yeah. Mom, Dad, and my little brother. And an aunt and uncle who are younger than me."

His brows shot up.

"My grandma remarried later in life, and she's one of those ladies who… you know." She cleared her throat. "So, uh, they had twins. Cutest things ever. Then there's my aunt and her family."

"You're much younger than I thought if your grandmother is still having kids. Are you sure I'm not robbing the cradle?"

"I told you, I'm twenty-five, you ass, unless this is your way of telling me you're fifty."

He grinned. "I'm definitely not fifty. So… I hope you have a swimsuit beneath that dress. I'm tossing you in whether you have one or not."

"I brought one with me, and it's adorable, so please wait until I've put it on first before tossing me anywhere."

Astrid stuck her tongue out at him.

Over an hour passed before they settled with their belongings unpacked. He prepared the grill while she mixed slushie piña coladas.

They were all alone in absolute privacy without a store or friends between them, and he hadn't touched her once. Not a single embrace, and she began to wonder if he found her attractive at all. Meanwhile, she often had to resist the urge to tackle him and rip off his clothes.

Maybe her man was the polite, old-fashioned kind of fellow. Chivalrous, like some modern-day knight in shining armor. An officer gentleman. She jumped to several outlandish conclusions before wondering if he scorned sex before marriage. Could she wait?

She'd waited twenty-five years. What were a few months or even years more?

"Those steaks look good," she told him as she set a tray of veggies besides the grill and offered him a frosty beverage. "Medium is great for me."

"I'm glad you agree, because that's what I do. Anything more is a ruined steak, and less is a slab of raw meat."

Astrid chuckled and arranged an array of veggies onto the grill. She'd brought asparagus, zucchini spears, and portobello mushrooms. Lots of veggies for a dragon.

While sipping his drink, he slouched back in the patio chair with sun shades in place over his green eyes. She hated them. His eyes were too pretty to be shielded. "So when do I get to see this swimsuit of yours?" he asked.

"After we eat."

She stretched out alongside him on the adjacent lounger. In her cutoff shorts and thin camisole, she felt sexy and desirable. Would he agree? Without a bra worn beneath it, the cool breeze tightened her nipples.

"So now that you know about my family, what about yours? Any brothers or sisters? Ridiculously young aunts and uncles?"

"Half-siblings. Mom and Dad split when I was younger, so he has a kid with his new wife. I have about a thousand cousins on Mom's side of the family too." He finally glanced at her, and his double take stirred a sense of accomplishment in Astrid.

She smiled smugly behind her glass and sipped again. "Divorce?" she guessed. "That's rough. My mom's parents weren't together, and her dad raised her pretty much from the time she was old enough to say she wanted to go live with him. I never met her mom. As for my dad…" She trailed off, gaze wandering toward the beach as she tried to figure out what to say. "His dad died when he was young, and his mom was a real mess afterward. It took her a long time to get over her husband, but she found a great guy in Max." Max was a name used by hundreds of men, so she figured it was safe. "He's great to her and a kickass grandfather."

"Sounds like your parents and grandparents are happy now at least, and that's what counts the most, right? It's great that your grandmother was able to move on. So, do they know you invited a random stranger out to their place for the weekend? Day," he corrected because nothing had been uttered about the weekend, technically. As far as he knew, they were leaving after dinner.

Unless she changed their plans.

"Of course, they do," Astrid half-fibbed. "When I asked if this weekend was okay for me to come up, I said I was bringing a guy along. Don't worry, no one's going to bust in and roast you for being here," she teased.

"I've dated girls with serious parents before. I don't need a dad and a granddad coming down on me," he joked back.

A cool, salt-scented breeze blew in from over the ocean, the surf only a few yards away from where they sat overlooking the sandy beachside. She'd never seen Nate in a complete state of relaxation before. He was a workaholic, always doing something on base.

"Did you have to take off work?" she asked suddenly. "Do you have the entire weekend?"

"I had Sunday off, but I was supposed to pull duty today. Don't worry. I have a friend covering me. Next week, I'll cover for him, and we'll be even."

She winced. "Sorry. I know it was short notice, but I..." *Couldn't wait to see you again*, she finished in her head while pushing her food around on her plate.

"No, it's cool. We do it all the time whenever something pops up on a duty day."

"So, I have something to tell you. Something you need to know before we go any further, I mean, if you want to go anywhere with this." She gestured with a free hand from herself to him and back again. "Because, truthfully, I really like you, Nate, and I want to keep meeting you."

His confident grin faded, dimmed by the shift in mood. "I like you, too, and I'm happy to be here. Honest. What's wrong?" His smile dropped away completely, and a look came to his eye. Guarded and closed.

What was he hiding from her?

"My last name isn't Ellis. Not really. That's my mom's maiden name. My legal name is Drakenstone. Astrid Drakenstone."

Her memorable, unique name was one of a kind, and everyone knew it even if they didn't care about his movies. Her father was Saul Drakenstone, the billionaire movie tycoon. Dragon. Son of their country's first lady.

Nate didn't speak or appear to breathe. She watched him grow still and visibly struggle with speech. "That's…" He took a drink. "Is someone going to bust in and roast me after all?"

"No." Astrid shook her head quickly. "My grandmother knows you're here and said she wouldn't tell the guys."

"The first lady. You know, you don't look the same as you did when you used to visit them in the White House. I remember seeing you on television when they were married."

"Yeah." Astrid's hair had been longer, much longer, and she'd filled out into a woman in the past few years, no longer resembling a coltish, pre-teen with gangly limbs and a flat chest. She'd been proud to develop breasts finally, even if her father lamented and pretended to weep when she and her mother came home with her first bras.

"Are *you* going to roast me?"

"No. No roasting from me," she said in a vague reply. "So, I wanted you to know, and I understand if that changes things. For you, I mean."

"No, it's not a big deal. I mean it is, but it isn't," Nate corrected himself. After an awkward lull, he jumped to his feet and set aside his empty plate. "You ready to swim?"

"Isn't there a thirty-minute rule?" she asked weakly.

"Myth."

He took it in stride, startling her with his unfazed reaction to her secret. She'd had boyfriends in the past who figured it out on their own, but they'd always changed afterward. She became a tool to achieve their goals instead of a girlfriend to cherish.

Nate wouldn't be one of those people. She felt it in her heart, but most of all, she prayed to her ancestors that he truly was the one meant for her. Her soul mate. All of her life, she'd been surrounded by adults who treated their mates with profound respect and unconditional love. Now Astrid wanted it for herself.

"Give me a moment to change," she told him.

Before he could reply, she sprinted away into a bathroom and stripped out of her clothes. Toni and Melanie had chosen the bikini, black boy shorts with a pearl pink bandeau. She wiggled into it, pulled her hair back and plaited it into a single braid, and then emerged to find he'd beaten her outside.

Nate waited for her on the patio in his shorts, his body bronzed and muscular with broad shoulders and a trim waist. She imagined running her fingers down the muscular contour and watched in appreciation while he remained blissfully unaware.

"I'm all finished," she announced, prompting him to turn.

"It's about time," he began to tease. "I thought you'd run off to buy a swimsuit before..." His voice trailed as he turned to see her.

"What?" During their first beach date, she'd worn a single piece with a revealing high cut above her hips and a playful but plunging neckline. It had revealed as much, if not more.

Less than twenty yards away, waves crashed over the beach. Their private yard provided a small area of sand free from the random passersby, a haven where she'd played as a child. Now the twins and her brother Brandt played together in the same sand. She'd brought them all herself one weekend and ran them tired for an afternoon while her parents and grandparents enjoyed time alone.

"Just admiring the view," Nate replied. He flashed her a cocky grin. "We going out there or not?"

A gate led to the public beach beyond. It was far from crowded, and only a few people had staked out seats further down the sandy stretch, giving a sense of privacy.

"Lemme think…" She feigned deep thought for a few seconds, only to take off in a mad dash for the water. "Last one in does the dishes!"

Swearing, Nate bolted after her for the shoreline. "Cheater!" he called.

"Hey, don't cry because you're too slow—oh!" Her lead on him evaporated. She'd expected him to be fast, but he closed the distance before she had the chance to find her stride. He caught up to her when they reached the shallows where the waves swept in and out, lapping warm water against their knees. Before she could escape and hurry into the open water, strong arms surrounded her. Nate lifted her in an effortless swing.

"Who's crying?" he asked.

"How'd you catch up to me so fast!" Astrid cried, startled. She groped at Nate with both hands and curved her arms around his neck. Impulsively, she wrapped her legs around him too and hung on.

Their eyes met and their gazes held, faces close.

Astrid had never seen eyes so beautiful. As she stared into them, she felt bare and exposed, stripped down to her emotions, as if every thought she'd ever had for Nate had glided to the surface for him to read.

Maybe they had. In the next moment, he claimed her mouth, curving one hand beneath each of her thighs for support as he tasted her lips. A trace of his tongue coaxed them to part, to yield to him, infused with sweet hints of coconut and rum.

A part of her screamed inwardly in triumph, her dragon recognizing its mate. The one. Nate urged, and she yielded, lips parting so her tongue could sweep in and tangle with his. With no one present to stare, she surrendered to the moment. It was her and him. No one else. He tasted like their drinks, but also something else. Something rich and new, deep and mysterious. Heat pooled in her gut, spiraling down to her core and spreading out to every limb.

Suddenly, she wished they'd stayed at the house.

***

Astrid was the softest woman ever to throw herself into his arms. She'd crushed against him, lotion-scented skin, and scant Lycra molded over subtle curves. Falling for her hadn't been part of his assignment, and now that it had happened, he couldn't undo it.

His hand glided over her thigh until he found her swimsuit bottom. He squeezed a handful of flesh and delighted in the way she moaned against his mouth.

Now he needed the cold water to hide the way she'd affected him. All pretenses and attempts to conceal his interest would become a dismal failure if she slid a hand between them and felt with her fingers.

When the kiss ended, he felt drunk, his brain too foggy to comprehend the motions needed for swimming. Thankfully, they were in the shallows with the surf crashing in and flooding out around his knees.

Kissing her heightened all sensations—the warmth of the sun, the kiss of the cool breeze whispering across his skin, and the tug and pull of the waves. Every experience intensified from the smell of salt and her skin filling his nostrils to her sweet taste overwhelming his senses.

Her eyes shone in the sunlight when they broke apart. Blue. The most dazzling blue, a sapphire jewel held in daylight.

Kissing her had been better than he'd imagined. He'd been positive he could remain neutral with his affections, maintaining a friendship without necessarily leading her on. A single kiss had abolished everything.

Nate claimed her mouth again, showing the restraint and tenderness he'd lacked before. The semi-private beach wasn't secluded enough to allow him to indulge in the fantasies in his head.

"Worth it," he murmured against her lips. When he leaned away, tilting his head back to look at her, he saw the telltale glint in her eyes, the ethereal shift of color, and instead of disgust, he felt only fascination. "You're beautiful."

He didn't know what made him say it. Beauty was a word she'd probably heard attributed to her looks since she was born, but it came out in a rush. Impulsive. For a moment, he thought he saw her and the dragon contained by her human flesh.

He'd been careful with her, reminded always they were from different worlds, and that duty took precedence over pleasure. Each of Astrid's hugs and smiles chipped away at his resolve.

Were they so different? It plagued him, making him wonder if any of his fellow slayers ever questioned their duties.

He and many of the younger ones wouldn't regain their true memories until they slew their first dragon, and doing that meant taking a life. The life of a dragon with a family, a lover, or even children. Someone like Astrid's father.

Without speaking a word, Astrid kissed him again, each moment as slow and sweet as the last. He savored each second as she ran her fingers over his closely trimmed hair and down his nape to the back of his shoulders.

Centuries ago, as a knight, he'd sworn to uphold a chivalrous code of duty against her kind, and yet he'd found no monsters in the Drakenstone family, only a gentle-hearted girl who cared about her loved ones. A girl who pleaded for him to brake so she could move a turtle to the other side of the road. Who took in homeless kittens and fostered them in her free time. And his dog Echo loved her.

The traitor rolled on her back for belly rubs whenever Astrid was near.

He ended one kiss with another, finding his thirst for her insatiable, unable to resist the lure of each subsequent taste of her lips. Finally, with a distressed sound in his throat, he forced himself to stop, arousal surging hard and heavy in his swim trunks.

"Sorry." She dragged in a shaky breath and dropped her forehead to his shoulder.

The waves rushed warm around their legs when he lowered her. He inhaled both the scents of her and the ocean and gave an uncertain smile. "Nothing to apologize for. I'm the one who mauled you. I think. Hell if I can remember anything before it now."

"I think we both were equal in the mauling department," Astrid said. She took his hand and tugged him further out into the water until they were a hip deep. Only then did she release him so she could fall back and give a splashing kick, grinning before she ducked beneath the water and swam perpendicular to the shore.

The shoreline wasn't as clear as the endless blue ocean he'd fallen in love with during his deployments, but he saw her silhouette ahead of him until he broke the surface. He'd eased out into deeper water where his feet no longer touched the sand. Treading in place, he grinned. "How strong of a swimmer are you? I guess that doesn't matter for you, though."

"What do you mean?" She had surfaced a few feet away, treading water easily.

Their make-out session may have scrambled his brains. "If your father's a dragon, doesn't that mean you're…?" He trailed off and glanced away in discomfort. Suddenly, his probes for answers felt inappropriate. He no longer wanted to know the truth about Astrid-the-possible-dragon. He wanted to get to know Astrid-the-girl.

"You want to know if I'll become a legendary monster, too," she said in a flat tone.

"Sorry, I just assumed with your dad being a dragon, you'd be one, too. We don't have to talk about it," he quickly said, only for her to provide the intelligence the slayers had sent him to attain.

"I am. I'm a dragon like my dad."

His expression must have changed, because hers did as well, though his attempt to release her from the conversation had become more truthful with each word. Turmoil rolled in his gut, the lighthearted enjoyment of their date threatened by his curiosity.

She ducked down beneath the surface again and came back up closer to shore. The waves rolled around her hips as she walked onto firm footing, a playful school of silver fish darting between her legs.

Nate waited for her to speak first, and when she didn't, he rushed after her. The water tugged at his board shorts, weighing them and the rest of his body down when he emerged from the water. In a few of his longer strides, he closed the distance and wrapped an arm around her waist from behind. "Hey. I'm sorry I asked."

"Why? You deserve to know. It wouldn't be fair for you to find out later and have a freakout." She forced a smile to her face, but the strain showed. "Like I said, I like you, and it'd be horrible of me to keep something as big as that from you if things progress further. Trust me. I'm used to it."

"I'm not freaking out," he lied. The freaking had nothing to do with her revelation and everything to do with determining what to do with the information. Technically, she hadn't confirmed Chloe was her biological mother. The big truth, the greatest question the slayers needed to know, was whether dragons were impregnating human women.

His left arm joined the other, trapping her back to his chest, palms flat against her skin. The tension melted from her stiff body and her lean curves settled in against his harder angles. "So... not worried I'm going to roast you?"

"More worried about your old man than you." He nudged his hips forward, then cursed himself. He was hard again, so impossibly hard the strain almost hurt. His breath skimmed over her ear, and he kissed the gentle pink curve. Now that he'd taken the first nip of forbidden fruit, he couldn't stop.

"My dad's a pussycat once you get to know him," she assured him.

"We don't have to talk about it at all if you prefer. I…" Liked her, too. And he couldn't bring himself to say the words out loud. It would make the situation and his conflict all the more real.

"No, I don't mind. It's who I am, and it'd be like saying I don't want to know anything about your Navy life." She rubbed back against him and made a small sound, part whimper and part moan.

Her moan did something to him, and his cock twitched, jumping beneath the sodden board shorts. All he could imagine was peeling her bottoms free.

For their sanity, he separated their bodies first, using willpower he hadn't known he possessed. He joined their hands instead, the gesture familiar and fond. "My Navy days aren't the best conversation material, to be honest, and some of the better stories are more depressing than anything. My job puts me all over, and I usually end up dealing with idiots." The shift in conversation helped get his mind off his dick.

"Idiots, right." She chuckled. "So why security? I mean… what made you pick that over something technical?"

"It's what my dad did, and his dad before him. We have a long history of military police in my family, so it was expected that I follow in their footsteps." There were no pleasant words to describe Kay. The man loathed all things supernatural, while refusing to acknowledge their own magical origins. If not for Merlin, they would all be long dead. There'd be no memories and circle of reincarnation.

The thought put a frown on Nate's face until he glanced at the sun and saw it had barely moved since their return to the sand. The breeze and summer heat dried the skin on his shoulders and freckled back while his brow wrinkled with consternation.

"Oh. But do you like it?

"I…" Did he? Most of his life had been what his father wanted for him. He lived by tradition, expectation, and understanding of who he was, or who he would become once he fully reawakened his dragon-slaying abilities. Did he like that part of himself? Not anymore. In as little as a month, Astrid had changed everything and provided a sense of humanization he hadn't wanted. Didn't need. Life had made sense before.

"No," he said with a quiet laugh. "I mean, I do enjoy life in the Navy, and I've worked hard to get where I am. I just think I might have chosen differently with my career path if Dad wasn't hell-bent on it."

Astrid led the way back into the private yard with its little stretch of beach. They used the outdoor shower to rinse the sand and salt from their bodies before they wandered inside.

"I'm going to go change back into dry clothes. We can watch a movie if you want," she suggested.

"Sounds good."

In the safety of the guest room, he peeled off his wet clothes and asked himself what the hell he was doing. Astrid was amazing, but she was also his assignment, and he'd compromised himself completely.

A tidy row of silver-framed photographs lined the antique dresser. One in particular caught his eye, and he stopped to squint at an image of Chloe Drakenstone holding a newborn against her chest. The room lacked hospital equipment, but her exhausted smile and sweat-slicked hair painted a portrait of recent childbirth.

Astrid was born from a dragon and a human woman. And he was falling in love with her.

He took an extra minute to clear his head before he stepped from the room. He found Astrid in the kitchen making fresh drinks, but she turned her cheek up for him to greet her with a kiss when he stepped alongside her. The skirt of her white dress skimmed her legs at mid-thigh, drawing his gaze down and back up again.

"I thought, after all that talk, some Bahama mamas were in order. I also queued up the family's Ultraviolet account. See if there's anything you'd like to watch."

He glanced into the living room and whistled. An impressive selection spanned the television, and more movies disappeared below the edge of the screen. He'd seen most with the exception of a few newer titles. "Pick something?"

"Go ahead. I don't mind."

He chose a superhero flick, compromising on a combination of action and romantic subplot, and he found himself drawn into the movie with his attention divided between the woman cuddled to his side and the extraordinary special effects. While there was plenty of room on the sofa, they squeezed together closely, and he draped an arm around her shoulders.

Superheroes fascinated him. It's what the Knights of Merlin ought to have been, seekers of justice and righteous knights fighting against evil. He sometimes wondered how he'd felt in previous lives. How many undocumented dragons had he killed? Had any been friends of Astrid's family and beloved by them? And most of all, he wondered, if one of the other slayers had been assigned his special job, would they still be able to see her as only a beast to be put down instead of a caring individual with a love for defenseless animals.

About thirty minutes into their movie, Astrid's stomach made an obnoxious, yet adorable grumble.

"That was man-sized," he commented while she flushed bright red. "Or should I say dragon-sized?"

"Definitely not dragon-sized."

Grinning, Nate hit the pause button and rose from his seat. "We were outside for hours, and we swam for most of it. I'd say a movie time snack is justified."

Outside, the sun was a hazy blend of gold against a deep cobalt sky. By the time the movie ended, it'd be a good hour to drive home, and his muscles were already stiffly protesting their long afternoon of activity. "If your folks are the kind to keep chips and cheese, we can make some decent nachos with the leftovers."

"Chips from the store are gross. I'll fry some tortillas."

"Great, I'll slice the steak while you—" His phone buzzed in his pocket, so he drew it out and noticed several missed calls and a current caller notification from his father. "Shit."

"Uh-oh, trouble at work?" she guessed.

"It's Dad," he replied with a grimace. "Gimme a sec to take this and I'll help you out."

Erring on the side of caution, Nate stepped outside into the fresh air to receive the call. While he trusted Astrid to respect his privacy, he didn't trust her ears not to pick up his father's voice.

"Hi, Dad."

"Why haven't you checked in? Do you know how much you've worried me? Son, we were on our way to blow that beast to hell."

Nate groaned and leaned against the wall with his head tilted back. He swallowed and thanked the stars he'd answered the last call.

"I'm sorry I've worried all of you, and I give my word that it won't happen again."

"Has it been hostile with you?"

"Not at all. She likes me."

His father remained silent for a time, then the man chuckled, only it lacked humor and warmth. "Not a surprise there. You've always had a knack with the girls, despite your disinterest in them. I guess even creature women can't help themselves. Report in at the conclusion of the mission. I want to know what this thing has told you."

He paced while outside, listening to his father's usual diatribe against the shifters, a reinforcement that Nate didn't forget his identity and origins.

"Then maybe you should allow me to return to her company," he spat. "As discussed during our last meeting, I will not report my activities to accommodate your schedule. You will hear from me when I have news to report. Do not contact me again during this weekend."

Without allowing Kay the chance to respond, he pressed the red 'end call' button and spent the next moments cooling off outside.

***

Nate's phone call changed his mood, and while he did help her in the kitchen, he worked in silence alongside her until they returned to the couch with their fresh nachos smothered in cheese and fajita steak.

She resumed the movie and settled in against the cushions, feet tucked up beneath her, and absently worried at the hem of her skirt. As a shadow fell over the evening, Astrid searched for a way to restore his cheerful disposition. She touched his knee and twisted to look at him. "Everything okay at home?"

"Just Dad being Dad," he said despite his strained smile. He startled her with a sudden question. "Are all dragon families like yours?"

"What do you mean?"

He gestured to the room around them. "It all looks normal, not that I was expecting humans in the oven and skulls on the mantle or anything."

"We're not much different from anyone else, I guess. Mom and Dad work at the studio together every day. Grandpa Max looks forward to retirement and spending time with the twins. Grandma manages a huge charity for foster children of all backgrounds from human to shifter. We have friends that are human, dragon, shifter, witch." She shrugged as if it were nothing abnormal. "Some dragons prefer solitude, but there's reasons for that, I guess. The rest are just living their lives, same as you and me."

With a thoughtful look on his face, he nodded. "Before meeting you, I guess I imagined all dragons living in caves and emerging to abduct princesses, not making families and raising little girls. Did your mother teach you to cook?"

She giggled. "Well, some *do* keep caves." That knowledge was common fact at least, but she didn't elaborate on treasure hoards or anything like that. "Actually, my grandma Ēostre used to tutor princesses. She didn't kidnap and eat them. As for cooking, yeah, I guess Mom sometimes did, but I learned more from watching Aunt Mahasti and Uncle Leiv."

His brows raised. "I didn't know Mrs. Emberthorn did that."

"Well, of course, you wouldn't," she laughed. "That was ages ago, back when we still had knights and castle and serfs." Relaxed again, she stretched her legs out, wiggling her pink-painted toes.

"Are your aunt and uncle dragons, too?"

"No." She hesitated a split second before adding. "My uncle is a shifter. His daughter and I grew up together."

"It must have been nice growing up with a big family at home."

"It was, I guess. But as big as my family is now, it wasn't always. I was… well, I was lonely as a kid until they got me some friends. Isolated. I was homeschooled, for one, and while there's nothing wrong with that, it didn't exactly lead to having many friends my age. What about you? Do you see your mother often now?"

"Yeah. I visit Mom in Los Angeles whenever I can get the time. I think we had this talk, but she's into doing stuff for the community and organizing programs to help out the urban youth in the less fortunate areas of LA. She got me involved in the Boys & Girls Club when I returned from my last deployment." He reached for another chip and scooped up a slice of avocado with the melted cheese and meat. The mood vastly improved, thanks to good food and her fruity, alcoholic beverage. "I think I've hit my drink cutoff if I'm going to drive."

"We could stay if you want…"

With a smile on his face, he shook his head. "As fantastic as that would be, I'm not going to abuse the kindness of the president by hanging out in his beach house all night. I should get you home."

"Sure, not a problem." She did her best not to let the disappointment show and took a sip of her drink to cover her letdown frown. "Your mom sounds nice. And I bet those kids looked up to you. Everyone loves a military man in uniform, especially one who will go play with them." It was easy to change the subject and turn the focus away from herself.

At least, for a moment it was easy. "What about your shelter thing?" he asked, directing the conversation back to her.

"I like animals," she answered, simple and honest. "Cats especially. Mom used to have a Savannah named Felix. She was so devastated when he finally passed on. Dad, too. In the end, Dad and I were using healing magic on him behind her back all the time to give her a few extra weeks together, but it was tiring Daddy out fast. So when Mom found out, she forced us to let him go. Dad had gotten used to the big guy and shed a few tears, though he'd deny it if you asked."

Nate said nothing at first, but his startled expression spoke for him. "I didn't know a dragon could do magic to heal others."

"Yeah, we both can. If you ever pull a hamstring while exercising, I'm your girl. I'm so used to having pets around, I foster kittens from the local shelter. It helps them get socialized and stuff. If you ever want to bring Echo over, I'd appreciate it. Kittens need a chance to get used to having dogs around, too." She bit her lip after the shy offer and glanced up at him. The shock had given way to a warm smile.

"Okay," Nate agreed easily. "Echo is well-trained, but I'd be wary of her breaking one of your expensive projects. Everything in your hoard looks as delicate as you do."

"She'd be fine at my condo. I don't bring them to work all of the time, allergic customers and all."

"Your condo?" He glanced at her sharply, his brows raised. "Yeah… we'd both like that."

Tidying together restored the beach house to its original state in record time. While the dishwasher ran, they chatted about the movie and enjoyed a final walk along the beach. He held her hand, and it felt right to be close to him.

When they embarked on their hour-long ride home, a belly of drinks and delicious food lulled her to sleep. She didn't stir until Nate nudged her arm. They'd reached downtown San Diego and neared her building. Rain pelted the windshield and stormy clouds swept in over the city, an evil necessity since they'd needed the rain.

"Here," she passed over her garage card and directed him to the entrance. "You can park anywhere."

Nate pulled inside and drifted through the parking garage until he found an empty spot. He killed the engine and glanced at her, a smile on his face. "Today was great, Astrid. Honest. Thanks for inviting me out."

"Thanks for coming out with me today. I know it was last minute." She hesitated, reluctant to leave when she had so much on her mind. So she blurted it all out in a nervous rush. "Look, Nate, if this is too much for you, I understand. I like you, but I'm not a normal human girl, and I get that the whole supernatural thing is still new. If you want to end things here, I'll totally understand. Really. It'll suck, but I'd get it. I just… please don't drive away and never contact me again, because even if you don't want to continue dating me, I'd at least hope we could be friends."

She was breathless by the end, expending all of the air in her lungs for a nonstop ramble. At first, Nate said nothing, reduced to staring at her while his thick brows drew together in a perplexed arch. "Did I say or do something to imply I plan to run away?" After a slow indrawn breath, he continued, "Today was great, and I've enjoyed every moment with you." He leaned in close enough to kiss her cheek.

Astrid shrugged. "You wouldn't be the first guy to skip off the moment he found out I was a supposed monster," she whispered. The touch of his lips didn't help soothe her fear; it was given with no real feeling behind it. Suddenly she was an awkward teen again, uncertain of herself, her words, or her actions. "Forget I said anything. I'll let you go." Tears burned behind her eyes as she fumbled with her seat belt.

As the seat belt snapped into its former place, he reached out for her wrist and caught her. "I'm not skipping out. I thought we had a great date."

And an even better kiss, she thought. As if she'd willed it to happen by the sheer force of her desire, Nate leaned in and kissed her again.

With one hand on her wrist, his fingers slid down the back of her hand and twined with her slimmer digits. His lips parted against her mouth, the kiss less coaxing, more demanding.

One kiss, one real kiss, was all it took to shatter the walls she'd been building up to protect herself, and suddenly the only thing in the world that mattered was them. In the secluded, dimly lit garage, they were completely alone. The outside world was silent, excluding the thunder and rain.

She made a small sound, a whimper of submission and a groan of need all wrapped into one. While one hand twined with his fingers, her other lifted to the back of his head and drew him closer.

The roomy Jeep allowed him to twist over the console between them, and as her arm raised around his neck, his other hand dropped from her shoulder, descending with confidence. She hadn't worn a bra beneath her dress, leaving nothing but thin cotton between his fingers and her tightening nipple.

A low, appreciative groan from him cried out to her, stirring her lust, hitting deep in her gut. She answered in kind, a soft growl she'd never made before as her fingers tightened in his hair and the other hand reached for him.

"Sorry," he murmured against her lips. His fingers toyed with the stiffening tip, teasing it in idle, playful circles. "You make it easy to lose control."

"Don't apologize," she breathed against his mouth before losing herself into the next kiss.

If she received only a single night with him, she'd treasure it beyond all the jewels in her hoard. One night of bliss with a man who wanted her for her, not for what she could get him. One night with a man who saw Astrid.

His hand delved lower, slipping from her breast to the crux of her thighs without going beneath her dress.

Without a single coherent thought, she maneuvered over the center console and straddled his lap. Her fingers tugged at his shirt, the need to feel his skin again an all-consuming desire, but it wasn't enough. Following instinct, she traced her fingers downward and boldly palmed his erection through his pants. Nothing prepared her for the heat radiating through the cloth, or the hard length of a well-endowed man with mutual desire. Their mingled pheromones filled the darkened car, and she knew without a doubt that she couldn't stop, couldn't pull back and walk away, not until he was hers.

"I think I have a condom." He fumbled behind him into the rear seat, searching clumsily while his other hand abandoned her for exposing his arousal to the open air. Tall and stiff, it jutted up without restraint.

Something primal and wild took over, frustration tossing good sense aside for the demands of the present. As if they were tissue paper, Astrid's panties ripped when she tugged them. She leaned over Nate and snagged the bag, so it came within his reach. Then her hand returned to where it had been, denim replaced by bare, hot flesh.

Hurry, hurry, hurry, she screamed inside, uncertain of her willpower when all she wanted was to sink down and feel him deep where no one had ever claimed her before. When her fingers surrounded him and failed to close, he groaned in appreciation, the throb beneath her touch frantic with his need for her.

Abandoning his fruitless search, Nate grasped a handful of her bare ass and jerked her forward, gliding the rounded, sensitive crown through the slick skin between her legs.

The tip of his cock notched against her clit, setting off an unfamiliar chain of sensations that left her trembling.

"Don't tease me," she whispered. With or without a condom, she needed him, and if he drew their liaison to an abrupt end, she'd combust on the spot.

"Shh," he muttered. "Give me a moment."

"A mo—ohhh," she moaned and swayed atop him as the thick, blunt tip of him dragged toward her entrance.

Then he did more than glide against her slick skin. He pressed inward, entering her with gradual increments. Her tightness surrounded him in a vice grip, seeming too shallow and narrow to hold all of him.

"You're so…so…"

"So what?" he whispered against her lips.

Astrid clung to him, her nails leaving divots in his shoulders, tearing his shirt. "Big."

Her body yielded over time, and just when she thought he couldn't glide any deeper, he filled her with a final, urgent thrust, melding their bodies close in the intimate embrace she'd craved since their first meeting at the cafe.

Cheek to cheek, she listened to his moans of mutual satisfaction while gasping against his ear. After the shock had vanished, her instinct kicked in, leading her into the first clumsy roll of her hips.

His head fell back. "Fuck," he groaned out, oblivious to the gift she'd given him, that she'd chosen him as her first. Her *only*. He churned with a few testing strokes. With tinted windows to guard their privacy, he pulled at her dress. "Let me see you. I need to see you."

She fumbled with the straps at her nape. After helping him yank the white fabric up over her head, she straddled him, nude from head to toe, her slim, toned body and small but plump and firm breasts on display. Perky, her friend Svetlana had teased her. Her blonde hair, knocked loose from its clasp, fell around her shoulders in a tumble of golden waves.

He tossed the dress into the passenger seat and spent a few moments gazing at her in awe. "Perfect. God, every inch of you is perfect."

She tugged at his shirt, wanting skin against skin. "You too. Get it off."

His shirt joined her dress after he adjusted the driver's seat and pitched them back into a reclined position. His jeans fell around his thighs, exposing him from the hips up, all lean muscle and hard, chiseled angles honed by training and daily athletics.

She peeked down, entranced with the lines of his hips and the flat, hard plane of muscle above his pelvis. Below her, she saw the root of his cock, so thick and perfect, glistening with her desire. "All of you. I want all of you." She needed that final inch.

He thrust up, grinding until their pelvises could be no closer. "How's that?"

"Good," she gasped, leaning forward with one hand against his chest to keep her upright while he reclined back, the other at her side.

The muscles surrounding his arousal ached with a subtle burn, but it hurt too good to stop. With sluggish strokes, Nate thrust deep, a full range of gliding motion meeting each descent of Astrid's hips. As she discovered herself, their tight rhythm became fluid, easier with each subsequent roll. He guided her hips at first, and once she seemed confident in herself, his hands traced over her lean curves, thumbs flicking the pink peaks at the tip of each breast.

When she found her pace, Nate dragged his dick from her slick embrace and slammed it home.

"Yes!" she cried.

He did it again, satisfying her new thirst. Each backstroke and subsequent return built pressure within her core, stimulating fine nerve endings she never knew existed. She cried for more, encouraging screams for his ears alone.

Over time, the Jeep grew warm, the windows opaque with steam, and a thin layer of perspiration glistened against her tanned skin.

"I'm so close," she wailed as she chased the elusive pinnacle gliding beyond her reach. Even in times of self-pleasure, she struggled to reach orgasm.

Don't let that happen now, please! she begged.

"Me too, baby. I don't know how much more I can take."

Nate leaned up to taste the tip of one nipple and trace the pale areola with his tongue. As she rose, he snuck a curved finger between them, wriggling until he found the source of her pleasure. He teased the small pearl and watched her face.

"I can't..." Frustration brought burning tension to her throat as her failure threatened to ruin the perfect moment between them.

No matter how good he felt, how deep he stroked, or how fast she rode him, the promise of orgasm hovered out of reach. "I can't. I can't," she whispered on shallow, hyperventilating breaths. She ground her hips against him, desperate.

In the back of her mind, she wondered if it was possible to die from lack of fulfillment.

"Nate, I... I'm sorry. Please come, baby. I can't. It's not happening."

"You can." He practically growled the words, voice raw with desire. "You will. Come here."

Seeking her lips, he silenced her protest with a kiss. Tender and patient, he coaxed her to lay against him; then he assumed control. He guided the frenetic tempo of their lovemaking, rolling her up and down with sinuous-paced movements of his hips. In and out he stroked while kissing her brow and running his fingers down her perspiring back.

"It's just the two of us. I want to feel you coming around me, baby girl. No rush."

She settled in as close as their awkward sprawl allowed, breasts flattened against his chest. He was tireless, movements slow and body tensed with self-restraint. And it touched her. It touched her so deeply that she turned her mouth back toward his and kissed him again.

"Stay with me tonight," she whispered as her body picked up his new rhythm and followed. The clawing panic subsided, the frustration dimmed, and renewed pleasure swelled in a bright fountain. But she waited.

Would a frenzied one-night stand in his Jeep be the end?

"There's nowhere else I wanna be, baby. I can't…"

Nate groaned, and on the next thrust, he broke—head tilting back and eyes shut. His abs flexed, and his pelvis bumped up, burying to completion, while the hand guiding her hips slipped around to her ass and squeezed, fingers denting into the pliable skin. The cry on his lips was purely her name.

With his words and his final stroke came bliss. Like a flower unfurling beneath the sun, it washed over her, coursing through her veins like wildfire. The experience was made all the more brilliant by his mutual release.

"Yes!" she screamed as she seized in orgasm. Her teeth nipped his jaw; then she whispered his name over and over amidst ragged breaths.

Her teeth sharpened and lengthened, her mouth hot with the desire to mark Nate and claim him with the Dragon's Brand.

No. Can't. Not without telling him. Discussing it.

Astrid held back and turned her cheek against his shoulder instead. From there, the sex became a blur. She lost track of the minutes while they rocked against each other, the connection of their bodies hot and slick. Tears leaked from the corners of her eyes, and her heart pounded long after she collapsed limp and loose atop him, completely spent. Blissfully satisfied.

Minutes passed before Nate moved, and when he did, it was to trail his fingers through her hair. "So much for being a gentleman," he muttered. "Completely worth it, though."

"I didn't want a gentleman. I wanted Nate. The real Nate. Unguarded and open with me."

"I wasn't the real Nate before?"

"Not always." She nipped his shoulder, grazing his skin. It wasn't the claiming bite her dragon demanded, but it was enough to sate the inner beast. That and his softening dick still speared within her. "I guess we should go upstairs."

Shifting beneath her at first, he protested moving with a low groan. "Fine, fine. Get dressed and I'll follow. Dragon or not, I think you'll raise a security guard's eyebrows if you wander across the lot bare-assed."

"Ugh, yeah, Charlie would probably glower a bit," she said, referring the usual night watchman.

Limbs shaky, she dragged her dress from the passenger seat. Once she'd crawled off him, she used her ripped panties to dab away the smear left between her thighs. She tossed them into a plastic bag she'd brought along for trash.

Almost shy again, she shot him a quiet smile and donned her dress. While he tucked himself away, she fetched the bags with their changes of clothing.

He joined her outside after zipping up his jeans. "Only a bit? Do you make it a habit of wandering naked around your building so much it only gets you a dirty look? Is there something I need to know about you?" He spoke lightheartedly with a smile on his face.

The smile she loved. The smile that made her knees weak.

"No!" A bright, hot flush crept up her cheeks before she ducked her gaze. "Besides, I've never brought a guy up before." The cement was cool beneath her bare feet as she carried her sandals by their thin straps. An elevator took them to the lobby, where they exited to take a second elevator to her floor. Charlie glanced over as they walked through the lobby. His nostrils flared.

The grumpy old bear probably smelled the sex on her.

"No one?" Nate asked with skepticism. "Not even your dad?" Passing the watchman, he nodded courteously and followed her into the elevator.

"Dad isn't a guy. He's Dad." She rolled her eyes at him and pressed the button. She lived on one of the top floors in a corner end unit.

"Is 'no guys in the apartment' one of Dad's rules?" he asked, lurking behind her while she unlocked the door.

"No." She peered over her shoulder at him. "I just haven't wanted to bring a guy up before."

A chorus of meows greeted them, and the three kittens dashed across the floor. Isis eyed the pair from the back of the sofa but didn't deign to come down and greet them. Instead, the older cat yawned and went back to sleep, considering her kitten babysitting duties complete.

"Just set the cooler down there," Astrid said, motioning to the kitchen area.

With the kittens on his heels, he did as she instructed. They must have smelled Echo on his jeans. They chased Nate relentlessly until he sat on the floor and let them pile onto his lap. Once they lost interest and abandoned him, he stood up and wandered to the huge windows overlooking the street.

"Make yourself at home," she said. "I'm just gonna go start the shower."

"Go ahead. Promise I won't steal anything." After his promise, he picked up a sketchbook from a nearby desk and idly turned the pages.

"You could join me," Astrid offered. She had a large sunken tub big enough for two, and a spacious walk-in shower. She'd bet money his ass was perfect and craved seeing him fully naked and wet beneath the spray. "I'll even promise to behave myself."

Nate froze with the sketchbook in his hands and glanced over his shoulder at her, blinking. Gently, he returned the book to the desk and studied her pensive expression while he approached. "I'd like that."

When he reached her, he seized her by the hips and leaned down. He coaxed her lips to part with his brief and playful, drugging kisses. She wrapped her arms around his waist and never wanted to let go.

"Go ahead and start the water. I'll be there in a second."

"Water. Right. Okay." Once she shook off the daze, she flashed an impish smile and turned to flounce inside the bathroom. "I hope you like your water hot."

Astrid hurried into the shower without questioning his delay.

Within seconds, water rushed from the dual shower heads, pelting down on the stone tile floor. For his benefit, she'd hunted through her bizarre collection of soaps until she found a non-floral aroma.

She jumped in first and rinsed beneath the steaming torrent to relax her nerves. In the heat of the moment, nudity hadn't troubled her. The poor lighting, her physical need, and weeks of longing had given her courage.

Nate would be seeing her again without shadows hiding her.

And she would be seeing him, too.

The glass door opened and shut behind Astrid. Anticipation struck, and when she glanced over her shoulder, it was to the sight of Nate approaching the second fixture. Water slicked down his neatly cropped brown hair and pelted his shoulders. He turned his face toward the showerhead, as if oblivious to the nude woman beside him.

If not for his visible interest, she would have thought him ambivalent to her altogether. His cock swayed while he soaped his body with the no-nonsense haste of a military man. And he grew harder by the second.

His arousal made her bold.

Without a word, she stepped behind him and stole the soap from his hands. She ran the bar over his back, creating suds with her fingers and reveling in the way his muscles shifted beneath her touch. Her fingers followed the trail of soap bubbles gliding down his spine toward his ass.

Yes! As predicted, her sailor was head-to-toe perfection, his firm, curved bottom designed for snug jeans and tailored suits. She gripped a handful and squeezed with delight, deciding his body was sin incarnate and created for her ogling. He turned before she could continue.

"Is this behaving?" he asked.

A flutter of pure lust clenched Astrid's core. "What?" she asked in a tiny voice, breath caught in her chest. She wanted to be sensual and coy and was failing miserably. "It seemed the nice thing to do after I helped get you all messy."

He nudged his hips forward and trapped his dick between their bodies. She gasped. Her failing attempts to appear experienced ended when her gaze dropped down. His rigid cock nudged in hard against her belly, a dark contrast against her fairer skin.

She'd wanted to see the real Nate, and the real Nate is what she received, playful and teasing, a soap thief who relieved her of the bar and treated her with tender care. His sudsy hands caressed the slick front of her, down defined shoulders and small breasts. His thumbs teased over the rosy nipples without lingering and traveled the gentle slope before descending below her ribs.

As restlessness stirred within her, bringing a craving for Nate that transcended physical pleasure. She stepped forward and pushed him to the tiled wall.

She took his cock into her hands and familiarized her touch with his length, hesitant at first, then more boldly. "I lied. I don't want to behave."

The soap hit the floor and bounced away.

"Like what you see?" Nate pumped his hips forward without avoiding eye contact. He met her gaze and held it, desire and ravenous hunger visible upon his features in equal measure. His cock twitched between her fingers, tense with apparent need.

Her tongue darted out and licked her lips. "I do," she answered, honest and without pretense. Her two-fisted grip slid up and down over his stiff skin as she figured out how snug a hold she could keep without causing discomfort. "Does that feel nice for you?" she asked in sudden wonder. "My hands, I mean. Is that nice for you?"

What the hell is wrong with me? She regretted the bumbling question and rushed forward without giving him the chance to reply. "I'm sorry for freaking out on you in the Jeep. I—" she swallowed "—I really liked... it's... I've never..." Goddamn. She either needed to shut up or just spit it out. "I've never had a climax like that before."

His hand slipped over her fingers and guided them, showing her how to curve her grip loosely but firmly, neither squeezing or timidly holding him. "Hey. No apologies, okay?"

A quick learner, she mimicked his earlier pump and stroked him long and slow, once, twice, and then a third time while picking up speed. The way his eyes glazed over made her toes curl.

His head fell back against the sandstone tile. "I—do we need protection?"

Did they? Astrid had yet to determine if she had a human or dragon's reproductive cycle. "I don't have any condoms, but if you trust me, I swear I'll pick up a Plan B tomorrow. I can guarantee you that I'm clean. Besides, I, uh, think we already jumped off that cliff, and I don't regret it."

"Thank God." Without elaborating for what he was grateful, he hefted her smaller body up, coaxed her thighs around his hips, and claimed her anew.

Words were lost, replaced by inarticulate cries for more. Gasped utterances of his name. Moans of unfettered passion. Eventually, their restricted position and slick footing led their coupling to the tiled floor.

Once they'd tired of the shower and craved a warm bed with clean sheets, they toweled one another on the fluffy bath mat and drifted to the bed.

"I'm glad we ran into each other at the coffee shop," she mumbled as they snuggled naked beneath the sheets.

A tender kiss to her damp hairline preceded a whispered, "Me too."

Exhaustion pulled her under, fighting the need to stay up and learn more. To taste him again. In the end, exhaustion won, and Astrid drifted to sleep with her head on his shoulder. In her dreams, she soared high above the skies, Nate astride her back. They were one heart and one mind—her mark emblazoned on his shoulder.

Chapter 6

Nate stirred once in the early hours of the morning, accustomed to waking with the dawn. Faint shafts of sunlight streamed through unfamiliar blinds. Blonde strands tickled his cheek. Astrid had snuggled beneath his chin, peaceful in her sleep with a slim arm tossed across his chest.

If she hadn't told him, he'd never believe an enormous, fire-breathing beast dwelled within her. He traced the curve of her shoulder and, for a while, was content to watch her slumber.

Beautiful, but impossible to keep. Fate had dealt him a raw hand.

Eventually, he drowsed again without shame. They'd swam for hours, drank, and had sex long into the night in a variety of positions. She'd been tireless, inexperienced but tireless.

She awakened him with kisses.

Somewhere on the precipice between consciousness and sleep, he roused enough to recognize a playful nibble to his left hip. His cock leaped, twitching as if to demand attention, too.

And Astrid gave it. His drowsy eyes opened to the sight of her lips tracing his length from tip to root, stirring him awake in more ways than one. The cheater. He rose steadily, swelling with arousal and renewed vigor.

Her kisses worked their way up back to the smooth, silken crown where she gave a delicate nibble against the ribbed edge, followed by a tiny lick. In an instant, he went from semi-flaccid to hard as a rock. Her gaze raised to his face as she took into her mouth.

He'd died and skipped the reincarnation cycle while deployed. Or maybe it happened on a mission for the knighthood. Something. He had to have, because he'd awakened in what could only be heaven, with an angel of his very own fantasies. He watched her mouth descend and the sweet warmth of her envelop the sensitive head. In one move, she had him as her captive audience. His fingers grasped at the sheets, and his hips jerked up.

Whenever he thought he had her figured out, she surprised him anew, her actions unpredictable. Endearing. He grew hard as tempered steel beneath her lips and swore out loud when the urgent need for relief robbed him of coherent thought. His hips worked independently of his brain, an automatic rhythm matched to the speed of her hand.

Although she was nowhere close to deep throating his entire length, her lips bumped against her circled index finger and thumb. And those weren't far from the root of him.

"More, baby. God, yes, more," he coaxed her. And this time, he had nothing holding him back from an orgasm. No need to hold back.

When his release came, her eyes shut and nostrils flared, but her hand and mouth didn't stop. She took all he offered, sucking his dick until he was a groaning mess on the bed, and his hips slowed their erratic pumps. Then, and only then, did she pull back, taking the time to lap up every bit of his seed before letting the glossy length of him slide from her lips.

It was the hottest thing Nate witnessed in all of his life, next to the sight of her pussy stuffed with every inch of him.

With her cheek pressed against his thigh, her eyes drifted shut, and a pleased smile crept onto her face. "Worth it."

Members of the order had debated before why humans found shifters irresistible, and now Nate had learned firsthand.

They became insatiable, wild beasts in bed. He sank against the sheets again with a groan.

"Not that I'm complaining, but what was that for?"

"Hmm?" she asked in a lazy, content tone. Her eyes remained closed, body still bent between his legs and cheek to his thigh. "I don't know. I guess… I wanted to do something nice for you. Something special. Why?" She stirred enough to lift her head and blink heavy-lidded eyes at him, golden hair rumpled around her face. "You liked it, right?"

He answered by running his fingers through her hair, his motion languid and lazy, but all of his affection was conveyed in a few simple brushes. As he moved tousled waves from her face and tucked them behind her ear, the reality of the weekend came crashing down on him. He'd not only slept with a dragon, his order's mortal enemy, but he'd loved every second of it.

"I think right now, 'like' would be an understatement, baby. Come here a second." He encouraged her to rise from where she'd folded her body between his legs, and sat up to hold her cradled on his lap instead. "Was last night the first for you?"

She lifted her ducked head, turning to look him in the eye. "I've never met a guy I wanted to share my bed with. Until you."

"Why me?" came the next question, a natural curiosity. His fingers trailed over her messy blonde hair, idly combing through the strands gliding over her back.

"I did it because you saw me—Astrid."

She'd given him her body, shared her bed, and he'd traded her gift with lies. The worst feeling came over him, guilt striking with a hammer's force. He should have treated her better. Should have given her roses and chocolates. He should have been another man who wasn't part of an organization hell-bent on the destruction of her species. Among those thoughts were a dozen more.

"Thank you," he said instead, "for bringing me into your life."

"Thank you for buying my coffee."

If only she knew the truth, that his gesture of goodwill had been a devious trap.

Their remaining morning dissolved into kisses and, eventually, another round of passionate sex beneath her sheets. This time, he gave her the lovemaking she'd deserved, what he would have done had he known she was a virgin, untested and untouched by any other man. With patient fingers, he explored every inch of her body in earnest, determined to repay a gift without a known value.

While she sprawled on the rumpled sheets in the afterglow of their sex, he showered alone, thankful she hadn't tagged along with him. He needed the time to think. Seducing her had been part of Kay's plan, never his, and now that he'd bedded her, he could only think of how much he wanted to spend the rest of his life beside only her.

What they had felt was real, and it had felt real long before their inappropriate parking garage romp. But why had he done it?

Nate leaned against the tiled wall and let the water careen over his shoulders. All of his life, Kay had smothered him with stories and tales of his heroics as Sir Galahad, raising Nate to meet an inescapable destiny.

Deceiving Astrid hadn't made him a hero; *he* felt like the monster.

Maybe the circumstances would change once he had a recollection of his "true self," but if hating Astrid was part of becoming Sir Galahad, he didn't want it. He'd happily live in ignorance as merely Nate.

Maybe he could.

The grim thought of leaving the Knights of Merlin sobered him, and he exited the shower soon after to find a towel awaiting him by the sink.

They'd never allow it.

Once he'd dried and exited the bath with the towel wrapped around his waist, he found Astrid setting the round, glass-topped table in the cozy kitchen nook. Vanilla bean scones and steaming coffee perfumed the air with their rich, sweet scents. Somehow, she'd known he liked his coffee with excess sugar. He enjoyed a sip before seeking his clothes.

"Where's my stuff?"

An adjacent grandfather clock told him it was nearing noon.

"In the washer. How do you like your eggs?"

"You don't have to cook for me, Astrid."

"I know. But I want to. Have a seat."

"I'm wearing a towel."

"I won't tell if you won't."

While she fried eggs and bacon, he sipped his coffee and helped himself to the plate of scones on the table. The conversation came easily over a casual brunch without lulls and awkward silences. He felt no pressing need to excuse himself from her home.

"What are your plans this week?" she asked him while loading his clothes into the dryer.

Nate chugged the rest of his coffee then shrugged. "Hell if I know."

Astrid nudged him in the shoulder. "Don't you have to catch up on work at the base or something?"

"Huh? Yeah, I'm sure there'll be piles of it waiting for me. I'll have to spoil Echo to make up for being away all weekend, too. Aside from that, I don't know."

He didn't have much of a social life aside from the occasional Saturday outing with friends. Military life and exercise filled his days; he devoted the rest of his free time to the knighthood.

While his thoughts wandered, the dragoness slid into his lap and wrapped both arms around his shoulders. He gazed up at her, snapped back to the present. "I'm guessing you aren't asking for the hell of it."

Astrid beamed at first, but the large smile was short lived, defeated by apparent uncertainty. "I wasn't. I kinda…" Her blue eyes shifted to the side, and a shy rush of color spread pink over her face. "If you're busy—"

The words came out before Nate could gain control of his impulses. "I'll make time," he interrupted, "no matter how busy I am this week. Just give me a call and I'll try to peel away from what I'm doing. In fact, there's a fireworks show over at Point Loma on the base tomorrow. It's bound to be crowded, but where isn't? Want to join me?"

Astrid's expression brightened. "I've seen their fireworks from a distance."

"Maria paid for a premium tailgating spot, and I'm supposed to be bringing brats for the grill. No idea which bands are playing, but the music is usually pretty good."

"You don't think they'd mind me crashing their party?"

"Nah, my friends liked you. Bring some drinks to share and they'll welcome you with open arms."

"Sound fun. I'd love to go with you."

"Perfect. I'll pick you up from your shop around five, and we can head over."

Hours later, when Nate left her company with cat hair on his jeans and Astrid's scent against his skin, he wondered if he could ever forgive himself for what he had to do.

By evening, he was prepared to face Kay and Bedivere's fury. The few members of the knighthood currently present in California awaited him at the stone table, while the others connected via a conference call organized over the computer.

Stoic faces watched him enter, Gawain the only one among them with a smile. Nate was the last to sit at the table, and the pervasive odor of flavored tobacco surrounded him, accompanied by strong coffee.

"I hope all of this time hasn't been wasted and you have something to show for your long absence," Kay said to him.

"As do I," Bedivere said. "So many weeks and not one iota of useful information gleaned."

Nate rubbed his face with the heel of his hand. "I gave fair warning. If you don't trust me to get the job done, you should have sent Pelleus at the start," he spat out.

"Hey, guys, chill with this arguing. We're all on the same side here," Lancelot said.

Nate shot him an appreciative look.

"He's right. Let's give him a chance to explain himself," Percivale said.

Kay grunted. "Fine. The floor is yours, Nathaniel. Consider us your eager audience."

Asshole, Nate thought while claiming his seat. He cleared his throat and launched into a vague summary of his time with Astrid, excluding acts of intimacy and tenderness between them.

"She revealed her true family name to me this weekend, but I can't verify whether she's a hybrid between our species yet. She wasn't that forthcoming with information," he lied.

"I see. But her trust in you has grown. Excellent. We may be able to use that to our advantage after all if it places you in a position to assassinate Emberthorn or Drakenstone," Gareth said.

Nate loathed the arrogant bastard, but he kept his thoughts on the matter to himself. Biting his tongue, he glanced away and took control of the projector.

"Back to the subject at hand. I may not have determined her species status, but I have learned that dragons possess magical abilities on par with the witches. You were right when you guessed that Emberthorn's miraculous recovery wasn't typical of their kind. Dragons are tough, but that explosion should have ripped his gut to shreds," Nate said. "It's healing magic."

Kay leaned forward eagerly. "Are they all capable of healing?"

Nate shook his head. "That I don't know, but we have an admission from her that Drakenstone was able to extend the life of a common feline for years beyond its lifespan by healing it."

"Christ," Bedivere said. "What else were you able to discover?"

"Further confirmation that there's a shifter also living at the Drakenstone compound. Their chauffeur is a bear, and likely the one responsible for the ass-beating she dealt Lancelot. She hasn't said much about his wife, but I know she's a paranormal entity of some kind since she's been with Saul Drakenstone's family for ages. Astrid is careful about what she says to me." Nate waited on the edge of his seat.

Aside from Lancelot muttering under his breath, no one challenged his observation.

"Excellent work, Galahad," Kay praised. "I see it now, the resolve you were always known for."

"Funny, I don't feel any different."

Bleoberis rubbed his chin. "I see it as well. Soon, perhaps."

"They're right," Lancelot agreed. "I see it, too."

Nate stiffened. He'd never used his powers to harm a creature in his recent life, but like the rest of them, the ability was there.

Would he awaken one day beside Astrid to perceive her as the enemy? He hoped to God he never saw her as anything but his girl.

Kay's smug smile widened. "When you take down this dragon, you'll remember who you are. You'll have your purpose again, son. Exactly as I've assured you."

"Do you have your next meeting set?" Percivale asked to bring the subject back on track.

"I do. She's joining me for the Fourth of July on base tomorrow. As for her being a dragon, I'm not entirely convinced. If she is a dragon, she's incredibly docile, as I've said before. Harmless. She's shown no signs of aggression toward me."

Kay ignored his praise of Astrid. "Good, good. Get more information. Ingratiate yourself into her family home. I expect updates in a month."

"I don't think it's necessary. These dragons aren't hurting anyone. Maybe it's time we open talks with Emberthorn or one of the other ancients for peace."

"Peace?" The word hissed out between Kay's clenched teeth. Blood rushed to his face, turning his cheeks purple with sudden and intense fury. The man was going to give himself a stroke. "We do not make peace with dragons. We slay them. One day, you'll remember that."

"Times have changed. We've changed. Hell, even the dragons are able to change. Don't you think it's time to stop fighting?" Percivale cut in.

Around the table, a couple of the knights nodded in agreement. Others remained stony-faced.

"He's right," Gawain said. "If dragons can run charities instead of hoarding gold, we gotta evolve and change our ways, too."

On one of the video conference screens, Sir Lucan shook his head. "No. You're both too young to remember how it once was between us. The only good dragon is a dead dragon," the elderly knight said. "You don't recall the wails of mourning mothers after the despicable wyrm Fafnir razed a village to the ground. The tormented screams of men caught in dragon's breath who weren't fortunate enough for a quick death. Their pleas for mercy from our Maker, because the pain is indescribable."

Nate and Gawain quieted.

He didn't have a riposte.

"Can you do the assignment or not?" Kay demanded. "Should I have Pelleus fly to America?"

"No," Nate gritted between his teeth. "Fine. But no more stunts. You hear me? You let me do this my way."

"Agreed."

Nate eyed his father, wary of his easy acceptance, but decided not to question it. He had the man's word, in front of everyone. It was more than he'd expected and enough to reassure him of Astrid's safety.

For now. In the meantime, before their next meeting, he'd resume his covert attempts to sway the rest of the knighthood to his favor. One man at a time, he could win them over to the side of peace.

Chapter 7

The months of July and August melted away, passing in casual dates and evenings in. Whether they spent time alone in her apartment or with mutual friends, Astrid cherished every second with Nate. Toni and Maria hit it off, much to Astrid's pleasure. After a time, her friends and his became *their* friends.

The final hurdle involved her family, and after enduring weeks of her dad asking about her new boyfriend, she decided the time had come to introduce everyone.

To save Nate the expense the long drive would cost him in gas, Astrid claimed financial responsibility for the drive. She had forced him to fold his body into her passenger seat without realizing he was too tall for the compact car. Every time she stole a glance at him, she giggled at the exaggerated dirty look he aimed back.

"Okay, so your legs are longer than I thought. We're almost there, though."

"I feel like we've been in this car for years," he mumbled. "Which isn't a bad idea. I'm not sure if years would be enough time to prepare for this."

"For the fiftieth time, babe, relax. My family is going to love you."

"Families are never okay with the strange dude boning their daughter, okay? Especially dads. He's going to eat me."

"Look, we've been dating for, like, three months now." Two wonderful months where they couldn't keep their hands off each other. She'd lost count of how many times they'd joked about buying stock in condoms. "Meeting my family is a cakewalk."

"Oh yeah, sure. Cake. Dragons and cake."

Astrid chuckled and ran a hand through her hair, tucking it back behind her ear. "Almost there."

The private road wound another five miles through the hills, stretches of light forest and green fields rolling past after a generous rain. She slowed as they approached an intimidating gate featuring a wrought iron dragon. It opened upon their arrival.

"Geez, he sure likes his privacy, doesn't he?"

"Wouldn't you? And not only because he's a dragon. Before all that came out, he'd get people trying to push screenplays at him, or wanting to complain about whichever movie recently didn't meet their expectations. Not to mention paparazzi and that sort of thing."

"Yeah, okay, I can see that. Fans get crazy. The press, too, I guess. So should I not mention any of his movies I've seen?"

"You can mention them. He's a sucker for praise. Just, uh, don't overdo it."

"Right. No ass-kissing the father for brownie points."

His anxious voice made her laugh, but she reached over and gave his leg a comforting squeeze. "There it is. Home."

"Holy crap. Your dad's estate is built into the rock. It's like a… a damned mountain stronghold."

Nate's eyes bugged out of his head. He leaned forward in his seat to stare, his discomfort in the cramped space forgotten.

Astrid grinned.

The front of the manor was all glass and steel, but equipped with a state-of-the-art security system with impenetrable panels that slid into place once the defensive system was activated. They hadn't needed to use it yet, but her father claimed it was for their safety if dragonslayers ever came to them.

He wanted his wife and children to remain safe.

Before they even parked, the front door opened and her parents stepped out. Nate sucked in a sharp breath.

"Your dad is huge."

"You're tall, too."

"Yeah, but his arms are like tree trunks. I think he can seriously snap me in half without the rawr and the grrr shifting."

His nervous humor coaxed another round of giggles from her. She put the car in park, switched off the engine, and leaned over to plant a kiss on his cheek. "C'mon, big guy. You can do this."

She slipped out and ran over to her mom, greeting her with a tight hug and kiss. Her father wrapped one of his brawny arms around her and kissed the top of her head.

"Welcome home, cub."

"I swear you are prettier every time I see you, sweetheart. I love your hair."

Astrid rolled her eyes. "You're just saying that because you get to deal with a messy toddler all day. Speaking of, where *is* Brandt?"

"He crashed on the couch in the solar. He was all excited you were coming home. He ran around collecting your favorite things, then passed out about twenty minutes ago with Toot under his arm."

"Aww. He's still playing with him?"

"Your brother loves that elephant."

Saul cleared his throat. "Our visitor?"

"Mom, Daddy, this is Nate."

At the prompting, Nate stepped up and offered his hand toward her father without missing a beat. After an elbow to the ribs from Chloe, Saul reluctantly took his hand for a wordless shake.

"Nice to meet you, Mr. and Mrs. Drakenstone. Thank you for having me over for Labor Day. Astrid's been gushing about your amazing barbecue for weeks."

"I have not," she muttered, cheeks hot.

"I'm pretty sure you mentioned copious amounts of beef and pork at least thirty times."

"And to think we once worried she'd be a vegetarian." Her perpetually friendly and engaging mother stepped forward and hugged him like a member of the family. "It's so nice to finally meet you, Nate. Astrid gushes about you, too."

"*Mom.*"

Chloe released him and stepped back to flash her daughter a big grin. "I can see why you do. He's polite *and* handsome. And he hasn't run from your father's glare yet. Saul, you promised to be nice."

Astrid breathed a sigh of relief. One down, three to go. If her mother liked him, there was a great chance her grandmother would as well. And once Nate won the two of them over, Grandpa Max and her father wouldn't be far behind them.

"Hello," Saul grumbled.

"An honor to meet you, sir."

"Please come in," Saul continued after another nudge from his wife. "The long drive must have been tiresome."

Chloe stepped between them and linked her arms through theirs, leading the way inside. Saul followed. Astrid cast a smile at her father over her shoulder, as well as a pleading look.

Saul never liked any of her boyfriends, but he'd shown more kindness to Nate in a few minutes of silence than any of the men before him, too. That had to count for something. He'd growled at the firefighter she dated and chosen to speak in an ethereal, reverberating boom like an angry god hurling down rules set in stone.

Literally. His theatrical side showed when he did everything but hand the man a tablet of Thou Shall Nots. Her father rarely used magic, but when he did, it was always to her detriment or embarrassment.

After a brief overview of the estate, including directions to and from the many bathrooms and points of exit from the home, Chloe released them to the veranda to find her early-arrival relatives divided between groups mingling beneath the gazebo and playing volleyball in the sandpit.

"Your family get-togethers are substantially less awkward than mine. No one's drunk yet. Or swearing."

"Give my Uncle Teo and Dad some time."

"Oh." His smile didn't waver. "Should I have worn my flame-retardant suit?"

"Nah, Uncle Teo exhales acid fog, so he isn't quite as free with his dragon breath as Daddy once he's had a few… dozen."

Nate shuddered. "I hope you're exaggerating."

"I am." She closed her fingers around his arm and raised to tiptoe, elongating her body against his side. "I promise, no matter what, you are 100 percent safe here from my family."

As she led him toward the gazebo, her uncle called out, "So this is the seaman in our Astrid's life."

A large, heavy hand dropped to Nate's shoulder from behind.

"Nate, meet Thor, my Great Uncle."

Thor chuckled and stroked a hand down his beard. "You will never know how much I appreciate that term and that everyone recognizes the magnitude of my greatness."

"Uh…" Nate blinked and stared. His eyes went large, and he was seemingly overcome with fear, which was standard when meeting one of the world's most renowned dragons.

"He won't eat you," Astrid assured Nate.

"No, I certainly will not. Humans are too stringy."

"Sorry. Good to meet you, sir." Nate extended his hand, but Thor grasped him by the arm and pulled him in for a manly backslap instead.

Her poor boyfriend was in for a culture shock. Everyone in the Drakenstone family, save for her father, greeted him with warm embraces and smiling welcomes. He stood in awe as Maximilian rose to his feet and approached him, secret servicemen in tow. One of them had the look of a fox, or even a wolf, with cunning eyes and alert features. He breathed in, nostrils flaring, bright blue eyes assessing the sailor in front of him.

Astrid hurried into her grandfather's waiting arms and hugged him tight. "So glad to see you, Grandpa. Where's Grandma?"

"She and Svetlana went to change the twins. They made the mistake of sneaking into Teo's pudding, and it didn't agree with them."

Memories of her uncle's kitchen nightmares made her wince in sympathy.

"But enough of that. Introduce me to this young man."

Her poor boyfriend had lagged behind, an expression frozen on his face between a cordial smile and terror. Max's arrival finished what Thor's greeting began, and reality must have crashed down upon him. Nate was shaking.

Falling back a step to place her hand on his arm, she waited until the moment passed. Max didn't press him or approach, accustomed to scaring humans with his sense of enormous presence alone.

Funny how Daddy didn't terrify him this way, and he is the aggressive one.

"It's such a pleasure to meet you, Mr. President," Nate said in a rush, recovered from his staring incident.

"At last, I get to meet the young man who has occupied our Astrid's time and kept her from us all. Though… have we met before?" Maximilian asked after a moment. "I find your face familiar."

"I don't believe so, sir."

"Are you sure? I usually have a good memory for faces."

A bead of sweat trickled down the side of Nate's face. "You made a visit to the ship I was serving on about three years ago, the Bonhomme Richard, but I didn't have the honor of meeting you personally."

Max's smile widened. "A fine ship. I think I recall now—you were standing watch when we came aboard."

"Yeah." Nate relaxed, the tension fading from his shoulders. Although weariness showed in his face, he flashed Astrid a reassuring smile. He was fine again.

"Come, Nate. Have a drink with us and share your tales of the sea. I am quite the boatsman myself, you know. Let me tell you about the time I battled the bull-headed serpent of the deep ocean." Thor took Nate by the shoulder, giving him little choice, and steered him away toward the gazebo where the rest of the shifter men had gathered.

"Your boyfriend smells funny."

Astrid turned at the voice and crossed her arms over her chest. "That's not a nice thing to say about someone, Javier."

The younger half-dragon shrugged. Despite standing as tall as Astrid, Javier still had a preteen's body and youthful face. Years ago, their fathers had hoped to encourage a match between the two. Instead, he'd fulfilled the role of an irritating little brother until Brandt came along.

But the damage had been done, and when she aged to adulthood first, all chances of connecting the Drakenstone and Arcillanegro families through marriage was lost.

He'd make some woman happy one day. Astrid was sure of it. His tousled brown hair, swarthy skin, and green eyes would only be enhanced by his dragon blood. She'd yet to meet a homely dragon.

"It's still true," Javier insisted. "He smells like the shaman we have on the island."

Astrid laughed. "Nate's no mage, believe me."

Javier shrugged again and stuffed his hands into the pockets of his cargo shorts. "Anyway, Aunt Chloe wants you inside for a second."

"Oh, sure."

"Don't worry, I won't tell him he stinks."

"So nice of you." She rolled her eyes and surrendered to the call of duty. Inside the manor, her mother set her to work chopping onions, potatoes, and a host of other fruits and vegetables for numerous side dishes and appetizers. Between food prep and observing Nate's body language from the windows for signs of his close-quarters dragon meeting going awry, she remained busy.

"I hope Nate likes apple pie," Chloe muttered. "Your father had me make three this time."

"I think Nate likes any pie," Astrid replied, chuckling. "He likes sweets."

"A man after my own heart," her Aunt Marcy said. "I love him already. He and Teo should get along well."

"And Grandpa. I dunno, he might give them a run for their money. I saw Nate put down a ton of cheesecake during a party. No idea where he keeps it all."

Svetlana came up beside Astrid and poked her in the ribs, her fingers cold. Astrid leaped and spilled flour over the counter.

"Jerk!"

"Heh, heh. You have such thin skin for a dragon. Why don't you take a break and enjoy the party?"

"I will, I will. Did you go over and meet Nate yet?"

Svetlana's dark hair fell into her face as she shook her head, revealing streaks of blue, purple, green, and pink in the underlayers. "No, not yet, but I got a glimpse of him in passing. He's cuter in person than his picture," she replied in a soft voice. "I like his freckles. They make his face a little boyish, but... whew, his body is all man."

Astrid swatted her. "That was awful, and you should feel ashamed."

"He kinda smells strange though."

Astrid frowned. "He smells fine to me."

"I mean, it isn't a bad smell or anything... is he a witch? Maybe he has one in his fam."

That was two of her relatives to point out an unusual scent clinging to her boyfriend. Had she never noticed it, too overwhelmed by the intensity of their attraction to take in the full package?

"No idea. I guess he could and not even know about it. He wouldn't be the first to be clueless about magical beings in his ancestry."

"True enough," Svetlana agreed. "Come on, let's get out of here before I raid the pies and your mom kills me."

"I heard that," Chloe called from across the kitchen.

Arm in arm, the two women abandoned the kitchen for the backyard.

"Where's Aunt Mahasti and Uncle Leiv? Why didn't they come?" Astrid questioned.

"Meh. They went to visit Dad's relatives in Moscow. I wasn't in the mood for it and stayed behind to see you guys instead."

"I'm glad you did. You need to come down to San Diego and visit me sometime soon."

"And intrude on you and your sailor?"

"Oh come on, it's not like we're living together."

"Yet." Svetlana teased. "So, what's it like?"

"What's what like?"

"You know." Svetlana glanced around their immediate vicinity, as if afraid one of the other adults would appear and overhear them. Or worse, Saul. Her cousin leaned closer and whispered, "Tell me about the sex."

"It's not like the dirty movies we used to sneak in your dad's cabin when they weren't home."

"What about the books?"

Astrid giggled. "Maybe a little like those. I mean, he makes me feel like I'm in a romance novel sometimes. He's so sweet, and he calls me at random times to ask how I'm doing and if I need anything when he's at the store, even though he's the one working at the big naval base."

"You're so lucky."

"What about you? No boys chasing you at the university?"

Svetlana shrugged. "No one interesting. There was this one international student, but he turned out to be a real jerk. He was dating four girls, not including me, all at once. So I dumped him."

"Ugh. Good for you."

"Speaking of guys, Yasmin's pissed you never remember to call."

Nate wandered over, having escaped from one of Thor's long-winded tales of battle and valor. Astrid thought he was handling himself well, all things considered. He hadn't panicked when a magical portal brought Watatsumi into the yard, which was a huge tick in his favor. She'd caught her father's surprised glance. He'd almost looked impressed at Nate's composure after the initial rockiness.

"Having fun?"

"I will never look at The Avengers the same way again. That man has fought giants and everything else."

"Don't let him fool you. He was beside himself with glee when he found out who was portraying him in the films." Svetlana laughed and held out her hand. "Hi, I'm Svetlana."

"Oh, hey, yeah. Astrid said you two grew up together."

"We're kind of like sisters, only about five years apart. Except she has scales and I have fur."

Svetlana had inherited the best of both parents, but she was a chimera with no discernible racial lineage. At a glance, she could be almost any ethnicity, and she liked it, playing up her ambiguity whenever possible. Thick lines of kohl edged her honey-colored eyes, and golden bronzer dusted her cheeks. She loved colorful eyeshadow, favoring jewel colors and bold shades. One day, she'd made her eyelids resemble a cosmic nebula.

The best memories of sleepovers at Leiv and Mahasti's cabin had been their girls' nights in front of the television with all of the makeup owned between their two mothers piled on the table. They'd watch horror movies, eat greasy food, splurge on ice cream, and give each other ridiculous makeovers. While her mother enjoyed subdued, natural looks, it was from Aunt Mahasti that Astrid inherited her love of bold colors, a love presented in her art as much as her makeup.

"Err…"

Svetlana grinned. She crossed her arms, and Astrid was jealous of her biceps. Genes had built her cousin like a kickboxer. "She didn't tell you?"

"I wasn't going to out you, you brat." Astrid bumped her hip into her friend's then swapped over to Nate's side. He wrapped his arm around her waist and pulled her in close.

"I wouldn't have minded. Unlike the rest of these big, bad beasties, I'm a bear shifter. Not as cool as a dragon, I know, but a lot less conspicuous out in the woods."

"It's crazy wrapping my head around it all," Nate admitted.

"From what I can see, you're doing a helluva job." Svetlana gave him a dimpled smile. "Have any brothers?"

"He's ten."

"Damn."

By evening, Astrid couldn't stuff another bite of food into her mouth and neither could Nate. After a few games of cards and rounds of charades with her family, they retired to separate rooms—whether she was an adult or not, she didn't trust her hands to remain chaste, and she wasn't comfortable having sex with her parents only a few bedrooms down the hall.

A restless half hour passed in her room. Astrid had showered and tossed on her nightgown but couldn't sleep without saying goodnight. She shrugged into the matching robe and crept to his door. Maybe he had become as aware of her as she was of him, because it opened before her knuckles struck the wood.

"Whoa. Hey."

Her eyes traveled over his white T-shirt and Incredible Hulk pajama bottoms with a grin. "Busted you escaping. Where ya going?"

"To say goodnight to you."

Goodnight became a kiss, which transitioned to both of his hands cupping her bottom. Without panties beneath her nightgown, only two layers of silk separated Nate's palms from her bare skin. He was her addiction, and one night of voluntary chastity was going to kill her when all she could think about was luring him back to her room.

"Damn. If I wasn't worried about trying your dad's patience…"

"Yeah. I know."

"Mm. It'll just make things better when we're back at your place."

But never his apartment. For all the time they'd dated, Nate danced around the topic whenever she brought up visiting him and Echo.

Did he have something to hide?

No, Astrid convinced herself. This was Nate, an honest and dependable man who accepted her, claws, scales, and all. She brushed aside the crazy accusations swirling through her thoughts and gazed into his green eyes.

Nate had never lied to her, and somehow, he'd weathered a storm of dragons instead of tucking tail and running for the California hills. He'd survived her crazy, bigger-than-life family. Better still, they'd *liked* him.

She had no idea how long she could resist the urge to brand him with her mark and bind their souls together. Soon, she hoped. She'd sit him down, tell him everything, and hope his heart yearned as deeply for her as she needed him.

Chapter 8

Cool, damp sand squished between Nate's toes and warm sunshine radiated against his back. Echo charged down the beach after the ball he'd thrown, kicking up water as she happily bounced through the waves washing up on the shore.

The day at the dog park and quasi-beach should have been perfect, but grim thoughts weighed on his mind. The leaders of the brotherhood planned to take action against the Drakenstone clan, and he wasn't sure he could stall them any longer.

"Three months with the beast is long enough," Kay had told him the previous afternoon, delivering a clap to Nate's shoulder reminiscent of a proud father. "You've done what no other dragonslayer could."

All his life, he'd wanted praise from Kay, and when it came, it invoked a sense of failure instead of accomplishment.

"Go get the ball, Echo!" He hurled the tennis ball down the sand. Once she'd clenched her prize between her jaws, the German shepherd shot across the sand to return to him.

She didn't slow, and instead, barreled past him with another target in mind.

"Traitor," Nate muttered.

Echo dropped her ball in Astrid's lap and lowered to her haunches, completely ignoring him.

"Silly dog. Who's a good girl, hmm?" Astrid set her phone aside so she could reach out and rub the dog's head and ears between her hands.

"Who you texting? With all of the smiling you were doing, do I need to pretend to be jealous?"

She laughed at him. "It was my mom, and trust me, I smile more when there's a message from you."

He dropped down beside her on the blanket and leaned over her lap to give Echo's head a scratch. "I have a bad feeling about this. Did it involve me?"

"Yeah. She said to tell you not to make any plans for Halloween."

"That's forever away."

"Fifty-two days."

Nate blinked at her. "Really? Let me guess, you're one of those people who counts down the seconds to Christmas."

She pushed at his shoulder. "No, that's Mom's shtick. And the reason she doesn't want you to make any plans is that she wants us to come up for the company party. Dad plans it out way in advance, and it's the best time ever. He gets the studio all set up with special effects and everything."

"Sounds fun. Guess this means I passed muster, huh?"

"Mom loves you."

"And your dad?"

"He didn't eat you. I call that approval."

"The rest of your family?"

"Grandma and Grandpa think you're awesome. Thor was thoroughly impressed with your tolerance for alcohol. You better be careful there, or he'll challenge you to a *real* drink-off, and we won't see each other for a week." She laughed and ducked her head. "Everyone liked you."

"I liked them, too." And his fondness for them had become his key dilemma. He *liked* them. The enemy. Once he'd stopped thinking of the friendly gang as dragons, he'd come to know them as people. He watched them play with their young children, helped cook on the grill while sharing stories, and discussed sports the same way he would have with any of his friends on the ship. Or his fellow knights in the brotherhood.

"I did have a question, if you don't mind, about something that came up last weekend during the cookout," Astrid hedged.

"Yeah, shoot."

"It's about you."

"Whatever it is, I didn't do it." He held up both hands and grinned, but inside his stomach knotted.

"No, nothing like that. It's just something Javier noticed. He said you smelled like magic."

Shit! The smile dropped off his face. "Javier's the kid your folks wanted you to hook up with, right? Maybe he's jealous."

"I thought so, too, until Svetlana said the same thing later."

If Maximilian and Ēostre had recognized him, they chose not to out him for reasons beyond his understanding. He'd been positive the water dragon had seen through the charade.

"What are you asking, Astrid? If I'm a shifter or something?"

"No. Baby, I know you'd have told me if you were. I just wondered if there might be a chance you had a witch or something in your family tree." She toyed with the frayed hem of her cutoffs. "I smell it too now. It's… it reminds me of mint. Fresh mint leaves and ozone. It tingles if I really breathe you in."

Nate tried to cover his discomfort with a chuckle. "So witches smell like a bundle of leaves?"

"Not always. Anyway, I was just curious. Whatever it is, I like it. It smells nice."

He couldn't lie to her face and dropped eye contact, focusing on the sandwiches they'd brought along in their basket instead. "I guess it's possible. I have this one aunt who everyone says is a little off."

"Oh, okay." The spark in Astrid's eyes dimmed, and her smile vanished. "Hey, let's grab ice cream on the way back," she said in an abrupt change of topic. "I know the best little shop near here. One of those hidden gems no one wants to share."

She knew. She knew he'd lied.

"Sounds good. We still on for a movie when I get back next week?"

"Of course." Astrid smiled up at him. "We can make it dinner and a movie too if you like. I figure you'd want to grab some real food after a week living on ship grub."

He chuckled and tried to push back the anxiety spawned by his lie. In truth, he was looking forward to the time away at sea, despite the activity bound to occupy every second. "It depends on who's cooking in the Officer's Mess, but yeah, I'd like that."

"What happens when you go out for your mini-deployment things?"

"Drills. The ship has to meet certain qualifications before they can deploy for real, so we go out and test their security teams. What are you going to be doing?"

"Same as usual. I have a necklace I've been commissioned to make, so I'll use the break to focus on that."

"Break, huh?" He leaned in and nuzzled her throat.

"Well, you are rather distracting."

Beside them, Echo flopped to her belly and let out a low groan until both humans gave belly rubs.

"Hey, what will you do with Echo while you're gone?"

"My neighbor will—"

"Leave her with me."

Echo's head lifted from the blanket and her ears perked.

"You sure about that? I mean, she's a bed hog and can get pretty vengeful if you delay when she wants to go out. She took a dump in my shoes once when she was a puppy. I'm *positive* it wasn't coincidence."

"Yeah, I do. Isis is lonely now that the kittens are gone, and this way Echo won't be bored until your neighbor goes to let her out."

"You didn't keep the one kitten? I was positive you'd end up adopting her yourself."

"I considered it, but this little girl came to the Kitten Korner in the shelter. Real shy and tiny thing. She didn't touch any of the cats at first, but Cleo scampered over and climbed right into her lap. The girl's smile made her mom cry. She's autistic and nonverbal, but she loved Cleopatra."

"You're incredibly soft for a dragon," he teased. "But I'm proud of you for letting her go. No better reason than to make a kid happy."

"Yeah, she was. So… Echo? Can she stay with me?"

"If you feel like it's okay, fine by me."

Astrid leaned against him and placed her cheek on his shoulder. "Great. I'll pick her up tomorrow night then?"

"I'll drop her off at your place tomorrow."

She frowned, and he knew she saw through him.

How much longer could he lie?

Better yet, how much longer would she allow it?

***

Astrid pulled her sporty little four-door coupe into the end of the estate's drive and glanced at her passenger. Echo proudly wagged her pink tongue from the rear seat.

"You ready for some good ol' fun in the sun, girl? There's so much space here and so many things to chase, you won't know where to run first."

She grabbed her purse from the front seat and slung it over her shoulder before letting the shepherd onto the driveway.

"Puppy!" Brandt rushed forward and wrapped his sticky hands around Echo's neck.

"Hey, little guy. C'mon, you know better. Always let a dog sniff you first."

To Echo's credit, she remained still and tolerated the toddler's manhandling. She sniffed his hair and licked the melted popsicle on his hands. He giggled.

"She certainly is pretty," Chloe said. "What a beautiful animal. Is it okay to pet her?"

"Sure is. She seems to love Brandt already." Grinning the whole while, Astrid watched the bonding between her little brother and Echo.

Perfect. Everything had gone according to her plan. She'd have time away from Nate to cool her libido and think without lust stirring her emotions, and she could also spend time with her family. Echo was a sweet bonus wrapped in black and brown fur.

Her father appeared in the doorway. "Your arrival is a pleasant sur—"

A snarl tore from the shepherd's throat. Brandt was forgotten as she twisted and leaped toward the open door. Echo charged with her jaws open, snapping toward Saul.

"Whoa, girl!" Astrid looped the leash around her fist and tugged back on the harness. Echo resisted. The dog's ears flattened back against her head, and she tried to lunge again. A deep, low growl reverberated through her chest.

In the months since meeting the dog, she'd become certain Echo was an enormous, soft-hearted therapy dog for Nate's PTSD or some other thing. She'd never actually asked why he had a service dog. In Saul's presence, she became a vicious attack hound, startling even her father.

Saul stepped back. "I believe I've upset her. She's quite protective of you," he said. "Certainly a sign of a good dog."

"Echo, no!" Another sharp tug on the leash dragged Echo back. "I'm sorry, Daddy. I don't know what's gotten into her. I should go."

As tears rolled down Brandt's plump toddler cheeks, he covered his ears and huddled close to their mother. Chloe swept him into her arms and took a few steps away from the angry canine.

"No, no. It's fine. I appear to be the only one she dislikes, and to be fair, I wanted to do the same to her owner." Saul grinned toothily but kept his distance. "Don't go, please. Your mother has looked forward to having you home for a time. I'll simply give the dog a wide berth while you're here."

"She's never acted like this before, I swear." She worried if distance would be enough. The dog's focus never wavered. With her teeth bared and hackles raised, she became the complete opposite of the playful companion Astrid had come to love.

Once her father was gone and out of sight, Echo remained on alert. Her ears pricked high, and she paced the immediate area, sniffing their surroundings as if some latent patrol dog training had come into play. She refused to step one paw inside the house.

"C'mon, girl, it'll be okay. You can stay in my room if you want."

One sharp bark preceded a low whine then Echo backed away from the door.

"I wish I knew what troubled her so much about Saul. Maybe she senses he's a larger creature?"

"Maybe," Astrid said. She nibbled her bottom lip and glanced from the shepherd to the door. "I'd ask if Uncle Teo would talk to her and find out what she wants, but if she's afraid of dragons…"

"But why isn't she afraid of you? You're a dragon, too."

Astrid shook her head. "I guess I have enough of you in me that I'm not as scary. I'll just make her comfortable outside then."

"Good idea. I'll set up her stuff over on the east side of the house."

During her childhood, they'd only had Felix for a household pet. And while he had been beloved, Astrid had been eager to convince her parents it was time to have a new animal in the house. A puppy for Brandt to grow up alongside.

So much for that. They kept no pet supplies on hand, but a single wish from Mahasti provided a spacious doghouse in addition to the canine's dishes. Another wish littered the area with toys of all squeaky shapes and sizes.

"C'mon, Echo, we can go see the zebras. Just don't chase them, hey? They'll stampede you."

The trio her grandfather purchased for her years ago had doubled. Safe on her father's property, with more than enough room to roam, they'd flourished and earned Astrid the respect of sanctuaries across the west coast. She'd accepted two more lame geldings since then, and she'd been present when the lone mare birthed a miracle foal her original keepers predicted she would never have. They had thought her sterile and the one stallion aggressive but lame.

By the time they reached the fenced pasture, Echo was at ease, with a spring in her step and a grin on her doggy face. After a brief hesitation, Astrid leaned down and unhooked the leash.

Echo stayed by her side, but her tail wagged, and she turned her face into the breeze.

"Go on, run to your heart's content."

With no one requiring her attention, Astrid took the opportunity to gather her thoughts. She climbed the fence and sat on the top rail, content to watch Echo chase dragonflies across the tall grass. The contrast between the current gentle giant and the hostile beast of a half hour ago stunned Astrid.

Her thoughts turned to Nate. She'd have to let him know.

Was he thinking about her at all, she wondered, or was he too busy with work? And why had he lied to her on the beach?

She kept turning the conversation over and over in her head. The way he'd avoided her gaze. Did he know something? Was he ashamed? Did he think she'd look down on him for being a male witch? Her inquiry had only led to more questions.

Despite his unusual act of dishonesty, one thing remained certain for Astrid: whether he was human or a witch in hiding, she would love him no less.

Chapter 9

Several breaths had passed before Astrid realized she'd awakened. The dream remained fresh on her mind and tears soaked through her pillow.

In gradual increments, she grounded herself in the reality of her bedroom. Her heavy, satin blanket. Moonbeams slanting through the window. A soft dog beside her, groomed and lilac-scented after an impromptu visit to the groomer.

Despite Echo's presence, she pushed her hair back from her face and sat up, unable to deny the incredible urge to sob. They came from her in great heaves and shakes of her shoulders, a sense of pervasive wrongness digging talons into her heart.

Something was going to happen to Nate. The sense lingered, compounded with a vision of living beside another man who had been his inferior in every way.

In a panic, she twisted around to stare at the glowing face of the digital alarm. A quarter to midnight. Earlier that night, Nate phoned to report his return to dry land. He wasn't at sea. He was home again and safe.

They'd chatted on the phone during his drive from the base to his apartment, and even after he crawled into bed. The conversation ended when his slurring voice prompted her to shoo him off to sleep.

Sensing her human's distress, Isis leaped onto the rumpled blankets. The Bengal's furred head bumped beneath Astrid's chin and her rumbling purr filled the dark room. She smelled like mint, the scent from a habit of rolling in the huge planter of it Astrid grew on the balcony.

"I'm so scared," she whispered against the cat's soft fur.

The dream clung like a burr, the sense of wrongness refusing to fade away. Every detail remained clear in her mind, unlike her usual nightmares. The tenacious, disquieting aura led her to reach for the phone and punch down on her contacts list.

The call connected after the third ring. "Grandma?"

"Astrid? It's nearly three in the morning here. What's wrong?" The drowsiness vanished, replaced by sharp words of alarm.

"What's wrong with Astrid?" Max asked in the background.

"I'm sorry. I didn't mean to wake you, especially for a dream."

"Don't apologize, sweetheart. Did you want to talk about it?"

"Yeah. Yeah, I do." Her breath shuddered from her lungs.

"Start from the beginning."

While recounting the events out loud to Ēostre, Astrid entered the kitchen and poured a glass of fruit-infused water from the fridge. "I was visiting Nate's grave at the cemetery to leave flowers, only it didn't feel like a dream. It was like a memory of something I've already done and lived. The sensations are still on my skin. I can still *smell* it. Have you ever had those, Grandma?"

"A prophetic dream? Once or twice," Ēostre said. "Do you believe you've had one?"

Astrid coiled a lock of hair around her finger and paced across the room. She wiped tears from her face again and struggled to control her voice. "Maybe. I don't know. I've never had a dream affect me this way. Ever. It was like reliving a memory."

Ēostre listened to Astrid's recounting of the nightmare, and after a moment of silence, she murmured, "It could be a true vision of your future. Were you able to see the date on his gravestone?"

"Yes." Astrid sucked in a deep breath. "Two days from now."

"Then tread carefully with each step you take, Astrid. Anything you do, or choose not to do, may be the catalyst to taking that path. Perhaps a reading with a witch could add the clarity you seek."

Astrid knew a handful of true witches with the gift.

"Astrid, I know this is delicate, but have you…?"

"Marked him? No. No, I haven't."

"But you want to."

"Yes," she whispered.

"Tread carefully, hon, and call me if you need to talk. No matter the hour. Okay?"

"Okay. Thanks, Grandma."

She disconnected the call and tossed the phone onto the kitchen counter. "Witches, witches, witches."

Was Nate also a witch? She'd wanted to ask her grandmother and grandfather if they'd sensed the same magical aura around him, but she'd feared their answer.

Of the many witches in Astrid's acquaintance, she only trusted one with her deepest fantasies and secret thoughts. She scurried to her laptop and flipped up the lid to open a Skype video chat. The musical ringtone filled her room until a tired voice greeted her over the line.

"Little late for a chitchat, don't you think?" The video went from black to an equally tired young woman's face.

"Hey, Yasmin, long time no see."

The dark-haired woman on the screen scrunched her nose and twisted a tight spiral of hair around her finger. "That's because rumor mill has it you've been busy with some hunk of a sailor. I'm hurt you didn't share that tidbit yourself."

"Sorry, Yaz, I guess I did sorta get wrapped up in him… which is why I need your help."

Yasmin's hazel eyes brightened. "Yeah?"

"I think I had a prophetic dream, and I wanted to get your thoughts on it."

"Oh. Wow, you want a reading then. You sure you don't want me to get my mom?"

Astrid and Yasmin met during a supernatural enclave hosted at Teo's island ten years prior. Aunt Marcy, Chloe, and Yasmin's mother were old college pals, and when the girls met, they'd become distant but close friends who often chatted over the internet when they weren't meeting each other over the summer.

They had that kind of low-maintenance friendship that didn't require everyday conversation, but when they did reunite, they were inseparable.

We need to hang out more, Astrid thought. "No, not yet. I feel more comfortable talking to you about it."

"Okay. Understood. Let me get to the channeling room. I haven't done as many readings as her, and it's always easier there."

The image on the screen shifted to a bumpy visual tour of Yasmin's Texas home and a glimpse of her father in passing.

"Are you still on the computer?" he asked in an exasperated voice. "Do you ever sleep?"

Astrid winced. "Sorry, Mr. Silva. It's my fault." Until she met Yasmin's father, she had never understood the way her friends stared at Saul. With only the word "hunk" available to describe the sexy Brazilian man, she'd harbored a secret crush for years.

"Ah, hello, Astrid." His handsome face came into focus on the screen. Faint touches of silver showed up against his dark hair. "What did I say about calling me Mr. Silva?"

"Sorry, Zac."

"Much better. Now, what are you two girls up to? Are we hexing cheating boyfriends?"

Yasmin groaned. "I told you I wouldn't do that again. It's nothing to be worried about, Dad. I'm just helping her out with something, okay?"

"Fine, fine. Don't be up too late."

"Your dad is seriously dreamy," Astrid whispered to pass the time until Yasmin reached her destination. She didn't know him as well as her Uncle Teo, and considered him safe to ogle.

"Dreamier than your sailor?"

"No," she replied without hesitation. "But definitely dreamy."

Yasmin set the laptop on a table and struck a match. "I don't see it. He just looks like boring, fun-killer Dad to me," she said while lighting candles.

"Pretty much what I see when I look at mine, yet you were starry-eyed for, like, days."

"Shush or I'm gonna disconnect."

Astrid had needed the laugh. Her giggles bubbled forth, loosening the tight knots in her shoulders and easing the churning in her stomach.

The young witch settled in front of the laptop and dropped both hands to her lap. "So, tell me about this dream and everything that's bothering you. If there are circumstances in your life that could be affecting your sleep, I need to know so I can interpret the signs and any visions I receive."

For the second time that night, she repeated her dream to another soul and left nothing out.

"After I left his grave, I went home to my family, but I didn't recognize them."

"You mean your parents?"

"No, to *my* place. There was a man there, someone I cared about, and a little boy was with him. I was happy, sort of, but it was like a huge piece of me was missing."

"Nate. It wasn't how you feel for Nate."

"Yeah." Another tear slipped down her cheek, and she wiped it away, angry and confused.

"Anything else?" Yasmin asked.

"I think he's a witch or something, and maybe too ashamed to tell me. He's hiding something."

"Male witches don't exactly have the best rep in our community. For some reason, they tend to be psycho warlocks raising the dead and shit."

"Yeah, I know, but I don't get that feeling from him."

"Could be nothing then. Residual energy from an ancestor in his line."

"But why lie about it? I mean, I'm a dragon. It's not like I could judge him for being different."

"Like I said, male witches have it bad, girl. I probably wouldn't own up to it either if I were a boy. Sometimes just admitting it is enough to get you up shit creek."

"But my granddad made all of those laws—"

"Murderers and magiphobes don't care about laws, Astrid. And he's an officer in the Navy, right?"

"He is, yeah."

"Well, if that got out for any reason about him, he could probably kiss his career goodbye. He'll never get another promotion."

"They can't do that."

"No, they're not *supposed* to do that. They'll make something up to cover the fact that they're slighting him because he's a supe."

"Maybe…"

"Why does it bother you so much?"

"Because it's not like him to keep things. I revealed the truth about who I am. I took him home to meet my family. He knows everything secret about me."

"You act like you two are married already or something." Yasmin sighed. "Look, it's not that I don't sympathize—I do, I really do!—but maybe he just needs more time to trust than you did. Maybe he planned to tell you, but you took him by surprise and ruined his plot. He might have wanted to share the news with you over wine and chocolates or something."

Yasmin's outside perspective, while irritating, was correct. Maybe she was reading too much into his reaction at the beach.

"Okay, fine, but what about the dream?"

"Let's see what the cards have to say. I need you to focus. This is better in person, but we'll work with what we've got."

Yasmin shuffled an old tarot deck in her hands. The beautifully painted cards depicted thorned roses and twining vines on the back.

"Seven is a magical number, so I prefer to do basic, seven card spreads." Yasmin dropped her voice to a theatrical whisper, "I don't know how to do anything but burning questions because it's all Mom taught me. So focus on it."

While Astrid concentrated on her anguished thoughts, her friend cut the cards, shuffled, and spread seven on the table in three rows, one at the top and three in the two rows beneath.

Yasmin flipped one. "This card in the center, the Queen of Coins, symbolizes your question, and your desire to know the outcome of your union with Nate. She represents beauty and fertility, love and splendor." Yasmin's eyes shone amber in the dim light; then she tucked her chin and closed her eyes. "I see acceptance. And… something else. Hey, Astrid?"

Her heart skipped a beat. "What? What is it?"

"How much of your future do you want to know?"

"What do you mean?"

"How deeply do you want to know your possible future?"

Astrid thought back to what Ēostre had said about the potential to make a wrong choice. "Just enough to help him if I need to. I'm… I'm afraid to know more. Watatsumi warned me against it."

"Okay. As I said, the Queen of Coins represents a woman who is nurturing and accepting. Don't press him. Let him come to you on his own. In time, Nate will reveal everything you need."

Yasmin moved to the next card and smoothed her fingers over it. "The Prince of Arrows tells of your obstacles and the influences regarding your query. Your misery is a short-lived burden, but Nate stands at the heart of it, a beacon in the foggy night. I see him surrounded by conflicts on all sides, emitting a radiant light. Honesty is the core value of his soul, and when he lies, it hurts him deeply. Especially when it's to you. Now, these two cards here on the right are your hopes and fears. The Nine of Cups is often thought of as the Wish card." Yasmin's fingers hovered above the card and her eyes closed. "Most of all, you wish for your dream to be a harmless nightmare, but it isn't."

Astrid swallowed. "So what I saw really was a vision?"

"It could be, yes. Prophecies are warnings given shape and form. Over here on the left, I see an older man entering your life as a guiding force."

"Who?"

"No idea. I've never seen him before. He's..." Yasmin closed her eyes and tilted her head, as if seeing something distant far away. "No—I don't know him."

"Damn. Okay, keep going."

"Your fates have become gnarled, and in the coming days there will be times when you feel trapped. Victimized." Her friend's voice trembled with each vague word. "Lost. But losing hope will only doom you to further suffering. You and Nate are both caught between opposing worlds headed on an unstoppable collision course. It's too late to change it. It's destiny."

"Opposing worlds? Collision? What the hell does that mean, Yaz?"

Yasmin chewed on one of her purple fingernails. "It means I can't speak anymore without upsetting the balance."

Astrid groaned and swept her hair back from her face. "Yaz, every day I am resisting the urge to bond with this man. I..." Her voice trailed off and she wrapped her arms around herself. "I don't want to lose him."

"Well, in that case, I'd say you need to go for it. If you feel the pull toward him, your heart knows best. And since shifters are out in the open, you have the freedom of telling him what's up and seeing how he feels."

"Is that what the cards say I should do?"

"That's what *I* am saying you should do. So get off the line with me, go splash some water on your face, and call your man."

"It's the middle of the night."

Yasmin stuck her tongue out. "You called me."

"Yeah, but he has an actual job."

The young witch held a hand over her heart in mock outrage. "That'll be the first, last, and only reading I ever do for you, chica. Love you, night!"

"I'm sorry, I love you t—" The conversation blipped and went dead, effectively cutting her off. Frowning, Astrid crawled into bed with her phone and brought up her message window with Nate.

Astrid: Hey, are you awake?

A few seconds later, her phone chirped with a return text.

Nate: I am now. What's wrong?

Astrid: Are you okay?

Before a game of textual tag could ensue, her phone rang with an incoming call.

"I'm sorry I woke you up after making you go to bed."

"It's fine. It's not like I *need* more than two hours of sleep, right? So what's up?" After a pause, he chuckled, and she heard the grin in his tired voice. "Can't wait to see me after all? Need me to make a spontaneous, late-night visit?"

They had decided early on that they were far too classy to use the term "booty call," but Nate had paid a fair number of them to her apartment over the months since his first visit.

"I wish it were that simple," Astrid muttered. She sighed and gazed at her ceiling.

The humor faded. "What's wrong?" he asked in a softer voice. "Bad dream?"

"Yeah. Are you, um, due to be deployed again or something?"

"Not really. I mean, they want me to go out for another drill and inspection gig, but I haven't received an official assignment yet. I'll be gone two weeks max if I'm picked. Why?"

She twisted the sheets around one of her fingers and made a disgruntled noise.

"Astrid, what's wrong?"

"I care for you, Nate, and I realized we haven't talked about a lot of things or where this is going for us. I just wanted to… I guess I wanted to know if you think about that, too."

Nate sucked in his breath, and a pregnant pause, heavy as a cannonball, hung between them before he finally whispered, "I've never felt this way about any other woman, Astrid. Not this serious. I wake up with you on my mind, and I can't sleep without texting you goodnight. It's crazy. Thought about you the whole time I was away, and now I can't wait to see you."

"Can you come over now?"

"Baby, if I drive now, I'm liable to veer off the road. Look, I'll be over as soon as I can tomorrow and we'll talk. About *everything*. I promise."

Goose bumps raised on her arms and a pleasant tingle of anticipation crawled down her body. The promise of discovering his secrets brought a smile to her lips.

Success.

***

It was the last lie he ever wanted to tell her.

Less than a minute after the call ended, a chirp-chirp from the phone notified him of an incoming message. He opened the text to reveal a photograph.

She stole his breath away, literally and figuratively, while he stood beside his bed half dressed with his phone clutched in one hand. Astrid lay amidst her bedsheets, topless with one arm casually draped across her breasts. The photograph only captured her from lips to midsection.

Another message arrived.

Downloading.

The image revealed cotton panties and crumpled Tinkerbell pajama shorts on the floor beside her bed.

Astrid: See you soon.

Nate hoped so. He really hoped so, but it was about more than sex and physical gratification. As arousing as the image was of Astrid sprawled naked in her bed, warm and wet, waiting for him, what he truly wanted was to see her face. He would have traded both for a picture of her drowsy smile.

Which was why it was time to come clean.

He couldn't continue living the lie, but he had one last job to do.

Nate made the drive to his father's house in Los Angeles, unconcerned with the late hour and fueled on coffee. The late hour made the trip easier, leaving a distinct lack of congestion on the roads. What might have taken him three or four hours by day took under two.

He sent a text from the driveway and waited until a light flickered on in a downstairs window before heading to the door and letting himself in. He had his set of keys, but he never felt welcome in the house, and the last thing he wanted was to catch a bullet for entering at odd hours. Kay owned several pieces and stored them in unusual places around the house

"What brings you by at this ungodly hour?" Kay's voice called from the kitchen where Nate found him at the island counter with a bottle of scotch and two fresh glasses. He nudged one toward Nate and smiled, his green eyes crinkling. "You're lucky I haven't crawled in bed yet with Elizabeth."

"Yeah, I know. Had something on my mind and wanted to talk with you though. Face to face."

"Speak up then. What's up?"

Nate wrapped his hand around his glass without raising it to his mouth, too nervous for a sip of alcohol—or even a full shot—to quell the unrest in his heart.

"I'm done. I'm not going to spy on Astrid or the Drakenstones for you anymore."

"Excuse me?"

Kay had a voice like ice. He never shouted, and Nate had come to learn at a young age that the quieter his father's voice went, the angrier he was. Kay's voice now was near a whisper.

"It's not right, and she doesn't deserve all these lies. I can't do it to her anymore."

"I can't believe I'm hearing this from you, Nathaniel. You have feelings for this creature? You think that thing gives a damn about you? You're a meal to it. A plaything. It's like the cat we owned."

Nate sighed, able to predict his father's point. "She played with her food."

When Nate was a child, shortly after his parents split and his mother lost custody, she'd gifted him a kitten for his birthday. She'd told him, whenever he felt down, whenever he was missing her, to hug the cat tight and pretend it was her. And he had. Nefertiti had died a few years ago, waiting exactly two days after Nate returned from his fifth deployment. She'd been a better friend than the man who raised him.

"She did. She'd catch a mouse or a bird, and she'd play with it tenderly, didn't she? Then she'd run away with it, and we'd discover the body missing its head in our shoes the next morning."

"Astrid isn't like that."

"She's an animal. A dangerous beast. And one day, you're going to be that mouse. Mark my words, it's a matter of time

147

before you see how deadly they can be. If you had your memories—"

"I don't want them back," Nate whispered. The magical words had the ability to halt his father.

Kay's eyes blazed with fury. "Has she cast an enchantment over you?" he demanded.

"No!"

"You wouldn't know if she did."

"I would. I know what magic feels like, and she hasn't done anything like that. She wouldn't because that's not the type of person she is."

Kay sneered and looked him up and down as if he were a little boy again. "So you think because one of these beasts gives you a little pussy that it cares about you and has human feelings?"

"She does," Nate insisted. He straightened his shoulders and gazed into the face of his dictator, and in a clear, confident voice continued, "I won't hunt her or anyone else. I'm done. Cycle after cycle of vengeance and murder isn't worth this. What's the point?"

"She's a dragon. You're a slayer."

"She's half-human. That doesn't prove the monsters are infecting us. It proves we can coexist and live together in harmony. It means they're people, too!"

Kay slammed his fist into the top of the counter, shaking the contents of their glasses and the scotch bottle. His face went purple with rage, and his voice rose to a rare roar. "It means you've been compromised! And it means you're no brother of ours if you're going to throw your lot in with them. You need to make a decision now. It's the brotherhood, or it's these beasts."

"Then I'll choose the beasts. I'll choose her every time because at least they've come clean with the world. They're honest, good people, and they accepted me into their home like I was family. I won't betray them."

Kay's jaw clenched and hard, green eyes stared into Nate's face without breaking contact. "That so?"

Something wild and insane came over Nate, an emotion he'd thought had been trained out of him by a stern, unforgiving father figure and years in the Navy: defiance. He straightened his back and refused to break gazes. "That's right. I won't do it anymore, and if you send anyone else in my place to harass Astrid or watch over her family, I'll tell them everything. I'll tell them about all of you. Names and identities. All of it. Maybe I'll do it anyway just to see you sweat."

"Get the fuck out of my house."

"Gladly."

Steel-spined, he strode from the kitchen and cut a direct line to the door. His younger half-brother peeked down at him from the stairwell, the spitting image of Kay's current body with wavy auburn hair and eyes like chipped emeralds.

"Dude, why are you and Dad fighting? We could all hear you guys."

"Don't worry about it, kid. Go back to bed."

"He sounded pissed."

Nate paused at the door, hand on the knob, and looked back at his brother. "Just remember he doesn't own you. You have to make your own choices in life, Aaron, and you have to own up to the repercussions."

With no other pearls of wisdom for Kay's favorite son, he headed back out into the night and drove away.

Nate stopped once to gas up and purchase coffee along the way back to San Diego. With two shots of espresso in his gut, he pulled into the lot of his condo and stared at the building.

He didn't want to go up there. What he wanted was a woman a few miles away, a devious minx who texted him a photo of her discarded panties on the floor. He wanted to tell her he loved her, and that he'd forsaken his people and everything he'd once stood for to keep her family safe.

Five minutes later, Nate hadn't killed the engine. He gave himself a pep talk; then he drove to Astrid's building and let himself into the garage with her spare parking pass. He nodded to the night watchman in passing on his way to the elevator, and once inside, he phoned her.

"Nate? It's almost five in the morning. Is something wrong?"

"Open the door."

"Huh?"

"I'm waiting outside."

A couple moments passed before the lock clicked and the door drew open to frame Astrid. She wore a thin, yellow silk robe trimmed in white lace. And he wanted it off. He didn't know what exactly came over him, but rather than greet her, he took her face between his hands, stepped up to her, and kissed her as if they hadn't made contact in months. Astrid made a startled squeak that gave way to a moan. She yielded, opening to him.

Her back struck the wall beside her door, and she writhed, trapped between it and his hard body. At that moment, he came to the realization that he couldn't wait. He fumbled to shut the door and turn the lock.

With one tug, her robe fell open, and the sleeves slipped down her arms, revealing the magnificent, naked body beneath. He dropped his hand to unzip his jeans, shoving them down enough to free his straining cock.

"Nate, wha—"

He claimed her in one stroke, her receptive body so wet, he would have thought she was waiting for him. In his haste to see her, he'd come unprepared without a single condom.

Even that didn't matter. Her thighs clenched and her head fell back, his name a moan on her lips. He slipped out to the tip with reluctance, only to feed every inch to her again with delicious slowness. On the next thrust, he adjusted the position of her hips until the angle drove his cockhead to the place that made her scream with lust. She squeezed her fingers around his shoulders and rolled her lower body.

"Nate?"

"I missed you," he huffed out between frenzied and wild thrusts, more urgent than any lovemaking they'd ever shared before. He hefted her up, bracing her with one hand beneath her thigh.

His rhythmic pace faltered, steady thrusts becoming erratic with the need for release. He nipped her ear and muffled his groan against the side of her neck.

"I want to come inside you, Astrid. So bad, baby."

He'd forgotten how it felt.

"Do it," she whispered. "I want to feel you again."

Freed by her words, he surrendered and threw caution to the wind. Their renewed thrusts slapped her ass against the wall in a repetitive thump, accompanied by their joint grunts and throaty groans. Release came with a hot spurt. Astrid quivered around him, silken muscles tightening over his dick in rhythmic squeezes and delicious aftershocks.

It was the best mutual orgasm he'd ever experienced in all of his life, and sharing it with Astrid only improved it.

She clung to him, eyes closed tight and breaths shallow and fast. Nate dropped his sweaty face to her shoulder and struggled with his racing heart.

"Are you okay?" she whispered in the dark.

"Yeah." He fell quiet, and after a moment said it again. "Yeah. Now that I'm with you, I think I am."

Chapter 10

Stone lanterns lined the beach on Itsukushima Island. Their subdued glow cast small pools of light against the sand, transforming each grain into a twinkling, miniature star. The famous floating Torii gate arose from the black waters, a ruby jewel beyond the shoreline.

Watatsumi enjoyed his monthly stroll with his daughter. Their tradition had endured since her childhood when her mother, a water dragoness from the coast of China, grew tired of playing the role of a nurturer, and relinquished their cub to his care. She'd been what humans called a toddler, no higher than his knee.

And he had loved her mother. Had loved her deeply, but water dragonesses swam free and wild as the typhoons, disinterested in bonding rituals and a prolonged relationship.

So Toyotama swam out of their lives, and he'd raised their daughter to have the compassion her mother lacked. She developed empathy and a love for humans and all small things, but she was also shy. Painfully shy. Although he had hoped she and Astrid Drakenstone would bond one day, all efforts to coax Otohime to visit his friends across the ocean had failed.

"It saddens me to see them starve. Why can we not feed them, Father?" she asked, her voice pulling him from his musings. He glanced at the four deer lying on the beach, huddled close together for warmth.

"It is how they believe the problem must be addressed," Watatsumi replied. In his heart, he agreed with her, but the deer on the island had grown dependent on human interference. With the ban in place, they would starve.

"It's an awful rule, and a cruel thing to do to any animal. A slow death by starvation is no way to treat them."

"Perhaps you should do something about it and speak to the humans who oversee the rules and laws," he suggested, though he knew his suggestion was wasted breath.

Otohime did not speak to humans, and only adopted her human form to travel alongside him. Their walks were the highlight of his month, and he'd hoped to continue their tradition for centuries.

Some hopes, however, he knew could never come true.

"Maybe I will," she retorted, sensing the challenge in his words.

"We both know that will never happen, my child."

"I may."

What would she do without him? he wondered. With exception to the hippocampi herd of Teotihuacan's island, she'd made no friends over the centuries. She had no mate, not even a passing lover. Her entire life had been grief.

He envied Saul's ability to play the part of the overprotective father, guarding his daughter from all men she encountered, because he would give anything for Otohime to trust someone again. Or better yet, for someone to enter her life willing to earn her trust.

But how could that happen when she'd devoted every breathing second to life beyond the waves?

He frowned.

"What's wrong?" Otohime asked. Her brows drew close together. "I didn't mean to upset you with my complaints."

"Your complaints didn't upset me," he assured her. "I have other things on my mind. And a request for you, my dear."

She tilted her head. "Yes?"

"Reconsider meeting Astrid Drakenstone. She is a kind young woman, and you have many things in common. She loves the animals of the land as much as you love those of the sea."

"California is dry," she murmured. "And crowded."

"Please."

Otohime paused midstep and stopped to level her eyes at him. They filled with suspicion. "What are you not telling me?"

"I hesitate to speak of it to even you, though I wish I could. It is a burden I must carry alone."

His daughter released an exasperated breath. "It is always the same thing with you, Father. Cryptic words and riddles. Mysteries. Would it kill you to speak straightforward?"

No, he thought. It would kill someone else and set off a chain of uncontrollable events beyond their worst nightmares.

It had to be him. If only he knew when his time would come.

Watatsumi placed his hands on her shoulders. Like him, when she wore human clothing, she favored traditional Japanese garments. She owned hundreds, if not thousands of kimonos in his island home. This one was beautiful, swirls of silver like water against sapphire blue.

A touch of magic swept past his defenses when they traveled inland away from the shore on their usual route through Momijidani Park. He caught a whiff of something foreign and strange in the air, mingled with the fresh ocean scent.

"Something is wrong."

"I noticed it, too," Otohime said. "Father, we should leave. Something is wrong. Something is very, very wrong here."

"Return home to the manor and call Ēostre for help," he said as a means of removing her from the situation.

"Help? Help against what."

"That doesn't concern you," he said sternly. "Do as I asked."

"No. Not without you," Otohime insisted. "If something is dangerous, you must come with me. You're no longer the great water god to fix the problems of all humans, Father. If something is the matter, leave them to it."

"Do you loathe the humans so much that you would have me leave them to the unknown?" he asked her.

She didn't respond.

"The one who hurt you, my daughter, is not worth this anger. One day you will love again. One day. It may even be another human."

"I will never trust another human."

"Time heals all wounds. Even the greatest pain of all."

The odor intensified, something darker and malevolent lingering in the area, falling over the island like death's shroud.

Her lips parted to respond, then a flash of light blinded him as their surroundings erupted into hell. Hidden fighters emerged from the trees in every direction. They'd been under a sort of magical concealment, something different from dragon's magic and the usual witch. Darker. More insidious. It laid an unnatural aura of negation over the area, smothering his magic. While he had fought it before, he had hoped never to encounter it again.

On top of their foul sorcery, the dragonslayers had laced the area with explosives. As the first detonated, he yanked his daughter against him and sheltered her from the blast with both his transforming body and his magic. The barrier shield manifested by his spell popped into creation in time to guard him against a high-power sniper round. It plinked against the magical barrier, then disintegrated into sparks.

"Father, what's happening?"

"Dragonslayers," he growled. "Dragonslayers are attacking the island!"

Alarmed cries shouted out from the town behind them, and lights flickered on in otherwise darkened homes and shops. Amidst the horror, Watatsumi realized one thing: their attackers didn't care about civilian casualties. The loss of a few humans to remove him meant nothing to them. There was fire all around.

"Go!" he urged.

"No, I won't leave you! I won't leave!"

"You must! Remember everything I've taught you. Remember that I love you deeply, Otohime. Now go and find help!"

His shield wavered, taxed by the onslaught of firepower. For as long as he held it in place, he couldn't open a portal to teleport either of them to safety.

Otohime remained, divided by her conscience and a desire to obey his command. She hadn't yet attained her full size and was much smaller, her scales compact and glossy as sequins, but no armor against bullets. He'd never expected they would come for him while in the company of a second dragon, and if he'd known, he would have canceled their outing altogether.

"I love you," she uttered in a thick voice. "I don't want to leave you."

"You must go and warn the others!" he roared to her. Her eyes grew large, and then she flinched as another mortar exploded beside them and tore the ground.

The barrier shattered, tiny specks of magical material flitting away on the smoky wind. Otohime dove away from him and transformed. One moment, she was a petite woman with Japanese features, and in the next, she had become the sinuous, lean line of a water dragoness.

And a target for the snipers hiding in the bushes.

As she rushed toward the northern shore, he threw himself between his assailants and his fleeing child. Another bullet bounced off of his tough side as he protected her exit from the storm of gunfire. Then a round from a high-power rifle penetrated his hide, ripping a roar of pain from his throat.

How powerful had they become to smuggle their arms into Japan? Despite strict gun laws, the Anti-Dragon Movement and Knights of Merlin had infiltrated his beloved country. It made him sizzling mad.

"Ignore the female and take down the target," the leader called out. "She's too fast."

The cunning slayers had been too wise to attack him by the shore where he would escape or use the water to his defense. Escape wasn't yet impossible, but he spied his target crouched beside an uninhabited food vendor cart in the once-peaceful park.

It wasn't uncommon for the dragonslayers to outsource aid from other sorcerers, and this mage held a totem fashioned from the skull of an innocent dragon cub. Darkness brimmed from it, creating dissonance in the air that disrupted Watatsumi's ability to cast spells.

Watatsumi narrowed his eyes and judged the distance between them. He didn't require sorcery to kill. All he needed were his teeth.

He leaped at the man holding the warlock's idol and opened his jaws wide, releasing a torrential jet of water. He regretted the destruction of the park's iconic stalls and the disruption to its natural greenery, but it was a necessary evil. Intense waves flushed several of their human shock troops away in a flood, and he hoped their heavy military gear drowned them all.

As the current swept a soldier past him, Watatsumi ripped him from the water with his teeth and tore him in half. He fought his way through the gunfire, swinging his tail and crushing men beneath his weight. They had come in force, dozens of humans prepared to throw their lives away to kill him.

If it hadn't been him, it would have been Astrid.

"Shit! Get the containment spell in place! We're losing men out here!"

"We've got his shields down!" another slayer called.

Watatsumi reached into the depths of his memory.

Kay. Though over a century had passed since they last crossed paths, Watatsumi couldn't forget the voice. Or the appearance altered by the modern age. He spied the knight across the distance, flanked by two more faces etched in his memory. Bedivere and Gareth.

Once, many centuries ago, he and Hermes had forged a temporary alliance with Bedivere, Kay, and Arthur to take down what legends knew as the Giant of Mont St. Michel. The true nature of the beast was more chilling than any fable, but history had a way of forgetting.

Magic, ancient and long forgotten, pinned him in place. His eyes flared wide in the glowing vermillion light emanating from an artifact he had thought destroyed long ago.

"You fools kept it. Do you truly believe anyone but its maker can wield it?"

Gareth stepped forward with the weapon held aloft. Pain wracked and twisted Watatsumi's body, a magical acid burning through his veins. He struggled to stay on his feet as the surviving soldiers of the platoon moved into formation around him with their rifles raised.

"I can, and I have," Gareth boasted. "I've conquered the cudgel, just as we'll conquer the rest of your race. This world needs no dragon gods, and it certainly doesn't need you."

"Arthur would never stand for this or what your order has become during his absence. You were once noble men."

While they had always sought dragons and killed them in honorable combat, the ones who fell to their swords had always been dangers to the populace, wild and feral, with no regard for lives beyond their own.

"Enough toying with the beast," Kay called over. "Kill him."

"With pleasure."

With his remaining strength, Watatsumi pushed through the magic binding and sprang forward, his muscles straining against the raw power ebbing from the cursed magical item.

Realization dawned slowly for Gareth. The knight's taunting smile transitioned to a panicked mask, then terror, and finally agony when Watatsumi's teeth closed around his upper torso. Snapping his jaws over the man's left shoulder resulted in a satisfying crunch, despite the blistering, electric arcs exploding in his maw.

"Fall back!" Kay cried.

"But the weapon," Bedivere argued.

"Leave the blasted thing. It's lost to us now. At least the beast will go down with it."

With no loyalty to their brothers, the two leaders rushed into the wilderness. Bedivere followed behind Kay, covering their exit with gunfire while they sacrificed their human pawns. Nearly a dozen armed men had survived Watatsumi's counterattack, and of those who remained, they all opened fire.

Gareth lost control of the cudgel, releasing the unrestrained primordial energies. He screamed and pushed at Watatsumi's snout with his remaining arm to little avail as the scalding force of magic swept over the area, incinerating all in its path. The knight's dead weight pulled at his mouth, but his jaw had fused shut, teeth blackened and skin blistering.

Knowing one's fate did not make it any easier. As agony spread through his limbs, he took comfort in the knowledge that his daughter would live.

Chapter 11

During their early morning romp, Nate had revealed a new side of himself. A hungry, animalistic side thirsting for her. She'd been delighted, and despite the risk, she'd given in at the end.

Her mother would have called it irresponsible, but Chloe wasn't the best person to judge someone else for having unprotected sex. Neither was her father for that matter. Careless sex was how they conceived Astrid, after all.

Awakening before Nate, she spent a half hour curled against him in bed, listening to his steady breaths, and the strong beat of his heart. What would it be like to have his child one day?

Would he want one? She thought so after listening to his stories of playing ball with the underprivileged kids in his mother's area. He enjoyed mentoring, but it didn't mean he'd want to be saddled with his own kid.

Astrid plucked her cell phone from the bed and glanced at the screen. Dead. After plugging it into the charger, she shuffled to the shower to wash the dried sweat off her skin. Nate had been a tireless bundle of insatiable energy, making love to her in a host of new positions. Still, he'd never taken her on her hands and knees, and the bestial part of her soul craved it.

Afterward, she wrapped herself in a fluffy terrycloth robe and slid a pair of raspberry scones into the oven, hoping the sweet scent would awaken him.

It did.

"Morning, sleepyhead."

"Morning, sunshine." Nate wrapped his arms around her from behind and nuzzled her neck. "Smells delicious."

"Me or the scones?"

"Mmm, both."

He nipped her ear then stepped away to pour himself some orange juice from the fridge.

"So, want to tell me what this was all about? Not that I'm complaining, mind you, but I thought you were worn out from your ship time."

"After I shower and brush my teeth. Promise."

He kept a toothbrush over at her place now, practically living with her most days. Charlie had teased and asked how long it would be before her boyfriend kept his spare dress whites and uniforms at her apartment, too.

He kissed the side of her neck again then retreated for his morning routine.

It was as if her worries had been for nothing. Or maybe Yasmin's reading had been spot on.

The jarring notes of an incoming call pulled her from her cheery thoughts. She snatched up her phone and hit accept.

"Hey, Mom, what's up?"

Her mother's voice filled the line, thick and choked with tears amidst hyperventilating breaths. "Astrid, we need you to come home. We need you home right now. Ēostre is going to open a portal for you as soon as she and Max get here."

"Mom?" Her heart slammed against her ribcage. Each beat seemed closer to bursting from her chest. "Mom, what happened? What's wrong? Is it Dad?" *Please don't let it be Daddy, please!*

"The dragonslayers killed Watatsumi."

"What?"

"Watatsumi is dead," her mother repeated. "Pack your bags. Your father and I want you to come home until we can figure out what to do with the slayers."

"When?" she croaked. Her knees wobbled so she sat down, hard, on the edge of the couch.

"A few hours ago. Otohime only contacted us moments ago. She's scared, Astrid. She's so scared. She hid for hours in the ocean, afraid they would find her."

"No, no, noooo," she wailed. "This can't be happening. It can't be real." Not her uncle. Not her beloved uncle.

Nate gave her a concerned look from across the room. "Astrid?" He crossed to her in a few strides and supported her with his arms when her world began to spin.

"How's Daddy? Is he okay?"

"He's in his hoard. I... I don't think he wants me to see him crying again."

"I don't... I can't..." Tears welled over and tracked down Astrid's cheeks.

"Your grandmother and grandfather are on the way from Washington. I'll phone back once they're ready to send the portal. I need... I need to check on your father. Don't go outside. Don't answer your door for anyone."

"Okay, Mommy."

Numbed, she pressed the little red button and dropped the phone on the table to sob.

"I have to go. I have... They killed Watatsumi, the slayers. It's not safe for me here. It's not safe for you if they come after me."

His eyes widened. "What? Are you sure?"

"My mom wants me to come back home now until they figure out what to do. Watatsumi's daughter told them dragonslayers killed him. It must have been while we were sleeping."

"Astrid—"

"I'll just bring you with me to the estate. Grandma can send you back to your base or apartment from there, maybe. I don't know. I don't know what to do, Nate. I'm scared."

"I swear, nobody's going to hurt you if I have anything to say about it."

A sense of helplessness overwhelmed her, and then the tears came without mercy. She cried while Nate held her with a hand on her lower back, the other cradling her head against his shoulder.

"Astrid, there's something I *have* to tell you. I don't want to do it now while you're hurting, but I've got to."

"Now?"

"Yes." Nate had thrown on his clothes again, but left his shirt unbuttoned and untucked around his jeans. He released her to pace nervously, wearing a track on the floor while Isis and Echo trailed behind him. "It's not easy to say."

"Then don't. It can wait."

"No. It can't."

"Nate, you're scaring me."

"When you asked me if I had magic, I wasn't entirely honest with you."

"I know, but Nate, it's not import—"

"But not a witch's magic," he pressed on, giving her no chance to wave him off. "It's something else, something older than witch's sorcery and different."

She watched him through a haze of tears, his features blurry. "I don't understand. Are you saying you're something else?"

"Yes." He hesitated. "It's dragonslayer's magic."

No. All the blood and warmth drained from her body, leaving behind a frigid husk. She stared at him, repeating his words over in her head, but her mind rejected them.

"Tell me you're joking," she whispered. "Tell me it's a sick joke in poor taste. Please."

"It's not a joke," he said in a quiet voice. He reached for her, but she jerked her shoulder from beneath his hand.

Her world had tilted on its axis. Everything she knew had warped, a twisted lie and a joke with a cruel punchline. Nausea rolled in her stomach.

"Astrid—"

"No. Don't touch me." She rose from the couch and moved away. Her condo seemed suddenly too small, as if the walls were closing in around her.

"I've wanted to tell you for weeks because I can't do it anymore. I'm sick of them and their bullshit, baby. Being with your family during Labor Day made me realize I have an actual choice. Maybe I was born this way, but I don't have to be a dragonslayer."

"You're with them," she whispered.

"I was."

"You're. With. Them," she repeated, her voice rising with each word. Echo whined and lowered to her belly beside Nate's feet.

Her eyes darted to Echo and understanding dawned. In Saul's presence, she'd become Dr. Jekyll and Mr. Hyde, sweet one moment, trained attack beast the next. *No wonder she hated Daddy.* Was there something in Astrid's blood Echo didn't recognize? Something she'd inherited from her human mother?

"Baby, not this time. I wasn't involved in Watatsumi's death. You have to—"

"I don't have to do anything! You're a slayer! The enemy! Your people killed Watatsumi!"

"I didn't know, or I would have warned you last night. I would have had you warn your family and tip him off to what they were doing. I swear I had no idea."

"Why should I believe anything you say when you've lied to me from the start?" Her voice raised shrill and sharp, reaching a scream at the end.

"Because I…" He had no reason, none that would suffice for a valid excuse in Astrid's opinion at least. "Because I love you," Nate concluded.

"You don't love me. You're infatuated with me," she said bitterly. Because of magic and instincts and everything that went together with being fated. But it wasn't love. What her mom and dad had developed over the years was love. What her grandparents had together was love. They'd never lied to one another.

Even from the start, Saul Drakenstone chose to tell his human lover the truth about his draconic identity, placing their future in her hands. And she'd accepted him for who and what he was.

"Why? Were you spying on me? Spying on *us?*"

Nate swallowed. "Yes," he whispered. "I was assigned—"

She held up a hand, cutting him off. "There's nothing more to be said between us. A friend of my family is dead. A peaceful dragon and a good, generous man. Gone. We can never get him back. My father is beside himself with grief. My grandparents are mourning. And all you can bring to me are half-assed apologies? Go."

"If I'd known, I would have warned you. I didn't know!"

She leveled her eyes at him and stared. "I have no reason to believe you anymore, Nate."

Astrid turned away and opened the door.

"I love you, Astrid. I love you so much I haven't known what to do. I've debated telling you—"

"Get the hell out of my house and never come back. If you do, I will take pleasure in tearing you to pieces myself. I'll be whatever you murderers think we are."

He stilled, and the hope left his eyes. "I'm sorry. I never meant to hurt you."

Nate stepped into his shoes, leashed Echo, and walked out the door.

For a while, Astrid huddled in the beanbag and sobbed. The catharsis of her tears helped to mend the immediate pain, but did nothing to soothe the sense of betrayal. All along, he'd been reporting information about her family. No matter how happy he'd made her during their short time together, she could never forget what he'd done. Or forgive.

Chapter 12

Nate brushed his damp palms against his jeans and approached the front door, traveling a stretch of driveway lined by perfect flowers. With any number of lethal, terrifying creatures beyond the estate's doors, he imagined he was walking toward his death. Bear shifters with sharp claws, dragons able to bite him in half, and an angry woman who would allow it to happen.

He took in a few breaths and calmed his nerves. Once he found the strength to continue, Nate rapped on the door.

"Saul, no!"

A woman's shriek reached Nate through the heavy wood and metal, as well as panes of colored glass. He flinched as the door swung open to reveal Saul Drakenstone, the man appearing more beast than human, nostrils flared and eyes slit in fury.

"You dare to approach my home."

Chloe grabbed her husband by the bicep and pulled ineffectively.

"Mr. Drakenstone, I—"

"Leave. You aren't welcome here." Saul took a menacing step forward. Nate gave ground and retreated two paces. "I should eat you where you stand."

"I didn't come to challenge any of you. I came because… I want to make things right."

Saul's face went purple, and every fiber of Nate's being wanted him to turn tail and run from the dragon's wrath. Chloe emerged from the home on her husband's heels, wearing an impassive expression.

"Astrid doesn't want to see you," she said. "And I'm not so sure I want to stop him from shredding you to bits, so I'm hoping you have a damned good reason for showing up here after what you did."

"I'm not here for Astrid. Not exactly," Nate said, although his honest declaration sounded like the stupidest thing he'd ever said in all of his many lives.

Others spilled outside to witness the spectacle. Nate recognized their faces from dossiers the knighthood maintained about every known dragon. Facing down Saul and his family was bad enough. The dragon who joined him, Tlaloc, had a fearsome reputation of his own and an aversion to humans in general. He'd already met his son, Teotihuacan, who followed with the President of the United States at his side. Max had no kindness in his eyes this time.

Nate rubbed his sweaty palms against his jeans a second time.

"Then what do you want?" Ēostre stepped out from the open doorway. According to their files, she was the even-tempered one and the wisest among their numbers next to Watatsumi. A dark-haired, unfamiliar woman accompanied her, a stranger to their immense archives.

"To help." He took a deep breath and prepared to verbally navigate a field of draconic testosterone. One wrong word and one of them would end his life in a quick gulp. "I want to offer my condolences for the loss of Watatsumi. I had no part in it. I didn't know he was an upcoming target. Apologies won't bring him back, but I can tell you what you need to know so the people who murdered him will pay."

Saul's scoff sounded like a growl. "Trying to barter for your pathetic life. Typical."

"No." Nate shook his head. "I don't care what happens to me anymore. You can hear me out and take whatever revenge you want if it'll grant you one iota of peace. I won't try to fight."

To Nate's surprise, Saul grew quiet and allowed Chloe to drag him back. "Then speak."

From the porch, Tlaloc growled in disapproval. "You allow this creature to disrespect your cub and live? Let the human tell you what he knows and be done with him," he said. "Or better yet, let me kill him if your heart has grown soft."

"My heart is not soft," Saul disagreed, "but if he knows something of importance to us, we must discover it."

"I do," Nate said.

His heart hurt, and self-preservation cried out for him to change his mind. Even if they killed him, death was only temporary. In a decade or so, he'd have a new life with a new family.

Or he could help the dragons end it all.

"I know how you can kill every single one of us. For good. No reincarnation. No coming back. There won't be any more slayers. You can go fight all of them and lose a couple of your people for a brief reprieve—people you can't get back—or you can stop them now and know none of them will be back in thirty years ready to fight you again."

Teotihuacan's brows raised. His father leaned forward, intrigued. Even Maximilian stared at Nate.

"I knew that I recognized you, Galahad, but I doubted myself. I thought my memory of our meeting weak and that I would recognize the stench of dragonslayer on your skin with absolute certainty—but our Astrid masked you with her love." Max's features darkened.

"I never meant to hurt her, sir. I swear it on my sword."

"You would tell us how to abolish them all? Participate in the genocide of your people?" Maximilian asked him.

"Yes. There was a time when we worked toward a noble cause. Those days are over, and it pains my soul to see it continue. I won't allow another person to needlessly die. Our time is finished."

"The days of Fafnir's rage against humanity was an awful period in time," Ēostre agreed. "His behavior, as well as the cruelty of many other dragons, led to the creation of your knighthood."

Nate nodded. "Yes."

"I loved him deeply, but even I knew he was wrong to terrorize the humans. I tried to stop him. I tried to use my influence over Fafnir to make him a better dragon, and when it worked, your people slew him anyway."

"I know," Nate said. "I can't recall those days in their entirety. I've been reborn, but my memories aren't all here."

"How would you regain them?" Chloe asked.

"By killing one of you. Much to Sir Kay's displeasure, I've never taken a life. I refused."

The dragons quieted. A window blind shifted to reveal Astrid between the parted curtains of gauzy ivory. Her large eyes studied him in disbelief, and her painstricken expression told him she'd heard everything from his offer to die with his brethren to his admission of lacking recent blood on his hands.

"Then tell us, how would we do this thing and kill the dragonslayers? What must we do?" the woman beside Ēostre asked.

"You'll have to destroy Merlin's body."

As the silent group of dragons stared at him, their expressions transitioned to varying stages of awe and disbelief.

Even the mighty Tlaloc, once believed as a god of righteous fury and anger, was shocked into silence.

"Then he truly is immortal," Ēostre breathed.

"He is, and we've kept watch over him for centuries. He's our true leader, asleep and resting in a state of stasis for years. He visits certain members of the knighthood in their dreams and guides the order."

Ēostre studied him. "Have you ever spoke with him?"

Nate shook his head.

"There may be truth in what the human says," Saul muttered.

The other dragons placed the interrogation in Ēostre's hands. "And what about your famed Arthur? Where does he stand on all of this?" she asked.

"He hasn't been reborn in this age yet. No one has seen Arthur since before the American Civil War I believe."

"I see."

"But I've been told by a friend, a good man deserving of my trust, that Arthur wouldn't stand for what's happened since your emergence into the public."

"What man?" Maximilian asked.

"Sir Percivale."

"We know the name." Saul regarded him with shrewd eyes.

"He slew Anansi of Ghana," Tlaloc said. "A murderer much like the rest of you. I have no res—"

"Good riddance," said the dark-haired woman beside him. "You know as well as I do of Anansi's temper and cruelty. He treated humans no better than ants and brought shame upon us all."

"Agreed," Ēostre said.

Tlaloc surrendered the conversation to the two women, but his expression remained aloof.

A quiet sound escaped Nate borne of both relief and realizing he could breathe again.

"Anansi lived in the past. Our council cautioned him many times. Even I warned him personally, though I can say he was no close friend of mine," Maximilian said.

"Then you understand why it had to be done. Anansi was top dog on our list of current threats, so Percivale did what *had* to be done. I don't know why they chose Hermes or Watatsumi—it doesn't make sense to me—but I know a meeting was never called to discuss it."

"Your leaders make the decisions, don't they?" Chloe asked.

"Technically, we don't have *leaders*. We have rules. Arthur decided to make us equal a long time ago, but that's not how Kay and Bedivere govern the table now. They call the shots."

Saul remained unconvinced. "And you expect us to believe you're just giving us a way to destroy your kind."

Nate nodded. "With exception to Anansi, dragon's live peaceful lives alongside humanity. The world doesn't need slayers now. There's only one way to sever our link to this world, and that means you gotta destroy Merlin. I think after his death, we'll be allowed to move on to whatever comes after this life. Or maybe we'll cease to exist altogether."

Ēostre surprised the other dragons by stepping forward first and taking Nate by both of his hands. While anger and a desire for retribution simmered among her companions, he saw only compassion in her silver eyes. "And you're willing to risk disappearing forever?"

"I'm ready for it." Nate quieted a moment. Astrid hadn't moved from the window. Her fingers gripped the curtains, blue eyes locked on him. "I may not remember my old lives, but I'm tired. I feel it sometimes, like the memories are present but difficult to access."

"Then you are a brave man."

"Mother, you can't believe—"

Ēostre cut her son off, barely glancing over her shoulder toward Saul when she spoke. "I feel we should trust him. If this is an elaborate plot to lower our guard, it is a clumsy one."

"And what he did to Astrid?"

"Only she has the right to offer forgiveness or withhold it, son."

Nate blinked a few times to lessen the stinging behind his eyelids. "I don't expect to receive forgiveness from Astrid. I don't deserve it. But I can do this for all of you, so she'll be safe in the future and nothing like this will ever happen again."

"Where is Merlin? I don't imagine it is as simple as you make it seem, strolling in and putting an end to his life," Tlaloc sneered.

"Show a little trust, my warrior," the dark-haired woman murmured, stepping up to his side.

"I'll show trust when we destroy his kind."

"Patience, Tlaloc," Ēostre chided. She turned her pale gaze on Nate and waited. "Well?"

"Disneyland," Nate replied. "His tomb has been beneath the King Arthur Carrousel since 1955."

***

Once the elder dragons and her mother convened inside the manor, Astrid crept down the stairs to eavesdrop on their determination. She'd overheard most of the conversation through the cracked window, divided between saving Nate from her father's jaws and bitterly hoping he'd smash him flat.

175

In the end, her relief won. Loathing Nate had been an exhaustive experience, overwhelmed by a pervasive sense of love creeping into her heart.

"We cannot trust this human cretin to remain true to his word. He's already irreparably damaged your cub's heart," Tlaloc said. "Why place further trust in him?"

"Excuse me," Chloe said between her teeth. "I'm human."

"My apologies, Chloe. I referred to this particular human cretin, not all human cretins. You and Marceline are a cut above the others."

The apology appeased her mother and made Teo snort with laughter.

"My father is right, however. How can we be sure this isn't a clever trap?"

"Perhaps he means to convince us to let down our guard, and by nightfall, his fellow knights will arrive to annihilate us all," Maximilian said.

Saul shook his head. "Only us. You've got the White House and a legion of secret service members to protect you. Where's Andrew by the way? You never leave without him."

"We ditched him and the others," Ēostre replied. "These are dragons' matters meant for our ears alone."

"We wanted to allow him plausible deniability," Max explained. "Regardless, we cannot make this decision alone if we choose to go to war. We must gather the rest of the council."

"And risk this opportunity?" Tlaloc snapped. "When will we ever have this chance again to destroy all dragonslayers? It is simple, one or two of us must accompany him to this sorcerer's lair—this Dinnyland—and see it is done. The remaining dragons will remain on guard."

"Disneyland," Chloe corrected in a mutter.

The black dragon waved his hand in a dismissive manner.

Ēostre, ever the peacekeeper, spoke up before he could cause any more tension with his disdain. "Tlaloc makes a good point. If we arrive in force, the slayers will realize something is amiss. Better to keep most of us here visible, in case they're watching."

"We must assume they have not left him unprotected. There will be magical wards prohibiting our entrance and their human guards on standby to keep watch over the attraction," Xochi said. "They will be vigilant."

Astrid reached the lowest step and entered the living room. "I'll go."

Seven startled faces turned toward her.

"Sweetheart, no, you don't have to do that." Chloe rose from the couch.

"You said it yourselves, there will be wards. But they never knew I was a dragon. Nothing about me sets off their magic. That's the whole reason Na—" Even saying his name hurt, and her voice caught in her throat. "That's the reason they sent a slayer to get close to me."

"No. Absolutely not. I forbid it." Saul crossed his arms over his chest and frowned at her.

"Daddy, it's my decision. Not yours."

"It's too dangerous for you."

Astrid shook her head. "Maybe this is what Watatsumi wanted me to do. The choice I have to make. Maybe Tlaloc is right and we'll never have the chance to do this again. I don't go and do this tonight, and end it all for you, there won't be a tomorrow for any of us."

"Perhaps we've had it wrong all along," Ēostre said. "Maybe Ascalon isn't only a dragon-slaying sword. Maybe it's also a wizard-slaying sword. Watatsumi spoke nothing of the prophecy to me. He only said there are some things that must happen to make a safer tomorrow for all of us."

Max jerked around to stare at his wife. "He meant his death."

"Yes. I believe Watatsumi knew he would die, and he allowed it to happen."

Max blinked. "And you said nothing?"

"She didn't know," Astrid defended her grandmother. "It wouldn't have made any sort of sense until after the fact."

Chastened, Max dropped his gaze. "Younger than us all and already wiser." He sighed, his shoulders sagging. "I think Astrid has the right of it, Saul. She has to be the one who goes."

"Aunt Mahasti can whisk me away if there's trouble."

Ēostre shook her head. "No. She can't. Perhaps you were too young to see at the time, but when I took you to Disneyland years ago, I noticed there is an anti-magic field unlike anything I had ever experienced in the past. I thought nothing of it at the time. Just a precaution against adolescent witches causing mischief and accessing the park for free. Now I understand."

"Well, he can't exactly run me through in a public place either."

"According to the slayer, Merlin's tomb is beneath the carrousel. I wouldn't call that public," Max muttered. He sank in his seat and made a frustrated growl. "I don't like the idea of you going alone."

Astrid ducked her head and fiddled with the hem of her shirt. "I won't let my guard down, but… he's had plenty of private moments to kill me if that's what he wanted. If anyone else shows up, I'll run. I promise."

Despite their trepidation, she gained the blessing of the elder dragons. The sword belt appeared around Astrid's hips by an act of magic, Mahasti summoning it from San Diego.

Saul and Chloe both hugged her tight, and at the end, she had to wriggle out from her mother's embrace. Astrid stepped outside, alone, and drew in a deep breath.

"Be safe, sweetie," Chloe called from the doorway.

"Tell him if you return harmed in any way, I will pick my teeth with his bones," Saul threatened.

Nate sat in his truck in the drive, the door open and music playing, but the moment he spotted her he jumped out.

"Astrid—"

She held up her hand. "I'm not here to talk about us."

"Fair enough." He returned to the driver's seat and buckled in. "No one's come out to eat me yet, so I guess this means all systems are go?"

"It means you have one chance to show you're telling the truth. For once." Nate's expression wilted after her dig at his honesty, and her stomach twisted with instantaneous regret. She slid into the passenger seat but kept her body angled away from him. "Since you all didn't take someone like me into account when you warded Disneyland, I'm going in."

"I don't think you should come, Astrid. Something tells me that visiting Merlin isn't going to be a walk in the park, despite the location of his wizard's lair." He glanced at her sword. "Do you even know how to use that?"

A flash of rage stormed through her body, turbulent and raw. "You don't get to make that decision," she told him. "Whether or not I go along isn't your choice to make. As for this sword, Uncle Watatsumi taught me how to fight with one himself."

"I don't get a choice? Astrid, I'm the slayer with access to the park. Even if you can use a sword, what exactly are you going to do with it?"

"Make sure it's done right. Report back to family." A cold knot of apprehension twisted in her stomach, heavy as a cannonball. It dimmed her anger and made her feel childish for snapping when he asked valid questions. Their reasons seemed flimsy. Certainly Nate could be trusted to follow through with his half. He was the knight with the experience. He could probably slip in without notice or danger.

"And your family is okay with you being in danger?"

"They aren't," she said, "but some of the others don't trust you."

"Okay then," he agreed in a strange, stilted voice. "Only because I realize there's a household full of dragons who will rip me to pieces if I say no."

"More important than my distrust of you, I think this is what Uncle Watatsumi wanted. He said something to me. That I have a choice to make. I've been told my entire life that one day I'm destined to make an incredible decision that will change everything for my people."

Nate swallowed and nodded. "I don't like the idea of putting you in danger."

"This isn't about you. This is about my people and our safety. It has nothing to do with us or our failed relationship. Nothing."

The words ate away at her, gnawing a hole inside her heart with every damning syllable. Nate faced forward and stared out the windshield with his jaw clenched.

Being close to him made her edgy, and her emotions tore her in half, dividing her between a need to forgive him and an equal desire to choke the life out of him for his betrayal. She settled for professionalism. Or, at least, she tried to. "Let's get going please."

"Okay," he said again, defaulting to the same response. Without looking at her, he fired the engine and directed the vehicle toward the stretch of road leading to the highway. He stared out the windshield without making eye contact even once, her silent driver.

Astrid gazed out the passenger window and watched the rolling scenery despite three texts from her mother at her father's behest. She assured both parents of Nate's good behavior and finally tossed the phone into the center console. His green eyes flicked toward her then away. He drove with his fingers white-knuckled over the steering wheel.

"Did you really bury Merlin in Disneyland?" Astrid blurted out. The idea should have been amusing, but all she could feel was disbelief. The grand wizard of all wizards was in the Magic Kingdom, a place meant for kids.

"Wasn't my idea. At least, I'm told Kay and Bedivere created that brainchild. He's always been there. The theme park is a recent thing to disguise the carousel's true purpose. My memories are vague, kind of like a dream that's fading hours after you woke up. Half the time, I don't know if I legitimately remember it or if I'm trusting the others to tell the truth."

"Lucky you, forgetting all the murders." The moment the words left her mouth, she regretted them, knowing they were too harsh. Nate flinched as if she'd cut him. Maybe she had, dealing the wound to his soul instead of by physical means. Any signs of him relaxing and losing the tension in his shoulders faded.

She shifted and stared out the window at the traffic they passed. "This isn't the best way to Disney. Where are you taking me?"

"Sir Kay will be at his son's soccer game right now with the rest of his family. I want his laptop. There's got to be all kinds of information your people can use once they crack through the security on it. Intel about the people in deep cover maybe. We may be their leaders, but once we go, I don't expect them to take their hatred quietly into the night."

"You didn't say anything about this at the house." She didn't think her dad would approve of the off-plan mission, no matter the potential reward, but she didn't call Mahasti to send an SOS. Not yet.

"It didn't come to me until now," he admitted. "Your decision. It shouldn't take me long to break in and get what we need."

"Fine. You're already headed that way." And if a squad of dragon hunters awaited her, they'd discover the rage of a scorned female dragon. For a while, she remained silent, but the heartache tore at her. His closeness. His scent. The vehicle itself was a reminder of their first intimate night. "Why?" she asked, voice quiet and more sad than angry. "Why did you do it?"

He clenched his jaw and focused on the road. "If I didn't, someone else would have. There's only one other single knight, and he's an asshole."

"So that's it? You did it because it was your job and there was no one else." She shouldn't have asked, and bitterness seeped into her voice. "At least I could have handled an asshole and sent him off with a black eye."

"I didn't want him to hurt you," he said in a strained whisper. "I watched you for weeks when I returned from deployment. And... you were better than all of us. Not a monster."

"Yeah, you did a great job of hurting me all on your own."

"I was going to tell you everything."

They rode in silence until they reached their destination. Nate parked in front of cozy residence tucked inside Santa

Clarita's suburbs, far from humble with a two-car garage and a rear in-ground pool.

"I'll wait in the car. I don't want to go in there."

He tossed his phone into the console. "It's unlocked. Promise there's no sneaky knight plans there," he told her before he stepped from the car. "So you're welcome to have a look if you distrust me."

A pair of dogs ran to greet him when he entered the fence. Tiny, fluffy things.

She waited with her door open, ready to flee at any sign of further betrayal. His home was so... normal. It wasn't how she expected a slayer's home to look, especially the yappy Pomeranians. She'd expected barking, toothy Dobermans or shepherds like Echo. Whatever Nate hoped to find, she prayed he did so quickly.

The car ran the entire time, the low purr of a well-maintained motor accompanied by music set quieter than a whisper. The minutes ticked by. Five. Ten. Suddenly twenty. When he emerged at a brisk pace, he held a laptop case beneath his arm and wasted no time in shutting the gate behind him. He passed the laptop to Astrid. "Password is Camelot with an 'at' sign for the 'a' unless he's changed it recently. Now I need you to do something for me."

His audacious request swept her relief away. She shut the door then buckled back in before setting the laptop with its supposed precious data down at her feet. "Really? You want me to do something for you?"

"I want you to make sure my mom gets my dog. I don't... I don't know what's going to happen to me when we put Merlin to rest. Maybe I'll die down there with him. Leave me down in his tomb. I don't care about that. But Echo... she..." He inhaled an uneven breath then became stone-faced. "Anyway. Consider it a favor for her."

The drive resumed as Nate pulled the Jeep away from the curb.

Her expression and voice softened. "All right. I can do that." The tightness in her chest returned. Death. That's what he was talking about. Kill Merlin, kill the slayers. No one seemed to know how it was going to work for sure.

"Thank you."

"Mahasti, can you take the laptop please?"

"Who are you—"

The laptop shimmered away, leaving Nate staring at her. He nearly drove into a fire hydrant.

"Mahasti is a djinn," she told him.

"Okay… You have a djinn at your command and you're worried *I* might do something to *you*?"

"She's not a killer, and she can't interfere at Disney, thanks to whatever protections the knights put into place."

"Right. Djinn can't kill mortals." He appeared uncertain just the same. "I've heard of genies orchestrating deaths worthy of the Final Destination movies," he mumbled. "But if we succeed in our mission, she won't have to."

Astrid hesitated. She wanted to be furious with herself for letting go of her anger, but it became difficult to see anything more than his fear of death. "Nate… I don't think severing the link will kill. Magic doesn't work that way. It's tethering your soul. When you cut the link, your soul is free to go when its time, and won't be forcibly pulled back to this world."

"Maybe. This is your last chance to turn back. What if our arrival disturbs him and he awakens? He won't go without a fight. We're talking about the most powerful wizard the world has ever known. I don't even know what we'll encounter."

"More than likely then, he'll be aiming for me. You're one of his kind and he doesn't know you're there to kill him. Or to let me." She shrugged, and tried not to think about it. A million and one horrible possibilities flitted through her mind. "We'll see what happens, I guess."

"I won't let him hurt you." Minutes passed in silence between them while skepticism and misery warred within Astrid's heart. "I told myself if I had the chance to see you again, I'd have a hundred things to say to you. Nothing seems right. Nothing can sum up what you mean to me."

He may as well have punched her. "You don't lie to someone you care about," she whispered, afraid to look over at him. She'd lose her nerve, break into tears, and forgive him. "I…" How could she tell him they were fated? That her dragon recognized him as the missing half of her heart? "I cared about you, but it was all a lie. You used me, for them."

"Used you for them?"

Without another word, Nate jerked the wheel and tugged the vehicle to the side of the road, slamming his foot on the brakes hard enough to toss them both in the seats. "I didn't use you for them. I met you because of them, and I love you in spite of their bigotry and hatred."

***

He'd risked everything for her. In fact, he had been ostracized as he fought to de-escalate tension between his people and hers. He'd tried to work from within to diffuse it all, desperate to end the fighting between dragons and knights. He'd failed, but he'd never used her.

Having Astrid so near and knowing she hated him twisted his stomach into knots. In his head, he'd planned a thousand possibilities of how their reunion might go, from begging her on bended knee to her father ripping him into tiny nuggets on the front yard. Sitting beside her and losing his cool hadn't been one of the scenarios he'd dreamed up.

"I put everything I have on the line for you because I thought I could convince them dragons are also people, that you cherish your families, your children, and your friends as greatly as we do and with no less devotion or love. And I was winning." He didn't mean to yell, but the emotion bubbled to the surface despite his attempts to keep an even voice. "I was winning... that's why Kay and Bedivere did what they did. I got Lancelot and Percivale both over to my side. And more were on the way."

"Why wait so long to tell me, Nate? Why?"

The fight drained out of him, and he rubbed his face with one hand. "I know I should have told you, but I was afraid. And I'll live the rest of my life, whether it's six hours or sixty years, regretting how I lost you."

"You didn't ask me out because you wanted to, you asked me out because they ordered you to do it. And I was so stupid. You were keeping your distance, and I just threw myself at you because I liked you and because you're the one." Her voice rose to match his, only to choke off with a sob. She put her fist against her mouth and looked away.

"And I was honored to be with you. The circumstances don't change how happy you've made me."

"I don't want you to die," she finally whispered. "I don't think I could handle it... a world without you."

"If it has to happen, it's only fair. The time of the Knights of the Round table is past. There's no place for us in this world. Slaying dragons and fighting evil were our only objective for so long, but there are no more evil dragons. Tlaloc and Loki were among the last of the great and awful wyrms, and they've changed."

"You're right about the others changing," she said, "but there's still evil out in the world. I've never understood why your order focused on us dragons when there are vampires and black witches. What if destroying off the knighthood is the wrong thing to do?"

"We've killed our share of black witches and warlocks as well as dragons. Hopefully, your people are pulling everything out of our databases as we speak." His father was too cocky to believe he'd ever take anything from them and their entire history was available at the push of a few buttons. "Ending the order is the last thing I can do for you. If it comes down to a fight, I'll protect you. I've had twenty-seven lives, and this is the only one you've got. The only one you'll have."

"Max is probably working on it now. What is your dad going to do when he notices it's gone?"

Nate shrugged. "Don't know or care. You know, he isn't my real dad, right? Not the first one I've had. I guess it's why Kay doesn't love me the way he's treated his other son. He's known from the start I was a member of our brotherhood."

"That's no excuse to treat you like shit."

He smiled and smothered his bitterness with a quiet chuckle. "You're kinder to me than I deserve. I stalked you. I followed you for weeks... and I knew from the start you were as beautiful inside as you are outside." He'd loved her then, he thought. Even though he'd never met her, not in person, he'd loved her. His shoulders drooped. "I have to make this right, because if we don't end it, your father could be next. Your grandmother might be the next phone call, Astrid."

Astrid ran her fingers over the sheathed sword belted around her hips. "You should have told me, but I guess, in a way, I see why you didn't. I just wish… I just wish I hadn't fallen in love with you while we were in a lie. But maybe I'm just as much to blame. Maybe I lied too, because I didn't tell you what you meant to me. The moment we met, I recognized you for what you are—not a dragonslayer, but the other half of my soul and heart."

His brows raised. "You believe in soul mates?"

Astrid sighed. "Have you ever noticed that dragons tend to mate for life?"

"Yeah, I've noticed it but never put much thought into it." It seemed a strange change in subject from his imminent death and the end of the knighthood he'd served for several hundred years. "Why?"

"Dragons have soul mates, for lack of a better word. No, it *is* the right word. It's just become so cliché among the humans, but for dragons, it's very literal. That's what happened with Mom and Dad. For the first time, as far as we know, a dragon and a human found they were *destined* for one another."

Nate stared at her. *She can't be implying…*

"Some dragons wait centuries, searching for their true mate. When you see them, it hits you like a Mack truck. You just know they're the one for you."

"I'm not the one for you, Astrid. If you're trying to suggest it's me, I'm no one special."

"Don't say that, because you are special. Maybe not to your dad, maybe not to yourself, but you were special to me. Special enough to give my heart to. Special enough that I don't know if I can do this and *kill* you."

Facing death had never been difficult before. Knowing it would be the last time came as a turbulent mix of relief and despair. He reached for her but caught himself in time to drop his hand back to his lap instead. Touching Astrid, holding her, or even kissing her would make separating even harder.

Nate averted his gaze and put his hands on the wheel again. "We need to be on our way," he mumbled.

"Yeah, I guess so." The disappointment in her voice struck him like a railroad spike to the heart.

"I know my apologies are worth nothing, but it doesn't change the remorse I feel for this. I hope you're right, that we don't have to die right now. They've all got families, you know? Lancelot's got two kids now." Who were more brother and sister to him than the other son Kay had fathered. "The others, too. Percivale's a bachelor, but he takes care of his mother. She can't live alone."

After checking the highway, he pulled out into traffic again, and resumed their travel toward Disney. Something felt off, his senses ablaze with worry and anxiety, but he gritted his teeth through it, and drove ahead anyway. Maybe it was the promise of death and the true possibility of facing Merlin down in some dark, terrifying tomb. He said nothing else during the drive to the amusement park, content to focus all of his concentration on driving. Instead of panicking.

The order had passes to employee parking. They went through checkpoints with ease, and no one glanced twice at her sword, accustomed to sword-carrying dragonslayers passing through. As they walked through 'the happiest place on earth' he thought of everything he'd be losing.

Astrid's smaller hand slipped into his, startling him. His mind had been preoccupied with all of the good-byes he'd never written. "I'm sorry," he whispered, "but I don't regret falling in love with you."

Knowing it was possibly the last time they'd have together, he led her through the magical kingdom. With hours between their arrival and the park's closure, there were families everywhere. "Under normal circumstances, Kay has the park operators shut down the ride and clear the area. I don't want to draw attention to us, but I could try a spell to chase everyone away. Or one to conceal us."

All of the knights knew magic to some degree, though some were more talented and capable than others, able to draw their swords and armor in silver blazes of powerful magic, or create small enchantments and charms. A few of their number and some white witches in close association were responsible for the anti-dragon charms and boundary lines they placed around their property.

"I'd say go for concealment. Chasing them away will just draw undue attention to the ride. I can do a cloaking spell, no problem. How do you think I get away with flying around?"

"Then you're up. I trust your magic better than mine. You're the dragon." He flashed her an uncertain, shy smile and released her hand to approach the sword in the stone display in front of the carousel. "Tell me when." They were between spins at the moment, the current riders stepping down from their horses.

The world around them dimmed slightly, as if a gauzy curtain had been drawn.

"Okay, we should be good. Just try not to run into anyone."

"Strange that you're able to use your magic here when so many others cannot," Nate muttered under his breath. He closed his hand around the hilt of the sword protruding from the anvil, and it glowed white.

In his hand, it moved slightly, like a lever, then he pushed it back into place. Just before them, the ground began to drop away, creating stone steps leading down into the darkness at a steep descent. He offered his hand to Astrid. She took it, and together they descended the steps into the unknown.

Chapter 13

Saul's personal office lacked the space to house the number of paranormal beings inside. He lurked behind Max's shoulder, one hand on the back of his chair, the other on the desk while he leaned close to look at the screen. "Do you know what you're doing?" he asked.

"I know more than you," Max replied.

Chloe and Ēostre had taken seats on a settee nearby while the two eager dragonmen potentially ruined their evidence. Teo and Tlaloc, ultimately useless when it came to computers, had no interest in poring through the laptop's contents. They had excused themselves to make use of Chloe's personal coffee bar.

"Gentlemen, maybe we should invite someone with the training for this kinda thing to peruse the slayer databases. Just a suggestion," Chloe said to Max and Saul.

Saul glanced at her and narrowed his eyes. "I know how to use a computer."

She raised a skeptical brow. "Is that why we had to pay three hundred dollars to the Geek Squad to recover all of your data after you nearly lost it while trying to upgrade your operating system?"

Her husband growled back at her. "That wasn't my fault. It glitched during the installation."

"Uh-huh."

Xochiquetzal chuckled quietly. She leaned against the wall beside the door leading to the balcony, the cool breeze rustling through her dark hair. She held a cup of deep, black coffee in her hand. Chloe had come to learn that Xochi, Tlaloc, and Teo practically lived on the stuff.

"Are you two not due to return to the White House, Belenos?" the earth dragoness asked.

Max shook his head. "The Oval Office can wait until Astrid is home safe." He leaned forward to squint at the screen, tapped the enter key, and grinned broadly. "This is surprisingly straightforward. Downloadable documents in their database, handily provided in ZIP format. I'm in their e-mail server at the moment and… Sweet ancestors," he said on a breath.

Ēostre hurried to the desk. "What?"

"They've gotten a dozen of their people into Congress. Over a dozen."

"Are there names or just discussion?"

"The cocky bastards are quite open, and while I haven't discovered a list yet, the e-mails are pretty damning," Max said.

"Your Secretary of Defense," Saul said. "Look. They're keeping an eye on you through him. He isn't yet part of the Anti-Dragon Movement but certainly considering his stance."

Max swore under his breath. "With this, we can root out and interrogate dozens of their agents."

"Do you still question whether the young slayer's intentions are legitimate?" Xochi asked.

"I certainly do not," Ēostre said.

"Okay, so like, I get that he's a reincarnated knight, but have any of you crossed paths with him before?" Chloe asked.

"Once in the past," Ēostre said.

"Twice," Max replied.

"Has he killed anyone you liked?" None of the dragons spoke. "Anyone you even *knew?*"

"That means nothing," Saul said. "Dragons were once plentiful. It was impossible for us all to know one another on a personal level. His kind has changed that."

"Your kind have as well." She hesitated and toyed with the edge of her shirt before saying in a softer voice, "I killed Brigid, but no one holds it against me. Not even Max."

Max smiled sadly. "No, I do not hold it against you, Chloe. You are as much my daughter now as she could have ever been."

"Then how can we hold it against all knights for killing a few of you when you kill one another as well? Ēostre had to slay Mahuika. You men can't deny that you've fought over the years, too."

"She has a great point," Ēostre said.

"I know I do," Chloe said, beaming. "I think you're too hard on him. Yes, he did hurt Astrid, but we've *all* hurt each other at one time, right? What matters is he's putting his life on the line to help us now. We know nothing else about him."

"This Sir Kay, however, he is well-known to us." Max's fisted knuckles whitened.

The two black male dragons returned at the tail end of Chloe's pitch, the younger raising his brows curiously over his cup of coffee. "How so?" Teo asked.

"He is the knight believed to have slain my father," Saul answered, tone subdued.

"Then we must find him and rip out his spine," Tlaloc said, making a fist. "If he is in this California, we will send a message to all dragonslayers."

Xochi sighed, and Chloe empathized.

"If anyone gets to take vengeance on Kay, it's Ēostre, and only if she wants to," Chloe told them. "But that is a discussion for later. Right now, I say we let Max do his thing and get us all the information we need. Agreed?"

"Fine. I have no fondness for these trivial mortal conveniences," Tlaloc said imperiously before disappearing through the door.

Xochi trailed behind him, laughing at her husband. "You dislike them because they don't obey your commands."

"Lovely. Saul, will you join me outside a minute?"

"As you wish, my love." Saul left his post behind Max's chair to join her. Without prompting, he sought her hand and laced their fingers. She led him outside and shut the door behind them.

Fresh air was what she needed after all the tension and machismo inside. She drew in a deep breath, relishing in the breeze scented with wildflowers and roses, before rounding on her husband.

"I wanted to chat with you before Astrid is home."

Saul's brows rose. "About?"

"Her boyfriend."

"The one who is soon to die?"

"We don't know that he's going to die when they slay the wizard. For all we know, she may have another fifty years with him, Saul." After a dramatic pause, she added, "Fifty years as your son-in-law."

He bristled. "Over my dead body."

"I think she loves him," Chloe said, "and it's no business of ours if she does. We're her parents, not dictators. We can't make the decisions for her, and if she feels for him even a fraction of what we felt when we first met, we have to stand back and let her choose."

"He deceived her!"

"Yes, and you once did the same to me. Are you both so different? Did you tell me from the start you were a dragon? You *marked* me."

Her husband grimaced. "I will forever apologize and regret—"

Chloe touched her fingers to his lips. "I'm not asking for your apologies or regret. I love you, Saul Drakenstone. I understand that your instincts took over and carried you away. And I wouldn't trade this life with you for anything. All I ask is that you consider there are circumstances that sometimes change everything we think we understand about a situation."

He sighed. "Very well. I will not dismember the human when he returns."

"And?" she prompted.

He grunted. "I will attempt to like him."

"Thank you." She leaned forward on tiptoe to kiss him. "I'll be glad when this ordeal is over and Brandt is home again."

"He's enjoying his stay at the island with Svetlana and the twins. I'm sure he doesn't even miss us," Saul pointed out.

"Poor Marcy for having to wrangle three tikes though. She's earned her raptor training badge today."

Saul's warm chuckle huffed against her cheek. "The children are all safe and, most importantly, oblivious to the danger. We will make sure Marceline enjoys a well-deserved holiday when it is all done."

"I think we all deserve a little holiday after this."

Hugging her husband close, she tried not to worry about their daughter. Astrid was stronger than they all gave her credit for, and she had her own destiny to fulfill.

Chapter 14

The entrance sealed behind them and enchanted lights flickered on, old lanterns dangling from the ceiling of the narrow, downward sloping passage. Astrid swallowed back her trepidation and adjusted the sword belt around her hips.

"So what can we expect down here? I mean, is he in a glass coffin? A bedroom?" She didn't let go of Nate's hand, savoring every precious moment of affectionate contact.

"He isn't Snow White," he replied. His nervous chuckle did nothing to alleviate her unease. Something scuttled in the dark, and she watched him reach for a sword he didn't have. "I've never been here in this life."

"Do you remember anything at all?"

"Not exactly. Few of us ever come here to see him, except for Kay, Bedivere, and a couple of the older guys seeking guidance."

Their descent ended at a thick, wooden door. Carved vine motifs decorated the old oak, polished to a glossy finish with what smelled like beeswax. Magic hung in the air, heavy as jungle humidity. Something nameless, wild, and ancient was present, a sense of power she'd never felt from her grandmother.

Merlin. She could sense him, too.

"Merlin slept here long before this land was purchased by the park," he explained. "I think it was his idea to move to California when the greater wyrms began to relocate their hoards here. So he made this."

Nate stared at the door. When she reached for the knob, an electric buzz ran over the tips of her fingers and down her arm, like the static reaction of touching a television. He jerked her back before she made complete contact. "No. Let me."

"Yeah, of course."

She stepped back and let him take the lead. The door swung open to reveal a path littered with skeletal remains. Active runes and the scrawl of powerful enchantments created a kaleidoscope pattern of color in the subterranean cavern. Dozens of them stretched as far as she could see.

Nate sucked in a breath. "I feel like Indiana Jones right now."

An assortment of bones, both animal and human, lay scattered over the floor and piled against the walls. As they rounded a bend, a dragon embedded in the rock stood out beneath a mage glow. She fell back a step, heart pounding. It was more than Merlin's resting place; it was a mass gravesite.

"There may be traps in the walls. Some of these bones have been shattered," he said, "and there's no telling what activates them. Don't touch anything."

"Trust me, I didn't plan on it."

He proceeded, only to pause as if uncertain whether to keep Astrid to his front or behind him. In the end, he slid an arm around her shoulders and held her close. "Many have tried to locate him and found only death."

"Too many. There must be hundreds of remains here," Astrid pointed out.

"He's been living here a long time." They came to a divide in the path, able to go left or right. He froze; then his brows raised. "It's a maze. We all know the way, at least, we *should* know the path to him."

They turned and continued down an identical path with another two turns. Torches glowed with ever burning flames, and with each deviation they took, nothing changed.

"That skeleton there. It's the same one," he said. "It's the same bear. Look. And so is that one. There's bits of cloth left on the bones."

They were going in literal circles, somehow rounding back the same way they'd come even whenever they changed their path and took another direction. He made a frustrated groan and looked at his watch. It had stopped. "I don't remember any of this."

"If we're going in circles, maybe we need to turn around? Go down the other way? Or maybe there's a lever you're supposed to press?" It was disorienting, but she felt out with her own magic, trying to find a weakness in the confusing enchantment. The charm was unlike anything made by dragon hands or common, modern-day witchcraft.

"Maybe," he said with uncertainty. "Do you smell that?"

Astrid sniffed the air and turned a quizzical glance to him. "Yeah. It's earthy."

The air had a strange, musty odor to it like the scent of livestock and the cool scent of water.

"Now I know how the others died. Some of them must have wandered for days, weeks, until they were too weak." He gestured to an intact skeleton. "I wonder…"

"You wonder what?" Nerves made her snap the question out, followed swiftly by guilt. "Sorry. I'm just so unsettled. And nervous. Maybe… maybe we should go back. There has to be another way to stop your brotherhood."

"Like what? Asking them nicely? I tried that. No one was willing to hear me out but the two men I've talked to you about. Some more were on the fence, but Bedivere and Kay have clout I lack for as long as I'm without my memories."

"There has to be a way to stop them. I mean... you said it yourself, Arthur would be appalled. Maybe Merlin would be too?"

Nate flexed his hand again, holding it at his side. Since entering, he'd been tempted to draw his sword. The desire remained, simmering just beneath the surface of his thoughts until he flexed his hand again. "Step back again for a sec."

"Nate?" She moved back, but kept one hand on his waist, holding his belt.

"When called upon, I draw thee to defend the rights of the weak with all of my strength."

Astrid pressed her cheek against the back of his shoulder to protect her eyes from the blaze of light erupting around Nate's hand. When she risked raising her face again, the silver gleam dimmed to a pale sheen. He held a blade in his hand, glowing with unearthly brilliance.

It was beautiful, watching him use his magical gift. The sight of a slayer's sword should have struck fear into her heart, but seeing one in Nate's hand made her feel safe—not threatened.

"I wish I could summon mine magically. Did you notice no one seemed to see it?"

The tension drained from his shoulders. "Yeah, at first I thought it was because you were using a spell, or because I was with you, but no one even glanced at it."

He held the sword like a torch, and wherever he shone it, the shadows receded and fell back. Where there'd been only smooth stone wall, another tunnel led forward. There'd been an opening in the wall in front of them all along, visible only by the light of his enchanted sword.

"How does your gift work?" Astrid asked.

"We were all cremated in our armor with our swords, I'm told, by Merlin himself, so that our magic would carry on each time we were reborn. It's spiritually smelted to my soul."

"Is it hard? Not remembering, I mean. Or, well, half remembering." Taking a cue from him, she drew Ascalon from its sheath, doubling their light.

"Sometimes. I'm one of the youngest, so when the rest of the guys are reminiscing about old times, I get to sit there and look dumb."

The next hall had a short trio of stairs. It smelled dank and moist still, the same odor growing all the more intense. She hesitated as her foot bumped into bones strewn on the ground. "I have a bad feeling," she said.

The air smelled like animal, musty and wild—the rancid scent of an untended stable with hay left to mold among old urine. Astrid choked on it, and her eyes watered.

Nate turned left and right, casting light over what appeared to be a deeper cavern, its walls rough rock, and water trickling down into a pool. There was no light, no torches, only darkness. She drew in a deep breath through her nose and tensed.

"Something is alive down here. It's a weird smell. Feline, maybe, or canine. Reptilian, too. All blended." Her grip on Ascalon tightened. "Think hard, Nate. What sort of guardian did they put down here and how do they get past it? There must be something, or you slayers would be killed coming to get your directives from Merlin, right?"

"I don't know," he whispered. "If there's a guardian, it would know me. Theoretically."

Something scraped in the distance over the stone ground, and a clicking noise, like a dog's claws over the floor, made the hair on her nape rise.

"Maybe it won't smell me," she whispered. "Echo didn't."

"Maybe not," he whispered back, "but it's a dangerous risk to take, Astrid."

She swallowed, throat tight. The clawed steps drew closer, bringing a fresh wave of fear, not only for herself but for Nate. What mattered were the true feelings shared between them, love too powerful to be denied by past wrongs.

The thought prompted her into grabbing him by his belt and jerking him back. Giving him no chance to protest or argue, she pushed up to her toes and kissed him, hard, pouring her heart out to him.

***

Astrid pressed against him on her toes, her slim body stretched along his front. He slipped his arm around her waist and lost himself to the moment shared between them.

"I love you," he whispered against her lips. "So much it scared me."

"Nate, I—"

The noise drew closer, the creature investigating the intruder in its home. The moment lost, Nate nudged Astrid behind him. The light of their swords reflected off something glossy and large—an eye. Two feline eyes, golden and bright within a lion's maned face, then two gleaming, red eyes above it where a goat's head arose from its back with massive horns curling forward. A third head became visible at the end of the tail dragged behind it, hissing and flicking its tongue in and out to taste the air.

"Oh my God, it's a chimera." Astrid's eyes widened. She kept her sword down, but ready.

A flash of memory came upon him, too brief to grasp. "It's been a guardian for centuries, brought over from the Old World with Merlin."

"Maybe you can tell it to back off?"

He gave her a dubious look. "I don't speak chimera."

Still on his guard, he stepped forward to confront the beast. It didn't attack him, perhaps the first positive sign that the encounter could end without bloodshed. Leaning forward to sniff him, its feline nose came inches from his skin. Whiskers tickled his cheek and rank, hot breath breezed over his face.

Nate froze on the spot, clutching his sword hard enough to leave indents in his palms. He shuddered as the serpentine head came next. A trickle of sweat slid down his hairline and his palms itched, his fingers flexing around his sword hilt.

"We've come to pay our respect to Merlin," he said, with some vague recollection of it understanding them. The beast strode past and continued to prowl toward Astrid, sniffing curiously with its lionesque head, smelling with its nose almost against her neck.

"I come in peace."

"Did you seriously just treat this thing like an alien?" he whispered.

She shot him a look, unamused, but remained quiet.

Finding nothing strange, the beast turned as if to stalk away. Nate's relieved breath whooshed out of him, and he almost collapsed. So close. Merlin was so close. And suddenly, he felt so very tired of it all and ready for the ordeal to end. No more dragonslaying, no more cycle of rebirth. How many women had he loved and lost over the centuries?

"Let's go, I think he's fin—" The tail swung past when the chimera turned, bringing its head within inches of her. Stopping, the creature stiffened and the serpentine head hissed.

"INTRUDER!" the goat screamed, while the lion's head roared. The snake bit at her, lashing out. Whatever test Astrid had passed with the goat and lion, she'd failed with the venomous serpent.

Ascalon clattered to the ground and bits of Astrid's clothing fluttered around her. One moment, she'd been a girl level with his shoulders, and in the next, he was diving out of the way to make room for a dragon looming above him. She hunched over in the cavern on all fours, too large to stand upright.

The lethal fangs struck against the tough scales of her shoulder, narrowly missing a wing covered in gold and black feathers.

Even in the dark, Astrid reminded Nate of sunlight. He was reduced to staring with his mouth open, awed by her beauty. Then he snapped out of it and leaped up to his feet, swinging his astral blade.

"Astrid!" While sharp, the edge of his sword glanced off the chimera's scales. He'd have to stab it with precision. The lion turned its head toward him and roared. Nate struck again, swinging to give her time to adjust to her shifting, glancing another blow off of its claws and drawing first blood.

The chimera snarled as he feinted, backing into the wider area of the cavern. Scoring another hit, he laid open the skin between its lion shoulder and goat head.

"Betrayer," it growled.

Bigger than both Nate and the chimera, Astrid swept in between them and snarled a warning to the creature. "Stay away from my Nate." She snapped her teeth at the serpent tail and raked her claws against the goat's horns.

Her Nate? His brows raised. Astrid may have been bigger, but other dragons larger than her had already been bested by the magical beast.

"Watch out for its tail!" he called to her. An older dragon's tough hide was almost impenetrable, but hers looked soft and supple. Youthful. One bite from it's serpentine maw would be enough to take her out of the fight. Refusing to risk her safety, he lunged in again, brushing past her winged side, and aimed for the furred front of the chimera where he scored his second successful stroke. The blade slid in almost effortlessly, but it wasn't the killing blow he wanted. The chimera was only angrier.

Despite being outsized and outnumbered, the chimera held its own in battle against them. Nate had thought with two against one, the odds would be in their favor, but the Chimera had three dangerous heads and a pair of talons, each head thinking and working independently of the others. It clawed and bit, ramming its horns into Astrid's chest and slamming her into the cavern wall. Nate viciously swung at its hindquarters and parried a bite from the swift tail.

"Nate, be careful!"

She slapped the snake away and maneuvered around to the beast's other side to split the heads' attention. She drew blood again, crippling the lion head by finishing the slice Nate began, but not before its goat horns dragged down her side.

The horns scraped down Astrid's belly, enraging him. He saw red, and all sense of self-preservation drowned beneath the rising tide of his fury.

As Astrid exhaled a line of flames, he dove toward the beast and brought his sword down in an overhead swing toward its shoulder. In a rush to maneuver out of the way of his overhand slash, the chimera barreled into dragonfire, setting its fur ablaze. The goat head screamed; then the snake lashed out and swung around. It bit him before he could parry, the sensation like molten lead in his veins.

Astrid's roar reverberated through the cavern, showering them with a light rain of dust and brittle lichen. She hurled her body between him and the chimera, drew a deep breath, then exhaled a volcanic storm of fire laced with white lightning.

Nate stumbled to one knee but kept himself upright with his sword, planting the tip of it into the soft earth beneath their feet. The pain was indescribable, worse than anything he'd experienced in all of his life. And it was spreading fast. All around him, the cavern became aglow with light, heated from the fire.

The prolonged effect of lightning spilling into the beast blinded him, and he closed his eyes against the repetitive strikes of electricity. It shone brighter than the most radiant strobe light, and her unfortunate victim could do nothing but succumb. The chimera's goat head gargled an awful death scream until the last bolt split its scaled hide and a smoking carcass was all that remained.

In the next second, Astrid was above him. Her blue eyes filled with worry, fear visible on her draconic face. "Nate, no, no, no." She shifted, shrinking down to her human shape, naked and pale in the dim lit cavern. "Please stay with me," she begged.

His hold on the sword slackened, sweaty grip too weak to hold it any longer. As he collapsed, Astrid caught him in her arms and cradled him against her naked bosom.

"Hey," he rasped up to her. "He's just in the next room. You keep your promise, okay?" Heat flushed through his body from head to toe, an inferno burning in his lungs. "I'm sorry. For everything. Sorry I hurt you."

"No. No, I won't. I can't lose you, Nate. Not like this." Tears rolled down her cheeks. "I'm not leaving without you."

Everything hurt, and he wondered if he'd felt as much pain during previous deaths. No. He hadn't. He remembered the last, recalled dying an old man, peacefully in his bed, surrounded by friends and a few knights, but no children, because he'd never married. How ironic that as his current life ended, he finally began to remember more than snippets of his previous life.

The serpent had left twin puncture wounds, deep and oozing blood, in his torso just below his ribs. If the venom didn't kill him, blood loss certainly would. Despite it, he tried to smile. "It's fine, Astrid. Go finish this." The acrid odor of roasting chimera and Nate's blood filled the cavern. He tried to ignore both to focus on her face.

Something told him death wouldn't come for some time, not until he'd suffered and his insides melted with sickness. Before that happened, he wanted Astrid to leave.

He couldn't let her watch him suffer, no matter how much he wanted to hold her hand until the end.

"I don't give a shit about Merlin. I care about you. I love *you*. I will *not* allow you to die."

Astrid bent over him and placed her hands upon his inflamed middle. His torso had already begun to swell, reacting to the venom. A subtle glow of ivory interspersed with gold bloomed around her hands until it surrounded her, creating a rainbow nimbus of light.

She was more beautiful than any angel.

Magic swept through him, bringing cooling relief to the acid flashing through his veins. Then the agony was gone. He sucked in a deep, starved breath, and for several seconds, Nate lay in her arms too bewildered and surprised to move.

"Astrid?" he questioned in surprise.

The dragoness didn't answer. She threw herself down and embraced him tight. Warm tears leaked from her eyes onto his neck where she'd buried her face.

No longer fighting to breathe, he instead struggled to hold the naked woman sprawled against him. His arms enfolded

Astrid and he held her close. A ghostly remnant of the pain remained in his side, and even that rapidly began to fade.

"You healed me." It took a moment for it to settle in his brain.

"You could have been killed," she sobbed against him.

"Hey, it's okay. It's over, baby. You killed it." Somehow. Thanks to her, and only thanks to her, the beast was little more than a charred lump with embers floating up from it's smoking carcass.

"You big idiot, trying to be all noble."

"Nobility is kind of what I'm known for," he pointed out.

She lifted her face, eyes watery and nose red, and looked him over. "Are you okay? Did I get it all? Are you still hurting?"

He groaned and adjusted his position, but ultimately shook his head when the final twinges faded over time. In a much quieter voice, and after an awkward pause, he whispered, "You didn't have to save me. I was ready to die, Astrid."

"I'm not ready for you to die," she whispered in return. "Nate... I meant what I said. I love you. And I know it might not mean much to you, or that you insist you aren't worth anything, but I meant what I said in the car, too. You're my soul mate, and I knew it the moment we met. You're special to me, but not only for that, but because... you're you."

"That's where you're wrong, baby girl. It means everything to me." He sighed and stroked his fingers down her back. "Your family won't understand."

He certainly couldn't blame her fellow dragons if they took offense to her decision. They still hadn't solved the dilemma of what to do with Merlin or how to defeat the slayers hell-bent on destroying her race.

"I thought I was losing my mind when I felt more of a connection with you after one date than I ever did with any of my human exes." He sighed. "Everything I've done since receiving this mission has been to neutralize the shit going down between the knighthood and your people. I thought I could convince them you guys aren't a danger anymore. I did it for you."

She looked over her shoulder toward the entrance to the next room then back to him. "Maybe we can convince Merlin of it. Make him understand. Show him what you and I have—it's real."

"Kay says he's given them orders."

"But you said you've never heard orders in your dreams. Do you trust Kay?" Nate shook his head. "If he's been asleep all this time, then he doesn't know. So let's show him my kind have changed." She helped him into a sitting position. "Because I can't walk in there and just kill him. I can't walk in there and kill you."

"And if he can't be reasoned with, baby? If he wakes up an angry old wizard and we have to fight him? It won't be like this," he said, waving his hand toward the smoldering chimera remains. "He's the first among wizards and witches. He'll be awake and capable of defending himself."

With effort, he climbed to his feet and began to inspect the torn cotton covering his ribs. The skin was smooth, but two shiny, puckered indentations were scarred in his side.

"I can't go in there and murder someone in cold blood," she whispered. "What would that make me? If you did live, would you ever be able to look at me, knowing I killed someone without giving them even a chance? Would you be able to see past me being a murderer? I couldn't. I couldn't look myself in the mirror and forget what I've done."

"Then I'll do it, and your hands will be clean." He leaned over to retrieve his sword from the ground and glanced at her. "What's one more murder on my hands among others?"

Despite all of his bravado, Nate agreed with her. He didn't want to kill Merlin any more than he wanted to die along with him. Murder was never the answer.

"Nate..." She flushed, her naked body pink from head to toe.

Averting his gaze first, he shrugged out of his jacket and offered it while facing the wall. After Astrid had zipped it up, she plucked Ascalon from the ground and moved toward the door without giving the chimera a second glance.

"You're not killing him in cold blood either. Whatever you were in the past, you're not that man anymore. I believe in you Nate. *Galahad*."

From her, the name didn't sting like an insult. It felt right. He watched her move toward the opening in the cavern and clenched his jaw. "He's the one at the root of this evil. For centuries we've hunted your kind on his orders, Astrid. That man is indirectly responsible for your uncle's death. For your grandfather's death. Should we just forget that and live and let live?" He tried to justify it as much to himself as he did to her.

"We'll see when we get in there, but I'm not going to drive my sword through a sleeping man. And I know you won't either." She lifted her chin, stubborn to the end. Her eyes softened when his knees buckled, and she moved up to him and slipped one arm around his waist. "Lean on me."

With Astrid's support, they proceeded into the next chamber. The rough-hewn rock gave way to polished stone with glittering veins of quartz and amethyst streaked through. Mage lights glimmered, brightening the further they went down the corridor past paintings of landscapes, noble figures carved from marble, and wooden shelves filled with old books.

They entered a chamber flooded with light—its source a hanging star cluster shimmering from above. Below, in the center of the room, lay Merlin.

In a glass coffin.

Astrid blinked at the spectacle then turned to look back at Nate. "Called it."

Nate grumbled under his breath. "Just rub it in." Part of him had to wonder why a glass coffin of all things. Did they preserve bodies the way a fridge kept meat? He boggled before he stepped forward, the sword carried in his hand.

The wizard was as he remembered him in vague and fleeting memories, tall and lean in build, dressed in robes of soft velvet and silk with golden embellishment and stitching against purple, flowing fabric. His beard lay over his chest, stark white and long as the hair spread around his shoulders. He looked peaceful.

"Here, help me open it." The lid came off easy, lacking locks to clasp it shut.

"I expected... more," Nate said. He shuddered. The room felt strange. Stagnant air surrounded them in a malicious aura. It didn't feel like the magic of a white wizard.

"Maybe there is more."

"Huh?"

"There's magic radiating from him. It's like... like he's wrapped in a web of it. I can see the strands." Her brow furrowed and frown deepened. "Nate, he's bound up tight here."

"I don't see anything," Nate replied, bewildered by her observation. He leaned closer for a look inside the coffin and gripped his sword hilt tighter in one hand. One stroke. One stroke was all it would take. He didn't feel anything protective around the coffin, no wards or barriers preventing him from taking swift action.

"I'm telling you, it's magic. He's wrapped in a cocoon of it, bound to this room." She raised Ascalon and swung the sword seemingly through thin air.

"Why the hell would he bind himself in magic?" Nate demanded. "That doesn't make any sense. He's always just laid down to sleep and awakened again on a whim to discover what kind of world we lived in." He took her word for it and mimicked her with his sword, only to feel a strange resistance above him. Nate narrowed his eyes. "There *is* something here."

"Stand back. I'm going to try to slice through it. Then we can take him back to my father, if he doesn't wake up and try to kill us first."

"Here's to hoping he doesn't reward you with a face full of fireballs," Nate muttered.

He stepped back and gave her a wide berth, observing as she shifted her stance and swung with all of her might. When she cut the spell, his ears popped like a shift in the atmospheric pressure. The blanket of negative, oppressive energy that had pushed against him since their entrance vanished.

Light flashed above the translucent coffin. Astrid winced and pressed her palm to her right ear. "What's that sound?"

"I don't hear anything." He twisted around and searched until he saw a small camera tucked inside a shallow nook in the wall. "But we must have set off an alarm. Wards and an alarm."

His attention drifted around the chamber, only to notice another wooden door in a recessed indentation at the rear of the room. Torches flanked it, each one lit by a blue flame. "That's our exit. I can't tell you where it leads, but I recall as much."

Voices echoed down the long corridors of Merlin's lair. Familiar voices. He'd recognize Kay's stern tone anywhere.

"We've got company, too."

"Shit. How the hell did they arrive so fast?"

Before he could make sense of what was happening, Astrid tossed his jacket back to him. "I'm going to trust you with my sword. I hope there's open space on the other side of that door."

It felt odd in his hands. Heavy and unbalanced. How did she use the damned thing? A couple of seconds later, he had his jacket on and Merlin tossed over one shoulder. With Ascalon clutched in his hand, he hurried with her to the door.

"Down this way! They're in his chamber!" a knight called. Their footsteps thundered, the noise of many people traveling closely together in full armor.

Nate threw open the door. Beyond the enormous wooden panel, he saw only beautiful green and rock. He rushed outside and realized they were miles away from where they'd entered the wizard's underground lair, as if they'd emerged from a portal to another location entirely. Had they been underground long enough to travel so great a distance? He doubted it.

"We're at Irvine Regional Park. Astrid, we're miles from Disneyland."

"Right." Free from the confining tunnels, she took to her dragon form once more and claimed Merlin in one of her claws. "Climb on. You're about to get a crash course in riding a dragon."

He gave her a dubious look then glanced behind them into the open doorway where shades of blue and purple shone from within, highlighting an empty glass coffin. The knights burst inside, Kay and Bedivere in the lead with guns and swords at the ready.

Chapter 15

Within ten minutes of going airborne, Astrid's fight or flight response dwindled, and she remembered Mahasti was only a call away. In a blink, the djinn brought them to Drakenstone Manor, her flawless aim placing them above the front pasture.

The pain registered in Astrid's mind after she touched down on the grass.

Astrid released Merlin from her claws seconds before collapsing. Her father and family rushed out, a herd of dragons crowding the area around her within seconds.

Her mother appeared by her side as if by magic, hands tiny against her child's bleeding side. "Astrid? Astrid, baby, what happened?"

The assault from Kay and the knights hadn't been as harmless as she thought. During the flight, adrenaline had numbed her, and she'd flown with no other purpose but to deliver Nate and Merlin to safety. Exhausted from her ordeal, she turned her head to see Nate pinned beneath her father's massive claw. He didn't struggle, and for a moment, she feared Saul had already crushed the life from him.

"What did you do to her, human?"

"She's been shot!" Chloe called. "Ēostre! I need you!"

"Not his fault," Astrid groaned through her pain. She strained to see Nate and her father through a haze of pain and tears.

"Must be armor-piercing rounds," Max muttered. She hadn't seen him rush up to her with the others, but he remained in his smaller form to stroke her brow with human hands. "You hang in there, sweetheart. They'll fix you."

"I know," she whispered. "Grandpa, check the wizard, please."

"Merlin?"

"Yes," Astrid groaned. "He was under a spell. Please check on him. Make sure he's okay."

"Okay," Max reluctantly agreed.

"Forget the wizard. Who shot my cub?" Saul demanded. The tip of his claw rested squarely on the center of Nate's chest.

"The other dragonslayers arrived as we left Merlin's lair. The place was bugged with alarms. I didn't hurt her. I could never hurt her."

Saul relented, reluctantly. He abandoned Nate in the grass and hurried over to Astrid's side as any concerned father would.

"Merlin was trapped, Grandma," she said while Ēostre and Tlaloc's mate worked over her wounds. Relief came with a wave of magic, numbing the fire in her side enough for her to breathe easier. She laid her large, golden head on the grass and turned her snout toward Nate, checking on him. He crawled to his feet, dirt and grass clinging to him. "There was a chimera guarding the lair and it bit Nate. I healed him, but... Daddy, will you make sure he's okay? Please?"

"Be still, child." Xochi pulled a bullet from her scales and she flinched.

"I'm fine, Astrid. Your dad's right to worry about you."

Saul eyed Nate with a mixture of disgust and grudging respect. He gave a single huff, a warm plume of breath billowing from his nose, laced with magic to help ensure any lingering traces of poison were gone.

"Thanks," Nate murmured.

Saul barely acknowledged him. "You did well, Astrid. He will be fine. For now. But I suggest we all return inside and deal with the wizard."

"I'll take him inside," Max said. He picked the old man up and gave a nod of his head for Nate to follow.

Mahasti summoned clothes for the others. Astrid shifted last with only her mother and grandma in her company. They'd seen it all before, countless times through her childhood to adolescence.

"Take it easy, baby," Chloe cautioned as she offered out a sundress for Astrid to pull on. "You want to wait out here a minute?"

"Do you think Nate will be okay?"

"Oh, baby." Chloe stroked a hand over Astrid's golden hair. "I promise you, your dad won't hurt Nate."

"Agreed," Ēostre said. "Do you want to tell us what happened? Why did you bring Merlin to us here?"

"Because I couldn't kill him," she admitted in a tiny voice. Her shoulders shuddered, prompting both women to draw in close beside her with reassuring touches. "I think he was a prisoner, has been for a long time."

"Then maybe we *should* get inside before our hot-headed men do something stupid."

Once Astrid was dressed, they found the dragonmen, Mahasti, Leiv, and Nate in the living room where Max had sprawled Merlin on the sofa. With his arms crossed over his chest, the red dragon stared at Saul.

"No, young one. Astrid asked me to watch over him."

Saul made an exasperated noise. Astrid couldn't discern whether it was because of Max's disagreement or her decision to stand beside Nate and take his hand.

"We should slay him now, while he sleeps," Tlaloc said.

"I actually agree with my father on this," Teo added, earning a surprised glance from his parents. "He's too dangerous to allow to live."

Merlin looked weak and fragile, a harmless old man draped in wizard's finery. "I agree," Nate spoke up with the two black dragons.

"As do I," Mahasti said. "He is a powerful wizard, and should he awaken, my powers will be no match for him. He is the first, the originator of all human magic, but only the knighthood should be affected if he is destroyed. They are bound by blood magic."

"You see, Max?" Saul gestured to his supporters. "The only choice is clear. For our safety and that of our children, he must be killed for the greater good of our species. We have lost too many friends and good brothers to the insanity designed by his hands."

"Saul, what are you saying?" Chloe stepped forward and hugged her arms around herself. "We can't just kill off a sleeping old man. It's not right. What if there's more to this story? And what about what Astrid said, about him being bound?"

Ēostre spoke up in a calm voice while laying a hand on her son's arm. "Agreed. I can see the lingering web of an imprisonment curse around him."

"I am saying I value the lives of our family more than one old man. Or many dragonslayers," Saul growled.

"I will not be party to murder," Leiv said. He glanced at his wife, expression calm. "I know he is magic, but look at him. He reeks of frailty. Even if he did wake up angry, he could not take on a room full of dragons, let alone a djinn."

The supernaturals argued amongst themselves, husband against wife with the exception of Max and Ēostre. The older fire wyrm shook his head and raised his voice to be heard among the squabbling.

"Tlaloc, Xochi, Ēostre, and I were there when Merlin first organized the Knights of the Round Table," Max said. "Yes, his magic is great, but I cannot abide by murdering him as he sleeps. We must awaken the wizard and have him speak for his crimes."

"And you will not make the decision for us, Maximilian. You are the leader of human men only and have no power here. We have a right as much as you," Tlaloc snarled. "I say he dies."

"No one is killing anyone." Astrid slammed her fist down on the table. The wood splintered, and the table shook. "You're all five for five, so I'm casting my vote, and I say we wake him. We're not murderers. If he's truly guilty of horrible crimes, then he can answer for them, but he has the right to speak for himself. Because I am pretty damn certain that none of you, not even you, Grandma, can say that you were blameless in the past. The dragonslayers came into being for a reason—because dragons rampaged and acted like *gods*. You hurt people, you took what you wanted, and you made this necessary. We've changed over the centuries, but he doesn't know that. Not if he's been cursed."

Chloe gave her daughter a satisfied look and nodded when her husband's shoulders sagged.

Saul relented. "She is right, though it pains me to agree."

Nate sighed and slumped against the wall. He closed his eyes. "As far as I know, none of us are capable of true magic at this level. We outsource most spells to enchantresses and mid-level magicians."

Ēostre shook her head. "It smells like dark sorcery, nothing I've seen from any good witch."

"Agreed," Max said. "I know little of magic and spells, but whatever traps this wizard in his sleep is unnatural. What do you say Xochi?"

"It is a spell far beyond the scope of my control. Black mortal magic, a curse of some variety or another. I can tell you little else."

Nate shook his head. "That doesn't make sense. The knighthood doesn't condone black magic."

"But you do employ mages."

"A few, yes, for services like teleportation, health potions and tonics, and enchanted gear for our troops. No one involved in the sort of sorcery you're talking about. At least..." Nate paused and seemed to consider his words. After a moment's thought, he shook his head. "If they do, it's high level and the majority of the knights are unaware. It's against our code."

"Perhaps we should call on Loki," Ēostre suggested. "He's meddled with magic beyond even my understanding."

Max gave a vehement shake of his head. "No. My cousin only lives to cause mischief. He'll try and twist this to his advantage, if he can even help at all."

Nate's jaw dropped. "Loki is your cousin?"

"Indeed. A trickster and troublemaker who will be of no use to us here."

"I don't know if you've seen your cousin recently, but I have." Nate hesitated a split second before pressing on. "While on assignment. He was as benign as a kitten."

"Benign? Kitten?" Max stared hard at him. "I think you must have watched the wrong dragon."

"No. I'm certain. Another knight agreed, and he's been doing this a decade longer than me this life cycle," Nate insisted. "If the rest of you can change, isn't he capable of the same?"

"You speak with great wisdom, young one," Ēostre said.

Licking his lips nervously, Nate looked to each dragon in turn. "I can't believe I'm saying this, but for the past thirty years of my life, I've been raised to think the worst of your race. Astrid showed me a side I didn't know could exist—that you're people capable of change and great things. I've read the books on you, Mr. Emberthorn. Your hands aren't clean either. Even Tlaloc is known for receiving sacrifices atop temples, but he's changed."

"Mahasti, could you please ask Loki to join us?" Saul asked after several long minutes. "Tell him it is of great importance."

The rest waited in awkward silence as Mahasti teleported away. Through it all, Astrid had never lost her grip on Nate's hand. She'd hoped it went unnoticed and was sure it had until Saul glowered at her boyfriend again.

"Have you attempted to place your mark on him, Astrid?"

"Mark?" Nate's eyes widened slightly. "What mark?"

"No," Astrid answered in a soft voice. Saul seemed to relax until she turned to Nate. "It's part of what I was telling you about, with soul mates. Dragons... they—we, I guess—mark one another. It's a magical bond. I've resisted the urge to mark you because I wanted to tell you everything about who I am and what it means, first. Because I didn't want to *force* a choice on you." She shrugged and glanced away, aware of her father's stare.

After marking her mother in a dank, rain-filled cave, Saul had no right to remark on her relationship.

"Might I suggest saving this conversation for a more private venue?" her grandmother asked. The storm dragoness's warm touch landed at the small of Astrid's back. Ēostre's other hand settled against Nate's shoulder.

Astrid loved her grandmother even more for her unvoiced display of acceptance.

Before anyone else could speak, Mahasti and Loki made a surprising entrance to the dining room. Max made no effort to conceal his disbelief. Astrid knew what he thought of Loki. According to her grandfather, the sorcerer dragon was a loose cannon, an immature liability to them all.

"Loki, thank you for joining us. As you can see, we are in need of your expertise. Meet Merlin." Saul gestured to the wizard on the sofa.

A business suit clothed Loki's lean frame and he wore his dark hair loose around his shoulders. Astrid had never seen him looking anything less than his very best. He and her father appeared to be of similar age in their mid to late thirties, while she would never assume Max to be a day over forty-five.

Years ago, in her teens when she first became aware of the attractive qualities in the opposite sex, she'd harbored a crush on the dragon god of mischief, adoring his green eyes whenever she saw him on magazine covers and newspapers. She hadn't dared to breathe a word of it, as none of the adults ever spoke favorably of him.

Now she had a better man to adore. Her fingers briefly tightened over Nate's hand.

Loki studied their group with skepticism before his attention fell to Merlin. "And for what reason would you call me to the company of a dragonslayer and his master?" he asked, seeing straight through to Nate's identity.

Nate flinched and looked away.

"Supposedly, killing him will end all dragonslayers," Saul told him.

"Information Nate gave us freely," Chloe added.

"And yet the wizard is very much alive," Loki said dryly.

"I wasn't able to do it," Astrid said. "And when we entered his lair, I noticed Merlin was trapped in a spell."

"So I see. And you seem to believe there's something I can do to resolve the issue."

Max made a disgruntled noise of disgust in his throat. "As I said. Far be it for my cousin to think of anyone but himself. He hasn't changed, and shall always be—"

"I'll do it," Loki interrupted. He shouldered past Max without looking at him and moved up to the sofa bearing the wizard. His eyes narrowed as he watched the motionless body trapped in a state of stasis. "But it's more than a spell. He's been poisoned."

Ēostre's eyes darted toward Loki in alarm. "If it were poison, I would have seen."

"This is a different poison. A contamination of the spirit as much as the body. Call it a curse, if you will. You wouldn't recognize it unless you knew exactly what to look for." His index and middle fingers touched Merlin's throat, then pressed inward and parted the skin. It gave away like putty beneath his touch, but no blood flowed to the surface. When he withdrew his digits, the wizard was unharmed, his flesh whole again, but a golfball sized, glistening beetle twitched between Loki's fingers. It hissed, the noise a high-pitched, ear-splitting wail that made even Nate squint his eyes in pain and clap both hands over his ears.

Bile rose in Astrid's throat. She stared at the grotesque insectoid, stomach turning. "What is that?"

Loki shrugged. "A remnant of Salem, the souls of several black witches condensed into a single dark entity given physical form."

The agonizing wail came to an abrupt end, its source squashed in Loki's fist.

"Really? On my Persian rug?" Chloe put her hands on her hips, but it was easy to see her relief that the noise was gone.

"Perhaps you would have preferred if I set it loose in your garden? I'll reconstruct it if you'd like."

Chloe grimaced. "Um, no."

"Now what?" Max asked, more curious than gruff.

"He's still asleep, and will be for a short while yet," Loki answered. "With no way to determine how long he's endured the poisoning, he could be asleep for days."

"Then we should keep a watch on him at all times, at least three of us," Max said.

"I will take up the first watch," Loki offered. "I'd like to study our guest."

Before Astrid could volunteer her aid, Chloe turned to her and set both hands on her daughter's shoulders. "While the dragons draw straws to determine who watches over the wizard, I'm tucking you into bed."

"Mom—"

"You were shot, young lady. Dragon or not, you're going to rest." She glanced at Nathan. "And we certainly can't kick you out if you've betrayed your knighthood."

Saul stared. "Chloe—"

"They'll be looking for him, Saul. My mind is made."

Chloe dragged them both toward the stairs where she shoved Nate toward a spare guestroom.

"Mrs. Drakenstone, it isn't necessary."

"You're someone's son, and I'd want someone to look after mine if he were in trouble."

Accepting no further argument, Chloe guided Astrid along to her old bedroom at the end of the hall. "As for you, missy, I'll run you a bath if you'd like, and we can discuss Nate."

The door shut behind Ēostre, who entered behind them. "Ah, good, you read my mind."

Astrid groaned. "I can't handle this with both of you. This is a pain worse than bullet wounds."

"Too bad. Now strip and get in the tub."

Her grandmother smiled. "I agree with your mother, young woman. We may have used our magic to expedite your healing, but your body still requires rest and time to heal internally."

They let her settle in the water before they tag-teamed her, both women taking a seat at her vanity. Astrid wanted to sink beneath the bubble-covered water until they left, but she spoke her mind instead.

"I love him, and I'm not going to leave him if that's what you all want."

"Honey, I'm hurt you'd even think I'd ask that." Chloe gave her a wounded look, pouting.

"And Dad?"

Chloe sat up straighter. "Your father and I talked. He's agreed that you're capable of making your own choices."

Astrid's wary gaze darted between her mom and grandmother. "Then what do you two want to talk to me about?"

"Your Nate is human," Ēostre began. "His lifespan will be short, sweetheart."

"Mom's human. So is Aunt Marcy."

"Yes, but we carried dragon babies, and that's changed something in us. Unless things get crazy in the future, I don't see him giving birth in your place anytime soon."

"So what are you saying?"

Ēostre left her seat and settled on the ledge of the tub with a comb from Astrid's vanity. Her fingers glided over the damp, golden strands before she dragged the comb through her loose curls. "I came to say your grandfather and I are on your side no matter who you love, and not to waste one moment with your Nate."

Astrid blinked up at her. "You did?"

"I know the pain of losing your bonded mate. I also know the blessed fortune of finding a second. I want you to know that I will be here for you, no matter what happens."

"Fifty or sixty years with the man you love is better than none, sweetie. Do what makes you happy," Chloe said. "Honestly, your father never likes any of your boyfriends. Nate could be another dragon and he'd still side-eye him."

A laugh bubbled out, taking out the last, lingering remnants of tension. She swiped at her eyes and gave her mom a smile. "You think so?"

"Of course. You're his baby girl, and no man, ever, will live up to his dragon-high expectations." Chloe grinned. "At least, not that he'll ever admit. I'm pretty sure Nate's selfless attempt at sacrifice impressed him."

"Grandma?"

"Yes, darling?"

"You said you met Nate before in his other life… was he a good person then, too?"

"The legends say Sir Galahad was one of King Arthur's purest knights. For once, legends spoke truly. He was, and still seems to be, an honorable man," Ēostre answered.

"He really is," Astrid mused. She hesitated and spoke up shyly, "Mom, do you remember when you had the whole sex talk with me eleven years ago, and we talked about bonding?"

Chloe grimaced. "That was awful."

Sexuality was a large part of shifter culture and openly discussed, not some dirty secret to be shared in whispers only. She'd been fourteen when her parents sat her down for "the talk" and spared few details. Her father had been straightforward and honest, her mother understanding and sympathetic when Astrid asked why she didn't resemble other fourteen-year-old girls.

Contrary to her father's treatment of her boyfriends over the years, she'd never felt pressured to remain a virgin. They had told her only she would know when she was ready to have sex, to take a mate, and start a family of her own.

"But what about it, hon?"

"Well, you marked Daddy. I've seen his and Uncle Teo's brands, but do you think it's because you carried me or because you have part of Daddy's soul from your bonding?"

"I honestly don't know. I didn't even know I could until a few years ago," her mother admitted. "I don't know what came over me that day."

"Perhaps it was the years in Saul's company that allowed you to mark him during your anniversary reclaiming," Ēostre mused.

Her mother's wistful expression made Astrid uncomfortable. While happy for them, she didn't want to imagine her parents having sex. At all. She shuddered.

"I want what you both have."

"Then go for it," Chloe encouraged. "You never know, there's always the possibility that marking him and sharing part of your essence is what changes him."

"But you and Aunt Marcy—"

Chloe shook her head. "Looking back, I honestly can't tell a difference between Marcy's wedding photos and now. At least a couple of years passed between their bond and her deciding to have Javier. Maybe we've made the wrong assumptions all this time."

"Your mother is right, Astrid. Your situation is unique, and we'll never know until you try. But regardless of whether he can seal the bond in return to remain with you for more than mere decades, love your Nate now while the time is yours."

Sometime after her mother and grandmother excused themselves from the room, she rinsed beneath the shower and pulled on pajamas. She crawled beneath the sheets with hopes of confronting Nate with her feelings the next day. Ēostre was right; any time spent loving him was better than none.

For a long while, Astrid tossed and turned in her bed. With her rollercoaster emotions riding a cruel wave between anticipation and relief, sleep remained elusive.

Her parents would welcome him, and all that remained was Nate accepting them in return.

Around midnight, she shrugged into her robe and tiptoed to the stairs. A casual minute of eavesdropping picked up the sound of Max chastising Saul and Teo. Once certain most of the household had gathered around Merlin for the night's vigil, she returned to the hall and padded into the guestroom.

She had a loose plan, but it mostly involved getting it through his thick head that she was a big girl who knew her own heart. He could either accept that she loved him—truly loved him—or they needed a quick, clean break before she was hurt any deeper. She hoped he didn't opt for the second.

***

Nate's senses screamed at him, a reminder of the multiple hostile dragons downstairs. Tlaloc and Saul would have been happy to pull him apart like a battered Mr. Potato Head.

He'd tried to sleep unsuccessfully for hours before resorting to looking at his phone and willing it to ring. He worried about his dog and his mother, as well as the welfare of his friends. Percivale or Lancelot had been absent at the tomb and weren't among the shooters. He didn't want to blow their cover and put them at odds with Kay yet by phoning them.

A text to his elderly neighbor put his mind about Echo at ease. He made up an emergency and thanked them for taking her.

When the door creaked open just after midnight, he knew the intruder would be one of the big dragon's come to floss his teeth with Nate's pathetic human body. He didn't have the strength to fight one of them.

"Nate?" Astrid whispered into the dark room. "Are you awake?"

She didn't wait for him to respond. She shut the door behind her and crossed the room to sit on the edge of the bed.

"I'm awake." His bloody, torn T-shirt and jeans were on the floor.

After showering, he'd tentatively tested the genie's powers by wishing for an assortment of clothes in his size. She'd been unable to fetch anything from his apartment. The condo where he dwelled was one of the properties owned by the order, and so she wasn't able to cross the protective boundaries. To rectify the dilemma, neat piles of new clothes appeared on the dresser with the tags still attached. The genie had known his preferences down to size and brand.

"Good. We need to talk." Astrid drew in a quick breath and pushed on before he had a chance to say anything. "Marking a mate and making them yours isn't a trivial matter. It's also no minor thing to find the other half of your heart and soul."

Tension dropped like an anchored weight in the pit of his stomach. "Uh. Well, I see we're going to hop right to the point."

"Yes," she agreed. "Because I've spent months putting it off and I'm not wasting another precious second."

Anticipating this conversation, he'd rehearsed what he would say a dozen times. As he sat up in bed, the words came easily. "I hurt you very badly, Astrid, and I don't know if love can flourish from a relationship built on lies."

"I've been thinking about that, too. It wasn't all a lie. I still got to know you. Not you the dragonslayer of times past, but the real you now. Not Galahad, but Nate. You're still that man. A man who loves his dog and enjoys the beach. A man who chills with a couple drinks in front of an action movie and brings me groceries when I have cramps."

Back in June, he'd kindly dropped off Chinese takeout, eggs, milk, and bread for her while she languished in bed. The memory cut through the solemn mood, and Nate laughed. "That was months ago and only once."

"It doesn't matter. Once was enough to know you care. You impressed Charlie."

"Even if we did make this work, I'll be an old man one day. That's only if I survive this ordeal with the knighthood and Merlin doesn't snap the magic binding me to the living world like a dry twig."

"I'd rather enjoy my time with you—any time with you. I wouldn't kill Merlin in his sleep because it was wrong, but I won't hesitate to shred him to pieces if he tries to harm you."

"I know. I'm glad you didn't." Deep down, Nate didn't believe he could have run the old man through either. Did that make him a good man or a dumb fool? He sighed and dipped his head to look at the lavish, Egyptian cotton sheets pooled around his waist.

"You're too good a person to kill a defenseless man," Astrid whispered, as if able to read his mind.

"So I'm the model of chivalry and all that's right in the knighthood. So what? What happens when I die, Astrid? It isn't a matter of if, but when. Maybe the heir of Isildur can pull off marrying an immortal, but I've got a few decades in me if I'm lucky." His voice softened after his attempted humor. "Forever is a long time to live with a dead bondmate, Astrid."

"Your nerdy Lord of the Rings references are part of why I love you, you know." She paused a moment and her solemn gaze seemed to peer into his soul. "I had a dream. Call it a future vision, I guess. I had moved on past you, found someone else, but I wasn't happy. Not the same way you make me happy."

Nate sighed and, against his better judgment and all of his wisdom, eased his arm around Astrid's waist to draw her into his lap. The size discrepancy between her enormous dragon body and slight, almost waifish human form bewildered him. The only similarity had been the golden sheen of her scales and her bright blue eyes. "I'm afraid you'll resent me once I'm old."

"You don't think I'm scared? That I worry about what will happen to us? I do. But I also know I'd regret it my entire life if I didn't love you and spend whatever time we had together."

Could he bind her to a possible eternity of living alone, mourning her lost mate? He grasped at straws, seeking any wisdom in his memories to alleviate the difficulty of his choice. Nothing came. After a time of holding Astrid, he lowered his brow to her shoulder and sighed.

"I don't think I'm selfless enough to walk away from you, but I'd be lying if I said your father doesn't terrify me."

"He terrifies everyone." Finally, she laughed, a small little sound as she leaned her cheek against his head. "Really, though, all he wants is what any father wants—to see his baby happy. Protected. Loved." She lifted a hand to his face, turning his gaze up to hers. "You make me happy. Isn't that enough for us to hold on to?"

"I do love you. And I'd fight any of the knights to protect you." And maybe he'd have to in the end. Something told him they hadn't seen the last of Kay and Bedivere, or their lackeys.

His grip on Astrid tightened as he tried to think like the man who had raised him and anticipate Kay's next move. They wouldn't have much time before Kay brought the battle to them.

"Then please stop pushing me away."

There were many ways to show forgiveness, but kissing him was the best one of all. The gentle brush of her lips against his mouth followed Astrid's quiet plea. Her hands framed his face, thumb stroking over his jaw, and the shadow of dark brown stubble. His arm tightened around her waist, and at the end, he gazed at her with only the dim, silver light through the window highlighting her features.

"Then I'm yours." The words scared him as much as the possibility of fighting Kay, a dragonslayer who had already honed his powers and regained all of his knightly talents. Gliding his fingers over her ribs, he searched where bright stains of red had glistened against her dragon skin. "I'll kill them for hurting you."

"Better me than you. Scales are a lot hardier than human flesh."

"They didn't seem to help you that much," he pointed out. She'd flown for their lives while bleeding profusely from multiple wounds. The realization struck him, and respect for her leaped to a new level of awe. Suppressing the fears of what could have happened, he relished the warm and alive woman in bed with him now, fingers gliding over her legs.

As his touch traveled over fair, silky smooth skin, Astrid seemed to recognize his lack of clothing. Her palms smoothed over his bare chest and across his shoulders. In the next span of thought, she shrugged out of her robe and pulled her nightgown over her head, revealing herself to him.

He'd crawled beneath the sheets in only his boxers, and they were useless between them, a thin layer of irritating cotton between her weight and his arousing cock. He groaned against her lips, barely able to turn his face away.

"Your dad's downstairs." Hell, her entire family was downstairs.

Astrid pressed closer. "I don't care," she whispered. "I'll sleep with my boyfriend if I want to."

Her movement, whether intentional or not, teased the tips of her breasts against his chest. He cupped one gentle swell and circled the stiff peak with his thumb, ending his protests. "God."

"Did you mean it? About being mine? Do you really, truly mean it?"

"I'll never tell another lie to you again." A palpable rush of excitement sent his heart into a racing rhythm. Hers. Neither Astrid or her mother had described in detail the strange ritual that bound dragons to their mates, but anticipation overwhelmed the minute apprehension urging him to flee.

Kissing her was a sweet drug, each taste of her lips as delicious as the last. He delighted in every second, tracing her mouth with a subtle probe before his playful dragoness sucked the tip of his tongue.

Her kiss deepened, aggressive and claiming in the end, the ferocity of her desire taking him by surprise. He raised the stakes and guided her fingers to the opening of his shorts. Then sweet relief came when slender fingers curled around his cock and coaxed it into the open air.

"Yours," he repeated. "Every inch. You know what to do with it, don't you, baby?"

A rumble echoed through her chest. She ripped their garments with the ease of tissue paper, and within seconds, they were skin against skin.

"Mine."

"I need to teach you patience," he murmured against her lips, unsurprised to lose his shorts. At the same time, he should have known better than to expect restraint from her.

It was part of why he loved her, part of why she had become irresistible.

"Screw patience."

She took the lead, straddling his lap and guiding the head of his cock between her spread thighs. He found her wet and inviting, the heat beckoning him to plunge within. Before he could, Astrid thrust her hips forward, sheathing him in her body's tight embrace.

"Mine," she growled again. Her hips rolled, and he arched up beneath her, thrusting as the intensifying pleasure threatened to consume him. He groaned a pitiful sound, startled by her enraptured claim.

"I—fuck," Nate hissed out between his teeth.

How was she so wet so soon? They'd made love countless times, but he'd never experienced such frenzy or loss of control from her.

"Don't stop, baby," he encouraged while resting both of his hands on her hips. He leaned back, entranced with the fluid movement connecting them anew after each sensual lift. Whether or not they were doing the right thing ceased to matter. He needed her in all ways, as addicted to his lover's bestial side as her laughter and coy smiles.

Her head fell to his shoulder, face against his throat to deliver kisses and playful nibbles. She lingered over his pulse long enough to leave a pink mark, tasting its beat beneath her tongue. Then she moved across his shoulder.

"Mine," she declared again. Pleasure and pain followed a sharp nip. "Tell me you're mine again, Nate. Tell me you want me as much as I want you. Tell me that I'm yours."

At some point in their relationship, his fear of her teeth had vanished. Instead, he relished the moment and tilted his head. His dick had never been so hard in all of his life, and a vague sense of awareness lurked at the edge of his mind that something magical was unfolding. Something otherworldly and unlike anything he'd ever experienced in all of his many lives. The hairs on his arms rose, and his skin tingled, hypersensitive to each graze from her small teeth.

One thrust of her hips remained between Nate's hard cock and blowing his load, trapping him on the precipice of losing control. Part of him wanted to savor it, but the other half cried out to her for relief.

"Yours. All yours. I couldn't give you up, Astrid."

The bite seized him without warning. Hard teeth clamped down at the curve between his neck and shoulder, and she shuddered around him in the first throes of a powerful orgasm. His breath left him in a hiss. The crackling thrum of her claiming ripped through him, burning bright. Elation wrapped with burning desire flooded through every nerve ending.

Astrid's teeth startled him more than they hurt, but the pulse of her climax drew his attention from the pain. Contrasting elements of pain and ecstasy became his only existence. She'd never felt so sweet around him, so enticing and undeniable.

Long after the final ripple from her body, he was still moving, hard as a pillar of polished stone.

"I need more," Nate moaned. "What did you do to me?" The exposure of cool air against his shoulder burned as if he'd been scalded or out in the sun too long.

"I marked you. My soul and yours, one, forever bound together." Her voice came out as delicate pants against his skin, kisses making their way up from her brand to his jaw. "I've claimed you. Now claim me, however you want. Make me yours."

Shifting his weight to one side, he rolled to tuck Astrid beneath him and slid free. "However I want?"

"However you want. I want you to make me yours."

She did belong to him, and he didn't need more sex to prove it. Wanting it was another matter.

"God, I'm so hard," he groaned, both impressed and distraught with his own virility.

Her hand roamed until she found his cock, and he made a strained, inhuman sound when she caressed the slick skin and fondled his balls. "Mm, yes you are."

"Astrid, I'm not a shifter, I can't mark you."

"You can. I shared part of my soul with you, Nate. I don't know how it works, but…"

"But what?"

"We should try," she said shyly.

"I wouldn't know where to begin."

"Trust your instincts. Give in to them."

Instincts, right. Because that told him what to do.

"Okay," he agreed.

His instincts told him to kiss her, beginning with sweet lips and descending to an even more delectable body. His girl had breasts worthy of worship, so he sucked one tender peak into his mouth and lavished it with attention while his palm rasped over its twin. He prolonged her suffering and made her wait, even as the swollen ache throbbing from his groin urged him to guide it home inside her.

"Nate. I can't wait. I need you inside me again."

He didn't answer, his mouth occupied with shifting to the other nipple, making her a hot, writhing mess on the disheveled sheets.

Craving more of her, he slipped lower between her parted thighs. With a pause to kiss the slick pearl at the center of her pleasure, he flicked it with the tip of his tongue and savored her flavor. He breathed her in and buried his face between her thighs, devouring her with the gusto of a starved man.

Astrid cried out and jerked her hips from the mattress when his lips sealed around her clit. He circled it with his tongue, driving her to grasp the sheets wildly.

The desire to join with Astrid became undeniable, the throb in his dick intensifying to a violent discomfort. Whatever she'd wanted to do to him with her claiming—it had worked, instilling mindless need for satisfaction. Her mouth fell open, and her head tilted back as he entered her with two fingers to test her wetness. Soaked. So slippery they passed in with ease.

His hips returned to her pelvis, and he gazed down at her with reverence. "I wanted you from the first time I saw you."

He joined them again without rushing their reunion, despite the burning in his veins as if every nerve fiber had been lit aflame.

Control, he told himself, refusing to give in. He drew it out at his leisure, an inch-by-inch tease slowly stretching her to his girth, all the while worshipping her with his mouth, tracing the curve of her shoulders and the gentle slope of her breasts.

His dragon was perfect from head to toe. The realization came as a delight eagerly voiced for her.

"My dragon," he breathed against her neck. "I don't regret a thing, Astrid." If he hadn't taken the stupid mission, he'd have never met her, never fallen in love.

He couldn't allow them to take her away. He felt changed in an indescribable way with a new sensation of strength flooding through him. He became insatiable for her, hungering for the next kiss, desperate for each subsequent thrust.

He'd broken every rule. Lied to his brothers. Betrayed them. Protected her. And he'd do none of it differently with exception to telling her earlier how he felt.

***

"Yours, Nate. Forever, yours."

The desperate lovemaking three mornings ago—when Nate claimed her beside the condo's front door—came back to her in a rush of memory. She shivered. He'd been raw and primal, much like a shifter then, taking what he wanted from her, and giving everything in return.

This time, he was tender. Gentle. Thorough.

Astrid closed her eyes and writhed beneath him. The sheets scrunched up in her hands

Sweet ancestors, he had a demanding libido, her god of lust and debauchery. His fingers teased the tiny button his lips had kissed, coaxing her to orgasm before he even reached the pinnacle to join her.

The slick length of him slid free, and he withdrew to his knees between her thighs. Bewildered, Astrid flicked her eyes up to his face. Perspiration glistened on his broad shoulders and beaded on his temples. She watched his chest heave and the defined muscles of his torso flex as a trickle of sweat glided over his abs.

"Where are you going?" she cried out in protest.

"I'm not going anywhere," he growled, wiping his brow with the back of a wrist. "And neither are you."

Nate's strong hands flipped her over. The sheets wrinkled beneath her knees as he drew her back by a strong grip on her hips. Before she had a chance to ask anything else, he reclaimed his rightful place, spearing her full depth.

Yes!

Urges older than time had incited a craving for the position since they met—to be dominated by the man she chose and willingly hand over control.

She clung to the headboard with one hand as he pounded her from behind, startled by the enthusiasm of his thrusts. And so wet.

"Yes!"

"Yes what?" he demanded against her ear.

"Fuck me," she blurted out. Uttering the word was almost as satisfying as the deep, long stroke he gave in reward.

"You know how I love it when you talk dirty to me."

Heat surged to her cheeks, but the request seemed inconsequential considering their current act.

"Deeper," she commanded.

His next hard stroke brought stars to her eyes and made her toes curl up tight. The wood beneath her hands cracked and split, hardwood denting in her grip. Lights exploded in her vision, heat consumed her, and she lost herself completely to sensation. Nate didn't stop, a relentless and insatiable beast.

When she came, she didn't cry his name; she sobbed it in a shuddering breath. Her back arched and she pushed toward him with her hips, delighted by the blunt crown of his cock nestling against her sweet spot. Then his hand dropped between her thighs, and her world disintegrated into pleasure.

The experience transcended the physical aspects of sex and became more than their exchanged words of love. She felt him. His every emotion, his every guilt and passion, and his absolute adoration of who she was.

Any worry related to Nate's ability to brand her proved unfounded. As they joined flush on the next stroke, he seized her by the shoulder. The bite didn't hurt, but it seared her and left its impression on her soul. Her thighs trembled, and his arm around her middle became the only thing holding Astrid upright.

"Nate!"

Bliss. The only word to describe what she felt was bliss. Exquisite sensation ripped through her from head to toe, bringing a rush of euphoria beyond anything delivered during their previous couplings. Her legs trembled and shook as she was swept along for the ride.

One sharp tug on her hair drew her head back, the angle bordering on pain. Nate's mouth crushed down over hers with bruising force. His release brought an additional edge to her ongoing orgasm, a pleasure so strong it threatened to drag her under. When Nate released her, she gasped for air, and as one, they sank against the bed, bodies sticky with sweat. He moaned and buried his face against her hair, his body first stiff and then shuddering as he came.

"I love you," she whispered while they lay together in silence. "I love you so much, Nate, and I'll treasure every moment we have over any jewel in my hoard."

"And I love you."

Somehow they both found the strength to reposition, moving only enough to twine in close, face to face. Nate enveloped her in his arms and held her close against his chest.

"Why do I want you again already?" he moaned against her hair. "Every time I think you can't surprise me anymore, you prove me wrong, Astrid."

"Mmmm. That's either your desire… or mine. I'm not sure. But with the bond comes a sharing of self. I feel what you feel, and vice versa." She managed enough energy to lift her head and nip his chin, then fell back again and closed her eyes. "I just want to curl up with you and fall asleep. Forget our worries and go away somewhere."

"Being with you, Astrid, it's…" He sighed. "Good isn't an adequate word to describe how happy I am with you."

"I kinda want a shower," she muttered.

"Me too."

"But I'm too tired to move."

"I won't tell anyone if you won't."

Chapter 16

If the circumstances were normal, there wouldn't be anything in the world capable of dragging Astrid out of bed. Nate had managed to draw the duvet over them before she crawled against his spine and snuggled her face against the back of his shoulder.

Initially, Nate had laughed at her unusual preference for being the "big spoon" when they slept. Then he'd adjusted and grown accustomed to her arms around him. Her mate was better than any teddy bear.

A few dappled beams of sunlight penetrated the guestroom, gleaming between slats in the blinds. After a groggy raise of her head, she noticed a peculiar buzzing, the strange static sensation crawling over her skin.

"Nate?"

He made an incoherent, bearlike noise.

Although she had no desire to crawl from beside her new mate, she recognized more urgent matters required their attention. There was something in the air, an electric sensation raising the hair on her arms and neck.

She shook his arm. "Nate, get up. I think Merlin's leaving his sleep. Something changed."

"But I'm tired," he mumbled against her pillow. "So damn tired."

Astrid couldn't blame him. Shifting on the bed, she stretched her aching limbs and eased onto her back to stare at the ceiling. Everything hurt.

Crush

I hope Merlin doesn't wake up to have a temper tantrum in our living room.

What the hell was she going to do if he did? Hobble away from his lightning bolts and fireballs? Maybe they wouldn't hurt. She was part fire dragon after all.

For a moment longer, she relished her time in bed beside Nate with only a light duvet covering their bare skin. Then responsibility urged her to push onto an elbow and peer down at him. "Are you coming or not?"

"Did too much of that last night. That's why I can't move now."

Her brows furrowed. "Smartass."

"Part of my charm," he muttered. "Go on without me. I'll be there soon."

"Your choice, but do you want your beloved sage to awaken alone in a room full of dragons?" Astrid tickled her fingers across his ribs.

His feeble swat didn't remove her hand. "Someone else is welcome to receive a faceful of fireballs when he wakes up surrounded by the enemy. No thanks." She persisted until he raised his head to drowsily focus on her face. "Can I at least get dressed or are you going to rush me down there with my dick out, too?"

She leaned down and peppered his face with kisses. "No, I am not. That's for my eyes only, thank you very much."

"I promise I'm getting up, but it's going to take a second, and I wanna shower alone. I don't trust you to keep your hands to yourself."

Astrid sniffed in disdain. "I need to hop across the hall for my clothes so you are quite allowed to shower in peace."

Despite his teasing and slothful comments, Astrid sensed the truth beneath Nate's behavior. Apprehension rolled through him, and via their link, it reached her too. He was afraid, and with good reason, wary of what they would encounter below.

After she showered away the smell of their sex and donned fresh clothing, she emerged from her room to find Nate pacing the hall. She'd taken longer than usual, first dragging a brush through her hair then suppressing the queasy feeling created from his worries.

He smiled when he saw her. "About time. Weren't you the one rushing me?"

Astrid ran her fingers down the front of his shirt. "You misbuttoned." She corrected it then raised to her toes and kissed him. "I love you. No matter what happens, we'll get through this."

"You're right."

But it didn't make him any less nervous, and by proxy, it didn't help Astrid either. "Come on. The wizard awaits."

Their arrival couldn't be at a more appropriate time. When Nate and Astrid stepped into the living room, it was to the sight of the old man stirring on the couch and a group of intrigued, eager dragons positioned at various points in the room for a tactical advantage. Loki, Ēostre, and Max—the most powerful of them—stood closest to the wizard. The distrustful Tlaloc and his wife near the door, while Chloe, Saul, and Teo lingered at the room's edges. As a human, Chloe remained in Merlin's direct line of sight. Maybe they thought her presence would help.

"What place is this? How did I arrive here?"

His voice, gruff from disuse, wheezed and preceded a cough. He rose unsteadily, revealing the frailty of his old body. Or maybe he required the support of his staff. Without the famed item, his back appeared hunched. His gaze darted around the room, going from face to face, and settled on Nate.

"Galahad?" His brows furrowed. "No, not yet, are you… I see him there, in your face, but not fully in your eyes."

No magical explosions. No lances of electricity. Astrid took it as a good sign and stepped forward since Nate appeared to be in a state of stunned speechlessness.

"My name is Astrid Drakenstone. Nate," she squeezed his hand, "and I rescued you from your resting place, where magic imprisoned you."

Merlin stared at them. His gaze traveled from their faces to their joined hands, then to the other solemn figures around the room. "You are dragons. Have the knights, then, given up hunting your kind?"

Appearing to recover from the awe of seeing the great sage awakened and on his feet for the first time in his life, Nate spoke, "No, sir, far from it. We've been directed all these years, in your name, to finish exterminating them."

The old man blinked, then a scowl twisted his lips. "No, not in my name. The extinction of dragonkind was never my goal. Never my intention. They are as much creatures of magic as I am, and balance would be lost from the world should they all perish."

Everyone in the room let out a collective, relieved breath.

Nate started from the beginning. He told Merlin about the current order and their goals. Their targets. Their recent kills. Astrid remained at his side the entire time, aware of the thick tension rolling off the other dragons. Friends and loved ones had been killed, and while Nate himself hadn't been party to their deaths, their anger and pain painted him guilty by association. Tlaloc looked over twice, fury in his dark eyes.

Discussing Fafnir, Hermes, and Watatsumi tore open mending wounds, threatening the indifferent atmosphere.

When he finished his tale, Merlin shook his head and turned toward the nearest door. "There is much to do. Many wrongs to right. Betrayals to repay," the old wizard said with renewed vigor in his voice. "Kay's actions will not go unpunished."

Nate immediately side-stepped in front of the wizard. "I mean no offense, but you've been asleep for a century. You'll break a hip or something if you hurry out there," he said. "Why don't you sit down for a few while we catch you up on the last century?"

Merlin drew himself up into a proud, stiff-spined stance. His body creaked, and it clearly caused him discomfort. "I am Merlin, young man. I shall not 'break a hip.'"

Nate resembled a little boy, chastised and flushed. "I don't know how to tell you this, sir, but the times have changed since you last walked among humans. They've got cruise missiles, fighter jets, drones. Starbucks. It's dangerous out there."

Teo nodded sympathetically. "Starbucks is a great weakness for many."

"Besides," Astrid chimed in, "your robes would draw attention. No one dresses like that anymore unless they're going to Renn Fair."

"So I see…"

The wizard pursed his lips, looked around at the gathered men—Loki in particular—then clapped his hands together twice. Blue smoke swirled up from his feet and around his head. When it cleared, his robes were gone, replaced by a well-tailored, cream-colored suit. He wore an unbuttoned linen jacket over a rich, plum velvet waistcoat and lavender shirt with a purple plaid tie. Brown, Italian leather loafers, and a mahogany walking stick topped with a copper owl completed his look.

"Damn," was all Nate had to say.

Astrid stared, and beside her, Loki's mouth fell open.

"I hate you, old man," the dragon muttered enviously. "This suit was a one of a kind design." Grudgingly, he added, "But I must admit you wear it better."

"Agreed. Though I hate to say it, waist-length beards are not a thing anymore unless you're impersonating Saint Nicholas over the holidays or a member of the Amish community," Maximilian said.

"Or in a motorcycle gang," Chloe added.

"Ah." Merlin snapped, and his magnificent beard morphed into a neatly groomed shape around his jaw, two feet shorter in length. His hair became collar length silver waves. "Acceptable?"

"Quite," Saul replied.

"By all appearances, you are certainly prepared to re-enter society, but how do you feel?" Loki asked. "You've been under the effects of a violent curse for several human lifetimes."

"I've certainly suffered a loss of magic, but this is a temporary setback," Merlin admitted. "I require my belongings and access to my lair."

"If all of your spell books and tools are behind in your lair, they're as good as lost. I wouldn't put it past Kay and the others to have raided your hideout to cripple your effectiveness if we awakened you."

"That treacherous worm," Merlin said, "is to blame for my extended sleep. In my dreams, I saw him curse me with the aid of a dark witch."

"We suspected as much. Loki recognized the spell and removed it," Nate said. "If I may ask, why didn't you wake up to stop Kay if you saw them doing it?"

"I could not. I suspect he had prepared for a very long time. When I went to my rest, a great weariness came over me beyond what was typical. At the time, I thought nothing of it. We had defeated a great army, and I had taxed my magic to its limits. Now, though, I wonder if more was at play."

"Poison perhaps," Ēostre ventured.

Merlin nodded. "Yes, I believe so."

"Where is Arthur?" Nate asked.

Merlin's jaw tensed. "Kay has imprisoned him. He and the witch acted shortly after they incapacitated me and murdered him in cold blood. Through my dreams, I watched, incorporeal and helpless, as they bound his spirit in a stone."

Max and Ēostre made eye contact.

"Grandma," Astrid said in a whisper, "wasn't Grandpa Fafnir's spirit bound in a gem, too, by a dark witch."

"Yes. Agnes had a small collection of such objects, but we freed all the trapped souls we found."

"Which means Arthur's must not have been one of them," Astrid said.

"Then you know of the dark one who cast this foul curse upon me."

"She's dead. A dragoness murdered her to conceal those particular wrongdoings," Loki replied. Maximilian turned to him and opened his mouth, but his cousin waved it off with a soft-spoken, "This is a conversation for another time."

Nate rubbed his hand down his face. "I may have seen it, but I had no idea what it was at the time."

"Describe it," Ēostre requested.

"He wears this pendant with an enormous ruby jewel, and it's always dangling from a chain he wears under his shirt. I asked him about it once when I was a kid, and he told me it came from a lover he had in a past life."

Ēostre nodded. "It may be Arthur's bound spirit. We must acquire this."

"If Kay knows I am awake, he will take steps to ensure he remains in control. We mustn't allow him the luxury of time."

"Everyone isn't loyal to him. I think Percivale and Lancelot are waiting for something like this."

"The three of you and Sir Bors were always among the most dutiful and resolute of Arthur's knights, and I sense all four of you live at present. Can they be located and brought here?"

"Now hold on a moment," Saul protested. "While I have been forced to accept one slayer here, I am not certain I feel comfortable bringing his more experienced and bloodied brethren into my home."

Astrid stepped over and set her hands against Saul's arm. "Daddy, we need them. Go ahead and call your friends, Nate."

Her father grumped but offered no further complaints. Chloe patted his back in sympathy.

Nate remained silent as he fired off a text to his fellow knights. After several exchanged messages, his shoulders sagged and he glanced up at the others.

"They've agreed to meet and discuss it. They'll phone me when they decide what to do, but in the meantime, they're clearing out their lockers and getting the hell out of dodge where the order is concerned. Kay's been up to some shady shit."

While the other dragons expressed their skepticism, Ēostre flashed a sunny smile at her fellow dragons then Merlin. "Then I suggest we all use this time to rest and cool our heads. Preferably over tea." The epitome of serenity, she turned and strolled from the room. Max, and eventually the others, followed.

***

Once Astrid left Nate's company to chat with her mother and father about their recent bonding, the other dragons chose to assemble in the pastures to sate their immense appetites. Max had wisely suggested for Tlaloc to eat and return to his human form before the trigger-happy and paranoid dragonslayers arrived and feared they had been drawn into a setup.

With their shapeshifting new allies divided around the property, Chloe guided Nate and Merlin to Saul's man cave and left them unattended after serving them glasses of sweet tea. She promised to return with a meal for both.

Nate had to admit his new father-in-law had style. The leather sectional created an L-shape with an enormous chaise able to comfortably seat two or three people. At Chloe's insistence, or rather, the insistence of his new mother-in-law, he'd kicked back in one of the two recliners to enjoy his drink.

"The dragon's wife is courteous," Merlin remarked after she served them with hearty breakfasts of fried eggs, fat sausages, and English muffins. He glanced down at the armrests then in their general area in awe.

"She is," Nate agreed. Ravenous, he devoured his meal and swigged down a full glass of tea. He hadn't much to say to Merlin, while his emotions coasted down a turbulent road shifting between admiration and resentment.

"I imagine you carry many questions for me. You do not yet recall your lives from before."

Nate shook his head. "No, I haven't slain a dragon yet, and I have no intention to do so. My memories are locked away."

Merlin laughed, a deep, chortling sound. "Is that what he's been telling you all?"

Confusion knit his brows together. "It's what everyone says. What all the knights believe."

"As if I'd use murder to unlock your memories. Barbaric." Merlin scoffed and pushed his empty plate aside. "No, Galahad, each time a knight was reborn, all he had to do was sit in reflection at my resting place."

"But… how could we not know that? Why don't we remember? Percivale has been down to your tomb at least once, and I know in my heart he doesn't condone Kay's behavior."

"It is true that slaying a dragon would jolt your memories, but it has nothing to do with the target and everything to do with the scar inflicted on the soul. Any extreme act of violence would do the same. By the same token, true joy and love would also encourage those memories to come forward. The ties of family. That is why I designed the bond between the knights to tie you to one another whenever possible in each lifetime."

Nate snorted. "I hate to break it to you, but being Kay's son was a horrible experience. My memories should have returned to me when I was seven by that logic."

"It should never have been that way. I am sorry."

"Why didn't you reach out to us? You're Merlin. You're a legend."

"With the soul scavenger leaching away my magical reserves, I was unable to reach any of you to deliver an adequate warning." Merlin shook his head. "If only I hadn't placed my trust in Kay. If I had foreseen the evil that would fester in his heart, I could have prevented all of this."

"He fooled us all, it seems."

"What of you? I sense something different about you. A close tie to these dragons. Astrid in particular."

Nate spread his hands and sighed. If Merlin could sense their bond, then he wondered if the others would perceive the spiritual connection between them.

He decided he didn't care. "We're bonded. I love her. There isn't much more to say than that I suppose."

"Fascinating."

"Fascinating?"

"Indeed. Love between our kind, slayer and dragon. It is a beautiful thing, Nate, and a gift well deserved. There were times in the past when there was a tentative peace between some members of their kind and our own, but I would have never thought such a thing possible as friendship and even affection."

A delicate cough drew their attention to the djinn in the doorway. Mahasti offered them a pleasant smile. "Forgive the interruption, but your friends have entered the property. They will be here momentarily."

"Come. Let us meet them beyond Drakenstone's sanctuary and guarantee they have come in peace. I also imagine a dragon's abode is daunting, to say the least, even for a knight," Merlin said.

The dragons had beaten them to the punch. In their human shapes, they gathered outside to await the SUV coming up the private road. The vehicle parked several yards away, and Nate approached alone. Merlin waited beside Saul and Chloe.

"It's all right," Nate called out. He waved and stopped short of the vehicle. Three wary knights stepped from the SUV, bearing skeptical and reluctant expressions.

"Nate, do you swear on your sword and honor that this is no trap to lure us to the mercy of the enemy?" Bors asked.

"On my word, no harm shall come to any of you so long as peace is kept on our side."

The three men had dressed in military-grade tactical gear. They sported protective body armor and concealed weaponry, augmented by enchantments and a host of charms to repel fire and the elements.

They hadn't come without preparations of their own.

"No one is keeping me here against my will or making me lure you here. The dragons and Merlin only want to get to the truth."

"Damn. It's Merlin, after all." Lancelot hung back, staring at the assortment of dragons peppering the drive. "If you hadn't candid camera'ed a picture of him with the big black dragon in the background photo bombing the shot, I wouldn't have believed he was awake."

"Believe me, I'm still trying to reconcile it all, and I'm the one who busted him out of his cell."

Lancelot crossed his arms. "Yeah, about that. Kay is frothing. He's insisted that you're under a spell and beyond our help. Nate, he's issued a kill-on-sight order for you. Says you're a lost cause this cycle and you've got to be recycled to your next life to repair the damage they've caused."

Somehow he'd expected it, but deep down the knowledge stung. His flesh and blood father wanted him dead.

"I told him it was bullshit and I wouldn't be a party to it. That's about when you texted me."

"Thanks, Lance."

"No need to thank me for doing what's right. Though I was beginning to wonder if the dragon chick really did ensorcell you."

"It's true," Percivale agreed with a heavy sigh and drooping shoulders. "I had wondered myself, though she seems to have brought together a fine group of allies to help us make sense of this madness."

"The knighthood is completely divided, Nate," Lancelot said. "We're not the only ones who doubted Kay, but we decided for our safety, we had to get out before he realized we weren't part of his scheme."

"Tell me the dragons have a plan of their own," Bors said.

Nate grinned. "Why don't you ask them yourself? Merlin is waiting on us. All of us."

The great wyrm Tlaloc posed an intimidating figure whether in his dragon or human form. Percivale's approach faltered, eyes fastened to the black dragon's face until Nate encouraged him with a hand on his friend's shoulder.

"They will cause us no harm, and I've promised the same from the three of you."

"A truce," Lancelot agreed. "Nothing we haven't done before on occasion before Kay lost his mind."

"Exactly," Nate agreed, as a fleeting memory resurfaced, only to disintegrate like wisps of smoke. Watatsumi, Hermes, and Arthur had once combined forces in the past.

But why? He'd have to ask Merlin. He clung tenaciously to the memory and led the others to the wizard with the dragons as casual observers to the reunion.

"It is you," Lancelot whispered. He dropped down to one knee and bowed his head. Percivale and Bors followed suit. Nate remained standing.

"By the achievement of Sir Galahad and through no effort of my own," Merlin replied. He gestured with his hands for them to rise. "There is no need to bow before me. I have failed you most grievously over these years, and for that, I apologize."

Bors shook his head. "Perhaps we are the ones who failed you. If we had doubted Kay and challenged him sooner, we would have realized you would never abandon us, Merlin."

"None of this can fix what happened," Nate spoke up. "What's done is done. It's about what we can change now before anymore innocent people, dragons or otherwise, lose their lives to Kay's insanity."

"Spoken wisely, Galahad," Merlin agreed.

Percivale nodded. "Then we have to take the fight to Kay. It's our only option."

"Excellent. I hoped you would say as much," Tlaloc said. He grinned. "I look forward to dispensing justice upon this Kay."

Lancelot shook his head. "There are wards around our compound that will keep dragons from coming within five clicks of the perimeter."

"But not Astrid." Nate abhorred the idea of putting her in danger, but he wouldn't bench her either. Her eyes darted to him, widened with surprise, and then a satisfied smile came over her face.

"But not me," she agreed. "I'll fight with you."

"Excellent." Merlin clapped his hands together. "Once within the compound, I can unravel the magical defenses. Long years of cursed sleep have damaged my magical fortitude, and I will require time."

"We'll give you as much as we can," Bors said for them all.

"And we will be ready to move in when the barriers fall." Saul folded his arms against his massive chest and regarded them with cool eyes.

Lancelot licked his lips. "I know we all need to work together, but sending a horde of dragons down on our brothers?"

"We will not go in with guns blazing, so to speak," Max assured the knight. "Our focus will be Kay, and whichever knights stand with him after being given the chance to lay down their arms."

"There's going to be a lot of humans," Nate said. "They've been recruiting heavily."

"A lot of humans?" Bors repeated. "He's got his army there. Kay takes in anyone with a gripe against the supernatural willing to pick up a rifle these days."

Nate turned to his brothers and met their gazes without fear. "If he has an army, we better prepare ourselves to give him a war."

Chapter 17

Once Saul surrendered his office again to the knights and core group of dragons planning to lead the siege against Kay's compound, they squeezed behind the computer desk while Percivale slid into the chair and pulled up the facility map.

"We've got military grade weapons and tanks now. Kay stockpiles a lot of rejects from the armed forces. Some of the tech purchased by the huge defense budget tends to 'disappear' and wind up in our hands. You've got to destroy this storehouse before he can deploy any men to man the machines," Bors said, tapping a building on the screen.

"How the hell did you get all of this? Kay took all of the servers down," Lancelot said. "Claimed there was a malfunction for IT to untangle."

Nate grinned. "President Emberthorn hacked into the entire slayer database and downloaded all content before Kay realized I'd stolen his laptop and took the servers offline."

Max chuckled at the impressed looks from Bors and Lancelot.

"Then Loki decrypted some private electronic correspondence between Kay and some high-ranking members of the U.S. Government. They're trying to turn this into a second civil war. Those two are scary with a computer."

"You picked a helluva day to break in," Bors muttered. "Kay arranged a rally over a week ago. Everyone will be at the training compound. He's stirring up the Anti-Dragon Movement and prepping them for something."

"A protest or an attack?"

"As far as we knew, a protest. But after looking at all this…" Lancelot shook his head and let out a long, low whistle. "I think Kay's instigating a war."

"Hence the murder of Watatsumi. Start a war and force the government to take sides," Max said.

"Why now, though? You'll be out of office at the end of the year."

"My wager, intimidation. If he forces me to lose my cool, if he brings the horror of a supernatural attack to the public, he'll turn the citizens of the world against us. They'll beg the knights to eliminate us all."

"He nearly succeeded," Ēostre said. "Before Nathaniel arrived and offered his plan as atonement, we all considered flying to war against your people." She glanced at Nate and smiled softly, reminding him of his mother. "I am proud to know such a fine man."

"Yeah, we all are," Percivale agreed. "But I can't help but feel we're missing something."

"Agreed," Nate said.

"Hold on, what's this here?" Percivale's brows drew together as he clicked through a series of files. "This log here shows a withdrawal from the dark vault."

"The what?" Max asked.

"It's where we keep all the dangerous items accumulated over the years. Some objects are too powerful to be destroyed with ease and others too useful to risk losing forever. Like the amulet that controlled Mordred and the black knight's shield. Everything was tagged about twelve years ago and is automatically scanned if something passes through the door."

"What was taken?" Merlin asked.

Percivale double-clicked the file and read, "Crius's Cudgel."

"Why is that name familiar?" Astrid asked.

"Old Greek mythology," Loki replied.

Merlin nodded. "It is an ancient and black weapon that should not have seen the light of day. If it's been removed from the vault, it must be located and returned."

It was almost two centuries ago, though the exact date eluded Nate's memory. As Sir Galahad, he'd aged beyond having worth on the battlefield and was prized for his wisdom instead. He was a mentor then, a friend and advisor to the younger knights who regained their memories to take up arms against injustices.

Crius had been the last of the giants to walk the earth after clawing his way from the Abyss, and Arthur had entrusted his weapon to Kay at the end of the battle when Merlin was sapped of his strength. The old wizard, sagging against his powerful staff, had been aged even further by the ordeal.

Nate turned to Merlin. "It's the same weapon recovered by Arthur two centuries ago. You expended all of your power to bind it after Hermes and Watatsumi overpowered him. I remember it now. I remember *everything*."

"Indeed. We could not have defeated him without the aid of the dragons. It grieves me to learn of Hermes and Watatsumi's passing, as they were both good, kindhearted souls," Merlin said.

"Their murders, you mean." Loki pushed away from the wall and joined them by the desk.

The wizard's grim expression darkened, his heavy brows drawing close. "Yes. Their murders will not go unavenged. This I swear to you all on my honor as a wizard."

"By the description, that could be the weapon Otohime saw the night her father was killed," Ēostre said. She squeezed into a gap between Percivale and Maximilian, bending forward to read the screen

"That could explain the damage to his body before he dissipated into sea foam," Max concluded. "He'd been injured, but most of the damage had been centralized to his maw.

Merlin closed his eyes and sighed. "Then he has destroyed it and it is gone forever. Good riddance. When this is all over, I suggest we find a better way to secure such artifacts."

"Agreed," Percivale said. "Do you believe exposure to the items in the vault has somehow clouded Kay's judgment?"

"I do not doubt it," Merlin said. "There is a corruptive force related to the tools once held by the Titans, and if his soul has been blackened, he must be removed from your brotherly cycle. Permanently."

Nate swallowed back the sudden tightness in his throat. With his memories returned, the idea of losing not only one but possibly a handful of knights for all time was an anathema. Their numbers, few as they were, would suffer for the loss.

"We'll survive, man," Lance offered in a quiet voice. He wore a matching expression of disquiet. "I have a family to return to after this is finished." He glanced over Nate's shoulder toward Astrid. "And so do you."

"Then we better get this plan together," Nate said as Astrid joined their hands, interlacing their fingers together. "Everybody listen up. I have an idea."

It took less than an hour to plan and put Percivale on the road with Bors. The two knights returned without Lancelot to embark on a six-hour journey east. Then Nate and the original man who fathered him centuries ago raided a Los Angeles safe house for gear and weapons. Inside, they trashed the anti-supernatural wards prohibiting Mahasti's entry and tore down ribbons disrupting her magic.

She helped them transport an impressive arsenal to Drakenstone Manor within a matter of seconds.

Crush

To think of all the times I've endured layovers at Atlanta and Detroit when I could have been flying Air Genie, he lamented internally.

Using a pen and a terrestrial map printed out by Google, he pinpointed the location of the massive citadel then described the defenses their dragon allies would encounter. He left out nothing, relief casting the tension from his body when Tlaloc answered with a deferential nod.

"I admire your plan, human. And what shall we do if their soldiers attack?"

"Defend yourselves and take no prisoners," Nate replied. "But if they flee, do *not* pursue them. This isn't a mission to commit murder."

"Understood," Teotihuacan answered for his father. "I have not taken a human's life in many decades, but it will trouble me none to harm these."

Nate's cell buzzed in his pocket, prompting him to check the face and spy a two-word message from Bors.

They had reached their destination.

"It's time, Mahasti," he said as he passed her his map.

Excitement and fear raced through him, pins and needles traveling down his arms while sweat dampened his palms. He brushed both off against his jeans and then turned to face Astrid.

A solemn, blue gaze stared back at him. "I love you. I know what I'm getting into."

"You could be hurt," he said.

With a wistful smile on her face, she leaned forward on her tiptoes and kissed him. "I was meant to do this ever since Watatsumi gave Ascalon to my mother."

"Are you prepared?" Mahasti asked.

"Readier than we'll ever be," Nate replied.

The sensation of a teleportation grabbed him in the belly and hurled him hundreds of miles to the northeast from the air-conditioned office room to the sweltering desert. Lancelot and Merlin appeared seconds later.

The Knights of Merlin owned over a thousand acres of Nevada wilderness in the middle of the desert. They'd chosen the area for its tactical advantage and clear view for miles in each direction. There on the sandy stretch lay a compound as old as Area 51, and equally secret.

Astrid, Merlin, Lancelot, and Nate lurked at the edge of the perimeter.

"We've been placed northeast of the compound, and the dragons will arrive from the south. This should buy us some time to approach before we're spotted. Invisibility won't work here. They've got high-powered detection devices and radar."

"Percivale and Bors are inside the compound," Merlin spoke up. His gaze fixed on a point southward.

Lancelot glanced at his phone. "They're going to lay down the story for Kay about me jumping sides. After that, they'll disable what they can of the security defenses and automated turrets."

"Let's hope they buy it," Nate said.

Lancelot grinned and threw an arm around Nate's shoulders. "After the shit I said to him when I left, I don't doubt he will. No matter the lifetime, you'll always be my son."

Astrid studied the pair with a dubious expression, eyes squinted and brows drawn together. "You don't look anything alike, though you do look familiar."

"Er…"

"Lancelot is the one who—"

"Mugged me!" Astrid blurted as recognition dawned. "You were the hobo with the toy gun."

"Yeah. Sorry about that."

"Did you bust up my shop, too?"

The two men broke apart as Astrid advanced on them. Lancelot threw both hands up to ward her off. "No, no, I swear. That was Gareth, and I had no idea about it, okay?"

"Now's not the time," Nate whispered against her cheek. He stepped around behind her and drew her back with his arms around her waist. "We'll talk about it later, but if it makes you feel any better, I almost kicked his ass afterward."

"She did a fine job of that herself," Lancelot reminded him.

They returned to the task at hand and delivered another rundown for Astrid and Merlin's benefit.

"This is where the no-fly zone begins. Wards and hexes run the boundary of the zone, creating a hostile area to teleportation magic and anything airborne once you're within gun range of the complex," Lancelot said.

"Right. Automated sentry guns once we arrive," she said.

"Are you positive you can outmaneuver those?" Nate asked. "No shame if you can't. I'd rather have you sit out or dump us somewhere to make the run on foot than risk yourself."

"I can do it," Astrid insisted. "Just remember your part. Besides, if all goes well, Bors will have taken down at least one turret."

Merlin and Sir Lancelot—gentlemen who didn't try to peek or question her modesty—turned their backs while she disrobed and passed her tank, jeans, and shoes to Nate. He folded the garments into a bag and held her sheathed sword in his free hand while she transformed to tower above them in her majestic draconic body.

Nate touched the side of Astrid's face. In the heat of the moment during their battle against the Chimera, he'd lacked the chance to appreciate her. Her skin was warm and alive beneath his fingers, and despite her draconic skin, he could still see the beautiful woman beneath. As a dragon, she exuded radiance, the scaled texture of her hide polished gold beneath the setting sun.

"Are you ready for this?" he asked.

"As ready as I can be. Uh. Please don't lose my stuff. I haven't mastered Grandma's talent for shifting with clothes."

"I won't," he assured her.

"Time to gear up." Lancelot grinned and summoned his armor. Gleaming silver and white plate mail manifested around him, complete with a crimson cape. Their armor wasn't typical of the time, a creation devised by Merlin and forged by Arthur's finest smiths. With his magic and their talent, they'd crafted twenty-five suits of metal smelted from starlight ore, which was no longer present in the world, to safeguard their lives as they battled the wyrms of the ancient kingdoms.

In a few spoken words, Nate called upon the innate ability each knight had possessed since the time of their initial deaths. The summoned armor blazed around him in white-gold metal. His original clothing vanished.

Astrid stared at him.

"What?" Anxiety rolled a turbulent wave through his stomach.

"You look so…"

"Ridiculous?"

"Noble," she finished. "But I like your Dress Whites best. Where's your helm?"

"Long story."

Astrid crouched low, and he clambered up onto her back. Unlike their first flight, he had ample opportunity to adjust his posture for comfort and security.

Just like riding a horse, he told himself, unconvinced he wouldn't plummet to his death despite Astrid's assurances.

Unless she had her own gravitational pull while in flight, he pictured himself becoming a Nate pancake on the sandy dunes.

"We'll be right behind you." Lancelot revved up the ATV's engine and, behind him, Merlin grimaced.

"Absolutely no style," the old man muttered from atop his Arabian steed.

"It's faster than your ride, Gandalf."

"Who?"

"Never mind," Lancelot said. He shook his head, realizing Merlin wouldn't catch his pop culture references.

"Then away we go," Astrid muttered under her breath. "Hold on tight, Nate."

"I thought you said I was safe back here?"

"In theory…"

Her legs tensed beneath her as she leaned forward, gazing at the target in the distance. With the next beat of his heart, the wind rushed past them, and they were soaring in flight, cool air against his face despite the sweltering desert heat below.

The report of gunfire alerted him to the compound's security force initiating defensive measures.

"Here we go!" he shouted to warn her.

Bullets whizzed through the air in their direction. Astrid swerved and barrel-rolled, and throughout it all, he remained in place, proving he wasn't in danger. He'd been wrong to underestimate his mate, but he wished Mahasti had glued the seat of his pants to her back just in case. She banked left and twisted to the side as automatic fire ripped past them.

Whatever magic she'd used, it worked. He didn't slip off. With his courage regained, Nate sprawled forward upon Astrid's back and pointed the barrel of his rifle above her shoulder.

Several of the turrets were automated machines and attuned to their movement in the skies, but others were operated by living, breathing men who saw her as a monster to be eliminated. He didn't have a clear shot.

And he didn't need it. Just as he opened his mouth to cry out a warning, the world around them blurred and became radiant with golden light. In the next second, the distance between them and the compound folded. He glanced behind them over his shoulder and saw the gate of the heavy-duty perimeter fence reduced to shards of twisted metal. They'd blown right through it.

My girlfriend is the Flash. How the hell? No, don't question it. Don't question it. Just be thankful you're not somewhere back there on the ground.

"Whoa, whoa, whoa!" a turret operator shouted.

He dove from the seat as Astrid ripped the machine from its mounting with her rear claws. Cables snapped and metal shrieked, then she tossed the crumpled and useless weapon aside.

"Don't stand there, shoot her!" a man screamed.

She turned her head and exhaled a cone of fire. Nate's protective armor guarded him, though the ambient heat warmed the air, and he saw the sizzle of electricity flashing in the dancing flames.

Astrid became a force to be reckoned with. She pounced the automated gun adjacent to it and disassembled it with ease while Nate turned his attention to the men scrambling into position on the security deck to shoot at her.

He waited between wing beats, aligned his shot, and pulled the trigger without guilt.

Unfortunately, some of the men recruited by their order were also military men and trained to operate while under fire.

Another automated gun rotated to face them, only to deactivate and lose power.

"Someone's taken the defenses offline!" one man shouted. "Take cover and regroup!"

"Fall back! We can't best the beast with bullets alone!"

Nate looked over her shoulder and resumed fire, keeping their assault at bay.

"Got them taken care of down below, Lance?" Nate asked over the communication link.

"The way is clear," the other knight replied.

"You're safe to proceed, Merlin. We'll cover your arrival from the air. All eyes are on us now, Astrid. Make it count."

"With pleasure."

Nate jumped down from her back and helped to hold down the area from the guard tower adjacent to the main structure. A hot summer day beamed down upon him, the air dry and worsened by her fire. It raged around them, flames licking up at the sky from the corpses of the fallen.

So many lives lost. And for what? He shook his head.

Down below, Merlin and Lancelot rode beyond the tattered fence designed to keep out the civilian rabble. Not that they'd ever truly expected to find any in the desert wastes. Nate and Astrid had already taken care of the extremists on the ground level and cleared the way.

"Merlin and I are inside the main building," Lancelot reported over their comms line.

After she had shrunk to her human body, Nate tossed her the bag and kept a vigilant watch over the area while she tugged her tank over her head, and hurried into the rest of her clothes.

Ascalon gleamed when she drew the enchanted blade from its sheath. Nate joined her while loading another magazine into his rifle before leading the way inside the building's upper level.

"Abandoned," he muttered. Despite the silence, he proceeded with caution and led her to a closed stairwell.

"Can you blame them? We annihilated the first wave of their security force."

"All members of the Anti-Dragon Movement are advised to lay down your arms," Percivale's placid voice boomed over the internal system. "The Knights of Merlin are no longer under the leadership of Sir Kay and have formed an alliance with the dragons. Surrender and live. Continue to resist and die."

Nate grinned.

"Come on. The door at the bottom of this stairwell leads to the training yard. We can cut across and meet up with Merlin and Lancelot."

Glossy blue resin flooring and white walls gave the hallways the stark and sterile feel of a hospital corridor. Their footsteps echoed in the stairway as they made their way down two levels to the ground floor.

The barracks lay to the east of the immense facility, separated by a vast training yard. Four levels of open floor dormitories housed the support members of the movement with a fifth floor divided into apartments for its senior-ranking members: the knights. Nate had a place of his own there, though he never used it.

Nate pushed open a heavy metal door and led the way back out into the oppressive heat. The air shimmered above the concrete ground. They kept low and lingered against the wall while Nate scanned the area for hostiles. Five men stood on alert across the way beside a climbing wall.

"Merlin's done," Lancelot reported. The wards surrounding the training compound and the surrounding terrain dropped with a sensation reminiscent of a pressure change. Nate's ears popped.

The sky above them filled with dragons, each a shining jewel in the sunlight. The sight was both beautiful and terrifying.

Tlaloc and Teo landed in the center yard, pitch black scales repelling the pelting barrage of gunfire turned on them by the militant extremists. Teo swept his tail and knocked them to the side while his father faced off against a single knight.

"Degore!" Nate yelled. He stepped out from the shadows and moved across the open space. "Stand down and listen to me. We don't have to fight them."

"You're a traitor, bringing them here. You've destroyed everything we've worked for!"

Sir Degore, a short, balding man built of hard packed muscle, favored the battle-axe. His summoned weapon whistled through the air. Tlaloc avoided the first blow, and Nate intercepted the second with his blade. Degore stared at him over their crossed weapons.

"Why, Galahad?"

A strong voice brimming with ancient power spoke up behind them. "Because I asked this of him."

Merlin stepped into the courtyard flanked by Lancelot. While Teo and Tlaloc kept the humans pinned down, three more knights rushed to aid Degore but drew up short at the sight of the wizard approaching them.

"What sort of trick is this?"

"No trick, Degore. That's Merlin," Nate replied. He stepped back, free hand raised with his palm out in a gesture of surrender, and lowered his sword to his side. "We don't want to fight you, only show you the truth."

"Knights, hear me and lay down your arms." Merlin moved to Nate's side.

"What's to prove this is the true Merlin?" Bleoberis held his sword out toward the wizard. "We've tasted Loki's shape-changing mischief in the past. This is a farce and nothing more, an act of treachery to divide us."

"Foolish human, I stand right here," Loki heckled from the edge of the cement helipad. The light from the setting sun behind him set his black hide ablaze, each scale glowing ember on the edges. "Do you dare imply I would imitate your wizard?"

"Anyone with eyes can see *and hear* Loki is among the dragons." Merlin regarded them with calm eyes, standing at ease in the face of their weapons. Nate wished he had the same confidence.

"I have encountered the compelling illusions of the trickster in the past," Bleoberis spat. "If you are Merlin, prove your identity with spells. Surely a dragon couldn't mimic a wizard's magic in all ways."

Merlin swept a hand toward the three youngest knights. They flew across the yard like leaves in the wind, separating them from Bleoberis. As for the main knight, their mentor, the wizard tipped his cane forward, and a shockwave cut through the knight's defenses. It thrust him against the wall, and for one ridiculous second, he resembled a ragdoll in glossy armor. The back of his head cracked against the cinderblocks, and like any man handed his ass by a wizard, he staggered afterward in a daze, his eyes squeezed tight from the pain. Blood ran down the corners of the knight's mouth—he'd bit his tongue.

"Was that an illusion, Sir Bleoberis?" Merlin asked.

Degore, Tristram, and Lamorak hurried to their feet, and the hero worship blazed in their eyes.

"It's him," Lamorak breathed. "It must be him!"

"Of course it is, and I have no doubt Bleoberis believes my identity now as well."

"My apologies, Merlin," the man said, grimacing and evidently in pain.

The four knights lowered their weapons and dropped to their knees, heads bowed.

"Forgive us, Merlin," Degore apologized. "We thought you an imposter."

"Sir Kay is the one no longer himself," Merlin replied. He stepped over and drew each knight to their feet in turn. "Where is he?"

"The armory—but wait! Bedivere has gone toward the dark vault," Bleoberis said.

"I'll go after Kay," Nate said, turning to Astrid and Merlin. "The both of you need to stop Bedivere from retrieving another dangerous artifact."

"What of us?" Tristram asked. "What can we do to help, Galahad?"

"Assist Lancelot, Bors, and Percivale with the troops. Get them locked in the barracks if you can, or let them retreat, just so long as they stop attacking. If they don't, they're going to get themselves killed against these dragons."

"As you command."

"What of these?" Tlaloc asked. He held a man pinned beneath his talons. The others sat against the wall under Teo's watchful gaze.

"We'll take them to the holding cells on our way to assist Sir Percivale." Tristram stepped forward and approached the large black dragon. "Thank you for your restraint."

Tlaloc grunted and released the man into the knight's custody.

The situation could have gone worse. Nate gave a silent sigh of relief and relayed their situation over the radio to the rest of their dragon team.

"Fall back. We have them where we want them now. There's no need for more bloodshed."

Chapter 18

Astrid sensed the vault before she saw it. The room oozed power, sending out runners of slippery and cold malevolence to prickle her skin and make her heart race. Barely audible whispers intruded on the far reaches of her hearing. Promising. Tempting.

Save us.

Help us.

Release me.

"Do not listen," Merlin told her in a quiet voice. He exchanged a knowing look. "Whatever happens, try to touch nothing within."

"I won't."

The massive vault defied her expectations. She had imagined a bank with labeled shelves or a wall of secured drawers, but what she saw inside reminded her more of a museum.

Nine glass display cases lined the room's perimeter, all but one shattered. Bedivere crouched beside a heavy duffel bag, a large tome tucked under his arm.

Astrid hung back and tightened the grip on the sword hilt in her sweating palm. An abundance of energy charged the room, crawling over her skin and thickening the air. She'd never before encountered darkness of such tangible force that it choked the air and made her eyes water.

In the center of the floor, a corpse in a tactical vest lay dead, struck down by a single sword strike through the chest. The body looked no different from the men she'd already killed during the initial siege on the security deck.

Bedivere had slaughtered one of their own before raiding their vault.

"Bedivere, return the grimoire to its case. You know not what you risk by disturbing it."

"I always figured you'd wake up one day, old man. I told Kay we should have buried you under a slab of cement, but we had to keep up appearances."

The knight shoved the book in the bag and zipped it. He shouldered the heavy pack before rising to face them with a smarmy grin.

A glowing vermillion sphere coalesced between Merlin's hands and shot out at the knight. Bedivere remained where he stood, motionless, with a cruel grin on his face. The spell never reached him, fizzling out against an unseen barrier into harmless sparks.

Astrid tensed and leaned forward to charge with her sword, but Merlin held out his arm and kept her back.

"No, child. He is too strong for even you."

Her eyes turned to the wizard in question, but he faced forward to stare Bedivere down.

"Did you truly think you could stand against us, old man? When you betrayed our order to bargain with the dragons, Kay and I found a new leader. A power greater than you and all of the lizards combined."

"You cannot trust them, you know that."

"And we couldn't trust you."

Bedivere clutched a fist-sized emerald in his free hand, its faint pulse reminiscent of a heartbeat. He squeezed the stone and spoke in harsh, guttural tones that raised the hairs on Astrid's nape and arms.

The concrete beneath them rumbled and shifted. Astrid stumbled into Merlin and grabbed him by the shoulder as the center of the floor imploded, showering them with debris. Thrashing vines and gnarled roots thrust upward through the breach and engulfed Bedivere in a spiral, barely concealed by the cloud of grit. They closed around him in a protective shell.

Merlin thrust with his cane, but the network of plantlife whisked the knight and the artifacts away.

When the dust cleared, Bedivere was nowhere to be seen.

"What just happened?' Astrid asked. She coughed and brushed dirt from her hair, fingers coming away bloody.

"Bedivere has made a choice he will soon regret." Merlin rose to his feet and groaned. "Are you badly injured?"

"A scratch," she assured him. "I'll be fine."

"Then we should get to the others. Bedivere is lost to us, for now. The same must not happen for Kay."

***

Their armory occupied a sublevel in the sprawling desert complex. Deep below the earth, there were no windows and few exits. Like all the knights, Nate knew the building layout by heart. If Kay planned to escape, he would have to enter the main corridor to access the elevator or the stairs at the end of the hall.

Heavy doors that should have been closed hung wide open to reveal shelves of ammo boxes and live grenades. Nate stepped through with care and swept his gaze around the weapons racks. A shadow moved at the far end by a wall.

"So, the son shows his true colors." Kay turned around to face him. His heavy armor added bulk to his already imposing form.

But it was wrong, no longer bright and radiant, darkened to a cloudy gray like smoked glass.

"I'm doing what's right. Kay, it's not too late to end this. Hand yourself over to us. Give me Arthur. Maybe then Merlin and the dragons can help you."

"Make me their slave, you mean."

"You're the one making us slaves. You trapped Merlin. You've lied to us for centuries. What made you betray Arthur? How could you murder your brother, a man you once called your friend?" Nate asked.

Kay chuckled. "A friend? That spineless churl knew nothing of strength and leadership. I watched as this brotherhood became weak and decadent. He wanted to talk peace. To cripple our order and make us the docile pets of these simple beasts."

Another memory returned to Nate of Arthur's last days—their final discussion—flying to him like an arrow piercing his thoughts. Arthur had spoken of sparing Fafnir and pardoning the other ancients for their previous crimes. He no longer wanted to live in the past and wanted to embrace a future of peace for all.

"Arthur made a truce with Watatsumi. That's why you killed him. He succeeded in negotiating his truce, and then you murdered him to cover up the truth. Murdered both of them and slaughtered Fafnir to unravel their work."

"I killed that water beast to teach you a lesson." Kay sneered. "Falling in love with the enemy. An animal. She'll turn out exactly like the monster that spawned her father. You saw him at Rainier."

"You're wrong, and you're more of a threat than any of these dragons. How many people died needlessly in Japan when you three assassinated Watatsumi?"

Kay barked out a sharp laugh. "And how many humans have you murdered to reach me, Nathaniel? Did you forget those men on the roof and in this building have families and loved ones of their own? People to return to? Thanks to you and your little rebellion, I can take out your swarm of precious dragons all at once."

Nate's attention dropped to the launcher in Kay's hands, a tool developed under the president's nose by a covert laboratory and funded with government money. The initial phase of research began eight years prior when Kay realized Maximilian had a legitimate shot at entering the White House.

Only a single prototype existed. It came into their possession a year ago when Max investigated a trail of wasted money in the defense budget and tracked down its source. According to the scientists on the development team, one high-powered round would punch through a dragon's tough hide on the first shot. It had never been tested.

"You're not going to use that. I won't let you hurt them."

Kay set the weapon aside and summoned his great sword. The daunting blade stood nearly as tall as the man wielding it, with a serrated edge meant to intimidate.

"Try to stop me. I dare you."

Kay charged forward and swung in a mighty, overhand blow. Nate gripped his sword with both hands and rose to block, bracing himself against the incoming strike. Sparks flew from their clashing blades. He staggered back, forced to give ground.

"I've grown more powerful in this life than any others," Kay taunted. "Do you think you can stand up to me? You can't even kill a dragon."

Nate ducked to the side and knocked over an empty rack to gain himself a precious moment to breathe. Kay sliced through the obstacle with ease and kicked the tattered halves aside before advancing, each step heavy against the floor.

"Running won't save you from this," Kay called after him. "After I cut you down, your dragons will *burn*." He drove the tip of his sword into the ground and split the concrete. It broke apart and rippled through the room, tossing Nate off balance.

I have to destroy that thing. Even if he takes me out now, I can't let him get to the surface to hurt them.

Kay struck himself in the chest with his fist and muttered in a guttural, unfamiliar language to Nate. The senior knight's veins bulged, pulsing green and black beneath his skin, and a foul-smelling, choking vapor arose from his body.

Nate stumbled back, aghast by the physical changes. "What did you do to yourself?" he demanded. It was no spell or magic they'd ever been granted as knights, but something dark and insidious sending coils of nausea into his stomach.

It was a boon from the ancient and wild foe of the dragons: the Titans.

"I took what I needed, what I deserved for years upon years of service. Bedivere and I found a new master to appreciate our devotion and service, one who will not embrace our enemies."

Nate shuddered, but he didn't lower his sword.

"Join me, Nathaniel. You were great once. Let me help you achieve greatness again. Together, you and I will lead the knights in a victory against the dragons. We can take back our world from the plague infesting it."

"I'll pass."

An angry shadow darkened Kay's features. "You can't defeat me. You can only die."

Giving himself over to his training, Nate fought for his life. Their swords clashed together, steel against steel, magic against magic. Sparks flew in their deadly dance, Nate always on the defense. Kay's greater strength gave him the advantage, but his berserker rage lacked focus.

Back and forth across the room, they battled. Sweat trickled down Nate's brow and dampened his back beneath his armor.

Each step he took brought him one step further from the weapon he longed to destroy.

"Nate!"

Astrid skidded into the room, Merlin a step behind her. There was a fire burning in her eyes, and after a split second to assess the situation, his mate charged in with Ascalon. Kay shoved Nate back against the fallen racks, tripping him up, and spun toward Astrid. Ascalon flared white as their swords struck.

Scrambling to his feet, Nate returned to the fray. A perverse glee filled Kay's cold eyes. He fended them off with ease, overwhelming their offense with effortless blocks. The black veins beneath his skin spidered across his face, and the whites of his eyes glowed green.

Merlin's magic swirled through the air, but each attack seemed to absorb into Kay and strengthen him. Every blow Nate landed against his chest piece seemed like a single drop into an immense ocean.

Despite their combined effort, Kay held an advantage over them with his corrupted new gifts. Astrid's limited experience with her magical sword and lack of armor placed her in a vulnerable position. Kay pressed in on her each time he threw Nate off balance, forcing the younger knight to stay on the defense.

"Little girls shouldn't play with swords," Kay taunted. He kicked out, causing Astrid to falter, and followed with a downward strike. The blow glanced off an arcane shield thrown between the blade and Astrid's unarmed body.

Kay turned on the interfering wizard, snarling.

"You cannot protect them all, Merlin. I see the toll this magic has taken on your body. Did you enjoy the sweet dreams from the Sisters of Salem?"

"I will not allow you to harm Galahad or his family."

"Abominations," Kay hissed. "I'll exterminate them both now while he watches. Then I'll deal with you."

Red intruded on Nate's vision. He threw himself between Kay and Astrid as Kay's blade descended. The sword struck his armor and cracked it, leaving a deep fissure in the starlight metal. Nate groaned as blood welled to the surface, but he pushed through the pain and spun with a backslash aimed for Kay's throat.

The older knight leaned back and twisted his head, taking the strike against his pauldron. Nate's sword carved a groove through the tainted metal. While their armor could be destroyed, each piece materialized from their spirit and eventually regenerated over time whether it took days or weeks.

As blood ran down his back, Nate praised the powers above that Kay had struck nothing vital.

"You should have remained a good soldier and followed orders, Galahad. A pity I'll have to destroy—"

Blinding electric arcs struck Kay from behind, transferred down the length of Astrid's blade. Anger had provided the key to unlocking her potential with the weapon, and it sizzled with the magical currents, sending white-hot pulses crackling up and down Kay's body. He seized in his armor but kept his footing, body stiffening as her stroke emerged from the front of his chest piece.

"I'm not a little girl. I am a *dragon*."

Nate didn't have time to marvel at Astrid's magical feat in her human form. He used the opportunity her attack offered and struck. Kay's gloating face transformed into a mask of pain and disbelief. He stared down at the two swords piercing his torso. He'd been skewered, and warm, wet splatters glistened on Nate's face and armor.

"Son, don't do this," Kay begged. "Don't let her do this."

Completing the stroke, Nate shoved his sword through Kay's chest despite the growing resistance. The hilt grew hot, and then something gave with a discernible snap where the fallen knight's heart belonged.

Something unnatural resided there.

"You were never my father. You're nothing to me."

Kay collapsed to the floor when Nate and Astrid both yanked their swords free. His blackened armor disintegrated into ash, and his sword did the same seconds later.

"Nate!"

Astrid rushed to his side and supported his weight before his legs gave out beneath him. He slumped against her without shame.

"I'm fine, baby girl. I'm fine."

"You're bleeding!"

"Not as much as him."

Merlin knelt down beside Kay and clicked his tongue. The knight struggled to breathe, each gasp rattling in his chest. He tried to speak, but bloody froth bubbled against his lips instead. After a moment, his body stilled, went lax, and the light left his eyes as Merlin chanted over him.

The magic in the air swirled in a miasma of dark and light. Nate watched with a heavy heart. As much as he'd hated what Kay had become, the man had still raised him. There were good memories peppered among the bad.

He couldn't celebrate, their victory coming at too great a price.

"The Sir Kay we knew is no more, and he will never again be born into a new life," Merlin replied. His quiet voice carried the weariness of ages. "It is over. For now."

"But what about Arthur?" Astrid asked.

Merlin ran his fingers around the edge of Kay's collar, revealing a golden rope chain. The ruby pendant at the end pulsed when he touched it. "The jewel must be destroyed to free the spirit trapped within."

"Then I'll do it," Nate said, stepping forward with his sword.

"No. Only two swords in this existence possess the power to cut through this dark sorcery. One is Excalibur and the other..."

Astrid gazed in wonder at her sword. "Ascalon."

"Yes, but not here. There is too much darkness. Let us free Arthur in the sunlight." The gold chain popped. With the jewel secured, Merlin rose and led them from the armory.

They left Kay behind and made their way back to the others through deserted corridors. The remaining knights awaited them in the yard while the dragons perched on the building above.

"Nate, you okay, man?" Lancelot hurried over and took his weight from Astrid. "Where's Kay and Bedivere?"

"Bedivere escaped," Astrid replied. "But Kay..."

"Kay is dead," Nate told him. "Gone for good."

"Damn. I'm sorry I wasn't there to help you."

Nate shook his head.

Merlin held out the ruby with Arthur's soul for all to see. The knights all recognized the pendant, accustomed to seeing it around Kay's neck, and each and every one of them bowed their heads.

"All this time, Arthur was trapped among us," Degore said in a heavy voice. "We were all blind."

"It's time to set things right," Percivale said.

Bleoberis nodded. "Agreed. Merlin, what must we do?"

"The time of fighting the dragons is over," the wizard declared. "This order once stood for justice and honor. I would like to see it happen again, and I know Arthur would wish the same. When he returns to us in his next cycle, let us be a brotherhood he can regard with pride."

"Here, here!" Lancelot cried out. The knights echoed his cry.

"President Emberthorn." Percivale stepped forward and turned to the red dragon perched above. Max glided down from the rooftop and landed across from the armored knight. "Once, long ago, Arthur asked to forge a truce with your kind. I'd like to honor his wish."

Max gazed down at the knight addressing him. "A truce we would have were it not for Kay's treachery. On behalf of the dragons and our council, it would bring me great pleasure to end hostilities between our races."

"On my word, no harm shall come to any peaceful dragon," Percivale said. He offered his hand, and Max extended a talon to him in return. "So it is witnessed, so it shall be." Merlin tapped his cane against the ground. "Now, Astrid, if you would kindly do the honors. Arthur has been trapped long enough."

Nate turned his head and pressed a kiss against Astrid's golden hair. "Go on, I'll be right here."

With an audience watching her, Astrid approached Merlin and the stone. In the twilight, sun dwindling with only faint hints of gold at the edge of the horizon, she was beautiful, his sword-carrying warrior woman.

It was a shame their knighthood never accepted women. He watched her angle the sword to the ground and place the sharp edge against the glimmering ruby. When the tip of Ascalon pierced the stone, a hazy golden mist arose from the shattered pieces and lingered in the arid air.

Was that Arthur's face, or was it Nate's imagination? He blinked and the serene visage was gone. A shapeless light remained, the lost soul making a lazy skyward spiral, only to veer at the last moment and streak toward Astrid and encompass her in a radiant glow.

Startled, Astrid leaped back, but it was too late to evade it. From the corner of his eye, Nate saw Saul leap into the training yard and begin to rush toward them. He arrived too late to help. The dimming light consolidated to her abdomen and vanished.

"Peace, Drakenstone," Merlin cautioned. "No harm has been done."

"What was that?" Astrid stared down at her midsection.

"Arthur has chosen his next life, it would appear." Merlin set his hand against her shoulder and gave a gentle squeeze.

"Wait, what?" Nate snapped his gaze from Astrid to Merlin then back to his mate in wordless disbelief, struck too dumb to form a complete sentence.

"I think the wizard's saying you knocked your dragon girlfriend up and this time around Arthur's going to be *your* son," Lancelot offered helpfully. "Congrats, Dad."

Saul rocked back on his hind legs.

Astrid touched her hands to her flat belly. "But that means…"

"Your unborn child now has a soul," Merlin said. "This destiny is what I sensed between you and Galahad, one of the ties binding your lives and souls together. For the first time, our fate, those of the knights and the dragons, shall join as one." Merlin lifted his gaze to the astonished knights and dragons gathered around them. "Let there finally be true peace between us."

***

Astrid ran her fingers over her stomach and turned sideways to look at her reflection in the mirror. Nothing had changed, her tummy toned and slim as ever, and she couldn't estimate her pregnancy at a glance.

How long would it be before she saw the first sign of a subtle swell? Before she felt the first kick?

Hours after the death of Kay and liberation of the Knights of Merlin, restoring their wizard mentor to his rightful place as their advisor, she stood in her childhood bedroom while her friends and family waited downstairs.

They wanted to talk to her, but they'd respected her privacy and state of shock as well.

Nate hadn't left the shower yet, but he'd surrendered the bathroom first to her. An unusual silence had fallen over him since Kay's death and the discovery of Arthur's reincarnation as *their* child, but it finally occurred to her that no one had asked if he was okay. No one but her.

She pushed through the bathroom door and let the steam encompass her. Her mate soaked beneath the showerhead, face raised to the cleansing spray. Still nude from her shower, she stepped in behind him and squeezed her body against his back.

"Hey."

"Hey," Nate replied. He reached back and stroked her thigh. "You okay?"

"I came to ask you the same question."

"I'm good." His strained voice told her otherwise.

He'd killed his father. One of his brothers-in-arms.

Without asking him another question, she tenderly bathed his back. The injury inflicted by Kay's sword had closed, a tender pink line only healed on the surface. Her father and grandmother had tended him without her asking.

She kissed the back of his shoulder. "I love you."

Nate turned within her embrace then dropped his eyes to her stomach. His strong arms wrapped around her. "Even now?"

"Even more," she replied.

"I don't know what I've done to deserve you. I ask myself every day."

"Continue to be a wonderful man and you'll always deserve me."

He kissed her. Sometime later, they exited the shower together and dressed, a visit with her family looming over their heads. Hopefully, Merlin had answered most of the questions for them.

Nate settled on the edge of the bed, his pensive expression distracting her long after she dressed.

"I'm s—" he began.

Astrid whirled and cut him off. "Don't you dare apologize for this baby."

"I wasn't going to."

"Good.

"I was going to say I'm surprised your dad didn't break down into tears." He beamed. "As for our baby..." His voice trailed, and her heart did a nervous double beat in her chest when his expression sobered. "Are you happy with this? With our child becoming Arthur?"

"It's unexpected, but yeah, I am. This is *our* child, and from everything you've said, Arthur was a good man."

"I wonder if he'll be a dragon like you."

"I don't know, but shifter genes tend to carry down generations. Everything about this is new. What about you? Are you okay with this?"

"I truly am," Nate replied while raising his arms to curve around her waist. He kissed her stomach through the thin cotton dress and closed his eyes. "I'll love both of you with every day this life gives me. And when it ends I will find you again, Astrid. This I swear."

"We don't know yet if you'll age and die."

"I know, but it makes my words no less true. If it should happen, will you wait for me?"

"Of course, I will."

Love shone in his eyes as he kissed her stomach again. They joined hands and ventured from the room to join her family. At the bottom of the stairs, Saul paced a groove into the carpet, resembling a caged lion more than a dragon.

"At last!"

Nate grinned. "I'll give you two a moment." He kissed her cheek before parting from her side to join their guests in the next room.

"Where's Merlin?" she asked her father, peeking around him.

"Outside with your grandmother talking shop and detailing out how to reveal the knighthood to the American public."

Astrid wrinkled her nose. She didn't envy her grandparents for the work about to pile up on them.

"Is everything all right, Dad?"

"It is. I cannot say I ever imagined this is how things would turn out for our family but—" he drew in a slow, deep breath then released it on a quick exhale "—Nate has proven himself a good and capable man. I am happy that *you* are happy."

Tears stung her eyes. "Thanks, Daddy. That means a lot to me."

Saul enveloped her in a comforting hug. "Your mother is quite emotional. Fair warning."

She smiled, hearing the thickness in her father's voice. "Thanks for the heads up."

They walked into the living room together, arm in arm, where he relinquished her back into Nate's care. The symbolic gesture of her father passing her fingers back into Nate's hand made tears spring to her eyes.

"I can't believe my baby is going to have a baby," Chloe gushed. She sprang from her seat and rushed to her daughter. "How do you feel?"

"I feel… normal. A little queasy, but I thought that was nerves because of the fighting with Nate then all of the action with rescuing Merlin."

Saul grumbled and gave Nate a dirty look, though it faded over the seconds to grudging respect. "Now that your memories have returned, I expect you to take excellent care of my cub. You must have centuries of experience with fatherhood," the dragon muttered.

"Actually, no. I've never fathered a child," Nate said.

Astrid's head swiveled around. She stared at him. "Never?"

"We don't *always* reproduce during each lifetime, and we only reappear in the bodies of our male offspring. That's how it's worked for centuries," Nate said. "I've never had children, and neither has Percivale. It was all about duty for us. At least, it was for me until I met you."

"He's right. Marriage and children has never interested me. I will live to the final day of this life screaming at kids to get off my lawn," Percivale agreed.

"I've had all girls," Lancelot added.

Saul offered a reluctant but sympathetic, "My condolences. It relieved me greatly to discover our second would be a boy."

Lancelot grinned. "Thanks. I'm dreading the day they start dating, but I figure I can flash my armor at their potential boyfriends and ensure they're brought home on time."

"An interesting strategy." Saul rubbed his chin.

"So now what?" Nate asked Lancelot.

"Percivale is overseeing things in Nevada. The, uh, president brought in some military guys to make sure the compound is clear. Lots of arrests happened, but due to the extenuating circumstances, he mentioned issuing pardons to everyone, knights included, which is nice because I have a family and don't want to spend the rest of this life in prison."

Even Saul chuckled. "My father is quite kind and benevolent for a fire wyrm. You will see as you come to know him."

"Still, we're taking back any gear Kay and Bedivere issued out to the movement. It's gonna take a while." Lancelot rubbed the back of his neck.

"Hopefully, it isn't too late."

"What about you, Nate?" Chloe asked. "What will you do now?"

"I have a legitimate job in the Navy." And enough work accrued over his impromptu, emergency leave to keep him busy for the next month. He sighed. "But I need to make the drive into L.A. first this afternoon."

"Do you want me to come with you," Astrid asked. She stepped in close beside him and rested her cheek against his shoulder.

"Not this time. This is something *I* need to do."

***

The idyllic home of his childhood awaited him beyond a white picket fence. The two little dogs barked and played in the yard, but the driveway was empty. Kay's SUV would never grace it again. Aaron played a game in the living room, the television visible beyond three narrow windows.

"Nate?"

He glanced to the side to see Elizabeth, his stepmother, standing beside his driver's door peeking in at him through the half-open window. He hadn't noticed her arrival, her car parked behind him parallel to the curb.

Shit.

The woman held a bag of groceries in her arms and had her fingers looped around a few more. He hurried from the vehicle and took a few from the tired woman. Dark circles under her eyes and a haggard appearance told a story he already knew. She'd been awake all night waiting to hear word from Kay.

The front door opened to frame his lanky half-brother, Kay's biological son with strawberry blond hair, freckles, and a small, upturned nose. He shared their green eyes, but he'd never thought of the spoiled boy as his little brother.

He took a bag from his mother but blinked at Nate. "What are you doing here? Dad's pissed at you, you know."

"Go fetch the rest of the groceries," Elizabeth told him.

"Fiiiine."

While Aaron ran for the rest of the bags, Nate trudged behind Elizabeth into the kitchen and lowered the heavy bags on the counter.

"Daniel isn't home, and you probably shouldn't be here when he returns," she said. Then after a grudging moment, she added, "But thanks."

Nate hesitated. He glanced over his shoulder toward the open arch between the kitchen and family room, and then he sighed. "I know he's upset with me. We've talked since then."

The woman turned and began unpacking goods from the store, placing cool drinks and milk into the fridge, cereal into cupboards. "Oh? Everything forgiven then? He raged and stormed around for hours, claiming you stole something of value from him the other day."

"I did, but listen, Elizabeth, I…"

Aaron dropped a bag with packages of frozen meat into the sink. "Really? Dad forgave you? Sweet! Hey, wanna play this new game with me then?"

Nate blinked. He'd never thought Aaron liked him. "Not right now, Aaron. Hey, wait a moment and stay in here with us, okay? Sit down, Elizabeth. I gotta… I have to tell you…"

To tell you he's dead, and that I killed him, Nate thought. His mouth wouldn't form the words, but Elizabeth saw it in his face. She paled.

"No," she breathed. "Tell me you're here to talk to him again and make up for whatever silly thing you fought over."

"No, I'm not. I'm sorry."

"No! I won't believe it! He's a knight! He told me he wouldn't die fighting the dragons. He told me he could take them all on!" She screamed the words at him as tears coursed down her cheeks and her stunned son blinked in confusion.

"Dad's dead?"

Nate caught her as she stumbled; then she sobbed against his chest in hysterics. "I'm sorry, Elizabeth."

"How did it happen?" she asked.

Big tears welled in Aaron's eyes. "Was it a dragon? Which one of them did it? I'll get them back one day for Dad. I'll be a tough guy like you and him and take them out!"

The truth hung on the tip of Nate's tongue, but he couldn't force himself to utter the words. He and Astrid together had given Kay the death he deserved.

"He died for what he believed in, Elizabeth. He came to realize a truce was what we needed, and when he tried to call the entire thing off, he was killed."

"A truce?" Her glossy eyes blinked. "I don't understand."

"There's... something more frightening out there now, Elizabeth, scarier than any dragon. Kay discovered this and gave his life to protect us all from it. He died a hero." He glanced at Aaron, the little brother he'd always wanted, but never felt he had. He saw the kid's green eyes gazing up at him with hurt and pain. "You don't have to avenge him, kid. His soul is already at peace now."

He was Sir Galahad. And he never lied.

Until he was given no choice.

Nate remained long past dinner with them, chatting with Aaron about the boy's future. With time, he hoped to unravel the years of emotional damage and manipulation Kay had woven in his son's head.

"What about... will there be a funeral?" Elizabeth asked as she walked him to the door.

"Of course," Nate said. "I'll help you arrange it if you'd like."

"Yes," she whispered. "Please."

The woman, who never claimed to love him in all of his life, hugged him tight and thanked him for his support.

He drove away praying the circumstances of Kay's death would be the last lie he ever told.

Epilogue

Two Months Later

The rich scent of pumpkin spice filled the condo, a mouthwatering aroma circulating from the kitchen to satisfy Astrid's craving. Toni had supplied her grandmother's best recipe, and since Yasmin had brought a bounty of fresh pumpkins from her mother's Texas garden, the three women spent the early portion of the afternoon scooping out the slimy insides for sweet pumpkin pie, buttercream-iced pumpkin loafs, and anything else that suited Astrid's pregnant fancies.

Holding a squeaky, ragdoll toy in her mouth, Echo padded closer to where the young women sat on the living room floor with magazines and catalogs spread around them in a haphazard mess of designer baby goods.

"I can't believe he put the crib together on his own already," Yasmin said. "Why didn't he have Mahasti poof it all together for him?"

Astrid shrugged. "He said something about wanting to enjoy parenthood the normal way. I guess I can see his point of view. As fun as it was to snap my fingers as a kid for every single thing, it was kind of like Fred and George Weasley Apparating all over the Burrow in the Harry Potter books instead of walking from one room to the next. It's a cool novelty, but it doesn't replace doing it yourself."

Yasmin laughed. "Good point."

"I dunno. If I had a genie, I'd probably weigh about a thousand pounds now."

"Trust me, you get bored after a while of not doing your stuff anymore. Mom and Dad cook in the kitchen all the time now, and she's got him doing some of their cleaning."

Yasmin cackled. "I'd pay to see your dad bending over to pick up Brandt's toys."

Astrid shot her a dirty look.

"I meant that in a non-perverted way. So come on. Pick something. You've been holding the same catalog page open for like twenty minutes."

"I don't know. I can't pick."

"You have to decide eventually," Toni pressed. "Unless you plan to let the little tyke snooze beside you and Nate every night."

Astrid blew out an exasperated huff. "They're all pretty bedroom sets, and Nate's no help with choosing. He just repeats the same thing whenever I ask for his opinion. 'Baby, whatever you like is fine with me. It's about making you happy.' And then he head nods a few times while I describe the options and adds nothing useful."

All three women burst into laughter.

"Men." Toni rolled her eyes. "So glad I don't have that problem. Anyway, I like this one."

"It's pink."

"What's wrong with pink? Look, it's carousel horses and everything."

"Maybe the fact that I'm having a boy?"

Toni laughed. "True, true. You know, pink is a color for anyone these days. Abolish those gender stereotypes."

Astrid tried to picture King Arthur growing up with rose-colored bed sheets and flowers painted on the walls. She giggled at the imagery.

"Isn't Nate due back soon to take you to your ultrasound?" Yasmin checked her watch.

As if summoned by the mention of his name, Nate stepped through the front door and dropped his travel bag on the floor. He stopped short, raised his brows at the three sets of eyes that turned on him, and took one small step back.

"Maybe I should come back."

"Don't be a dummy, dummy," Toni called over. "Come look at all the stuff we picked out."

"I'm not sure I want to know how much my bank account is going to suffer."

"*Our* bank account will be fine, Mr. Drakenstone."

"I still can't believe you made him take your last name," Yasmin said.

"She didn't have to make me do anything. I was glad to be rid of Kirkpatrick," Nate said with a shrug, though he seemed well over the pain inflicted by his father's betrayal.

Abandoning her friends, Astrid crossed the room and wrapped her arms around her husband. "You're still my Nate, regardless of the last name."

He met her halfway, lowering his mouth to her lips. Kissing him never changed—it remained some magical, rejuvenating force able to set her soul aflame every time.

Toni booed and hissed. "Come on you two. Get a room."

"This *is* the room," Yasmin stage whispered.

"Ugh. Fine. We'll let you two lovebirds have space, but we'll see you both tomorrow for the baby shower. Svetlana will have all our heads if we don't get you there on time. That girl is scary."

"See you tomorrow. Mom's totally digging this new spell she perfected, so you'll be seeing a lot of me." Yasmin squinted at Nate. "You better be good to her or else. You never know when I might appear."

"Hopefully not inside my house. I'm not responsible for what you see if you materialize at random," Astrid said.

Yasmin stuck out her tongue and crushed a gemstone ampoule between her fingers. A colorful fog seeped from within it and swept her away to Texas on swirls of magic crafted by her mother.

"Damn, that is awesome." Toni stared at the spot where Yasmin had been. "Guess I'll make my exit the old-fashioned way. Later you two."

Astrid waved without releasing Nate. The door closed behind her friend, granting them time and privacy to unwind.

"How was your day?" Astrid asked as she pushed his jacket back from his shoulders. He made a quiet groan of relief. "That bad?"

"Tired. Lots of training to do. This two job business is harsh."

She slid her palms up and down his chest, then walked her fingers around his sides to his back to discover a mass of tension and knots from his waist to his shoulders. "Let me get you into the shower then. You smell like man and hard work."

"Ha ha. Funny."

While Nate wolfed down the plate of leftover lunch she'd set aside for him, Astrid started a hot shower. Pregnancy hadn't dulled her craving for him. If anything, it had amplified her libido, so she joined him to scrub his back. And his front.

"I think I pulled something lifting weights. Mind giving me a touch?"

"Already working on it," she assured him.

By the time the hour for her appointment approached, she had him in working order again. He rolled one shoulder then the other, exhaling a blissful sigh.

Her poor husband. Ever since the eve of Kay's final demise, he and the other knights faithful to Merlin's cause had their work cut out for them. The knighthood was in shambles, and with the help of Percivale and his closer friends, Nate had taken the reins until Arthur's return.

Astrid didn't know how to feel about it yet, raising a future king. She stroked the curve of her stomach and imagined a little boy with Nate's green eyes.

Would he have Nate's green eyes? Or would they be the eyes of a man who would despise her once he reached adulthood, a man with a soul older than his mother and a memory spanning centuries into the past.

Nate assured her Arthur would love her as much as he did. She hoped so.

"I love you, little guy," she whispered to her tummy while Nate dressed across the room.

"What's that?"

"Oh, nothing." She turned and flashed him a smile as he approached, pulling a T-shirt down over his abs.

"Everything go okay in Nevada?"

"Oh yeah, we cleared the last of the equipment out of the compound and returned a ton of shit to the government. Merlin collected most of his old artifacts from Disney and settled in at our old headquarters in Temecula. He and Loki spent the morning laying down new spells."

"Percivale still going to live there, too?"

"Yeah. They're best buds again. He's made it his personal mission to catch Merlin up on everything he's missed, and with

Lancelot living not too far away, and us, it should be educational."

"Any word on Bedivere?"

Nate raised a brow at her. "You're full of questions, but no, not yet. He's gone to ground." Her husband shrugged. "One of the other knights based out of Britain never answered our call to duty, so we have to assume he's defected and joined Bedivere."

"They can't hide forever, but this means we'll still be looking over our shoulders," Astrid grumbled.

"They'll take their time licking their wounds. But enough of that, let's get you to the doctor and meet our baby."

At the clinic, a sociable nurse in pink scrubs escorted them to the examination room where Astrid endured the usual vitals checks and frowned at the scale.

"I've gained more weight," she whined. "I'm going to be a whale by the time this baby is ready to be born."

"What? Baby, your weight doesn't matter as long as you and this child grow to be healthy and happy over the next months." He placed his hands over the meager hint of a bump curving her belly, her stomach muscles no less defined, but rounded at the bottom.

"All right, are you two ready to take a little peek?" The doctor greeted them with a smile and stepped inside the modest examination room. "Astrid, your vitals are looking good. Anything you need to discuss or should we get right to it?"

"I'm fine, Dr. Rourke, thanks. Anxious to know if I'll be decorating in pink or blue."

"I'm partial to greens and yellows. You'll find they're wonderfully neutral," the woman said. She winked and settled down on the stool beside the bed. "Okay, same as last time, this will be a little cold, but hopefully, that will get the little one moving around some."

"It tickles." Astrid giggled and tried not to wiggle on the table. Nate grinned beside her.

"Wuss," he teased.

"According to the measurements I've taken and the data I received from Dr. Thompson, if this is a standard, eleven-month dragon pregnancy, you're due to deliver in June. That means your little one was conceived in early July, give or take a couple weeks. Does that sound about right?"

Astrid glanced up at Nate. "I did take that morning after pill, you know."

"Those dosages are calculated for human women," Dr. Rourke said. "It doesn't surprise me that it was ineffective."

"I'm glad."

"Me, too." Nate lifted her hand and kissed her knuckles. "Let's leave out the protection and have a dozen after this one."

"Let's not get hasty," Astrid muttered.

"Now that we have the measurements out of the way, let's get to the good part, eh?" Dr. Rourke moved the probe across her belly and applied light pressure. "Shy little thing, but, aha!"

"Ready?" Nate asked in a quiet voice. "Bet you a back rub that it's a boy."

She swatted him. "Cheater." Then her eyes softened and her vision blurred with unshed tears. Knowing the outcome didn't dull the emotional effect of the momentous occasion. "We're ready," she said to the doctor.

"Then congratulations are in order, Mr. and Mrs. Drakenstone. It's a boy!" The doctor printed out a copy of the sonogram picture. "Do you have a name picked out for your little bean yet?"

Astrid's eyes darted up to Nate's face. "Arthur," she whispered as her husband smiled down at her. "His name is Arthur."

Crush

King Arthur would enter his next life as a dragon, and there would be no shortage of affection, respect, and good friends whether they soared on feathered wings or gleamed in shining armor.

Her baby was proof that two sides could do more than coexist. They could love.

About the Author

Vivienne Savage is a resident of a small town in rural Texas. While she isn't concocting sexy ways for shapeshifters and humans to find their match, she raises two children and works as a nurse in a rural retirement home.

www.ingramcontent.com/pod-product-compliance
Lightning Source LLC
Chambersburg PA
CBHW030532270626
47155CB00024B/2780